THE CHOICE
ARRANGED BOOK THREE

STELLA GRAY

Copyright © 2019 by Stella Gray

All rights reserved.

No part of this book may be reproduced in any form or by any electronic or mechanical means, including information storage and retrieval systems, without written permission from the author, except for the use of brief quotations in a book review.

ABOUT THIS BOOK

On the day my husband and I committed to each other, I didn't wear a white dress.

We didn't exchange rings.

There was no audience or minister to witness our union.

Only the two of us.

We swore to put each other first, to take on the evils our families had perpetuated together. Side by side.

But that was before the past returned to haunt us.

Now everything has changed.

Stefan can't have both his past and my future.

I can't ask him to choose.

ABOUT THIS BOOK

And neither of us can do what has to be done without the other. It's an impossible choice, but we've run out of time.

ALSO BY STELLA GRAY

∼

Arranged Series
The Deal
The Secret
The Choice

Convenience Series
The Sham - June 2020
The Contract - July 2020
The Ruin - August 2020

STEFAN

CHAPTER 1

"He's yours," Anja said, her eyes locked on mine. Her voice was barely above a whisper. "Your son."

I felt like I'd been shot in the gut, like the whole world had gone still around me.

I heard Tori gasp at my side, and instinctively tightened my grip on her hand. My gaze shifted to the dark-haired boy on the couch. This was...*my son?*

The shock was visceral. My whole body was cold, my pulse pounding in my ears, as if I'd just plunged under the surface of an iced-over Lake Michigan.

How was this possible?

Anja, the first woman I'd ever loved, the woman I'd lost, the woman I'd tried so desperately to find for almost a decade—I'd spent all this time searching for her, and this was the moment she chose to reappear? Right when things with my wife were finally coming together, when my plans to tear down my father and take over KZ Modeling were starting to coalesce?

Memories flooded back to me as I took in Anja's waterfall of black hair, her long legs, the wide eyes and sharp arch of her brows. Eight years later, and she hadn't changed a bit. It was almost like she was taunting me, the way she was suddenly sitting right here in front of me in my father's library. Looking at me with tears in her eyes and a hopeful smile. As if this was merely a reunion. As if no time or trauma had passed between us. With a child beside her that I was supposed to believe was *mine*. Was this the reason she'd disappeared all those years ago?

Eyeing the boy more closely, I could see that the kid had the same full lips as most of the men in my family, and similarly dark hair—but Anja had dark hair, too. With lips fuller than mine. I couldn't say with certainty that he was my offspring. But could I honestly say he wasn't?

The timeline made sense. Her disappearance made sense. Yet I still couldn't process it.

As something exploded in a bright flash on the kid's screen, he glanced up from the game he'd been absorbed in and our eyes met. It was only for a split second, but it was enough to hit me like another gut shot. His eyes were green. More of a blue-tinged green than my own pale olive color, yes, but maybe that was owing to Anja's mix of colors. Who could say for sure? But if it was true—if I did have a son—what did it mean for the boy, for Anja, for me and Tori?

I was numb, speechless, my mind blown. It was all so unreal.

My chest constricted and I sank into a chair, my brain reeling with all the questions I'd bottled up inside over the years. Even if I could form the words, they all felt irrelevant given the situation. Like pebbles to a mountain. Because the fact of this child sitting here—changed everything.

Looking up at Tori, our hands still locked together, I realized she still hadn't spoken either. And she refused to look at me. God, why did this have to happen now? As much as I wanted her here, I wished she had never come with me to my father's tonight. Because despite the fact that I loved her and needed her at my side, I knew this bombshell could destroy us, could destroy our marriage, could destroy everything we'd built. It was all crumbling in the wake of this impossible revelation.

And I couldn't lose her. Not after everything we'd been through. Everything that was still to come.

I needed to talk with Anja, but there was no way I could rehash my personal history with her in front of my wife. I would never subject Tori to that. But how could I just walk out the door now and leave Anja here? Especially with her son—our son—at her side? Even now, I could see my former love eyeing the huge diamond ring on Tori's finger, probably noticing the way my wife and I were holding hands so tightly. As much as I deserved an explanation, Anja probably had some questions of her own. And the boy—did he know anything about me? Did he want to?

There was no way out of this. No easy solution. I was trapped.

I looked back across the room at my father, taking in the familiar smirk on his face, and that's when I realized: he'd done this all on purpose.

Konstantin Zoric, ever the conniving, manipulative puppeteer. He'd arranged all of this—Anja, the boy, inviting me and Tori over for dinner just so he could pull off this surprise meeting—to cause maximum pain for everyone involved. The sadist. He'd stop at nothing to maintain his power over me, his control of the family business...even if that meant destroying my life and the lives of everyone around me.

"Look, son," he was saying now, his smug voice dripping

with self-satisfaction, "Anja's finally returned. Now you two can build a real family together, once and for all. Just like you always dreamed of."

I stood, my fists clenching. It was all I could do to keep myself from lunging at my father. My first instinct was to punch him in the face, but I couldn't. There was a child in the room. My child. But I was enraged in the face of my father's gloating, and even more disgusted by the way he was acting as though Tori—my wife—wasn't even here. Like she meant nothing, wasn't even worth a passing thought to him. But her grip on my hand only grew tighter, and she finally looked at me, offering a tight smile that I couldn't read.

Then she turned toward my father, and though I was grateful she'd interfered before I could engage in a full-out assault, I braced myself for what my wife was about to say.

"Konstantin, why don't we give Stefan and Anja a chance to speak alone?" she suggested, keeping her voice calm and neutral.

"What?" I blurted. I had no idea what I'd expected from Tori, but it wasn't that. Judging by my father's expression, he was just as surprised as I was.

"An excellent idea," my father said, quickly recovering his cool demeanor. "I'm sure they have a lot of...*catching up* to do."

Anja was looking at me expectantly, but I shook my head. "No. The last thing anybody needs right now is to—"

"Stefan," Tori interjected, cutting me off before smiling apologetically at Anja and my father. "If you'll excuse us for just a moment?"

"Of course," Anja said, her Romanian accent now just a hint of what it once was.

Then Tori gently led me out of the room and into the

hallway, closing the library door shut behind us. I slumped against the wall, grateful for the dim lighting, and rubbed a hand over my face.

"Tori. I don't know what to say. This is all happening so fast. I never—"

"Shh. Just listen," she started, looking me determinedly in the eye.

"No, you listen," I shot back, suddenly energized by my panic and grabbing her by the shoulders. "I don't know what the fuck is going on in there, but my father is obviously amusing himself by playing God—"

"It. Doesn't. Matter," Tori said, her voice soothing. "Your father *doesn't matter*. Okay? This isn't about him. It's about you and Anja and that little boy in there. Regardless of your dad's role in making this happen, it *is* happening. And now you have to move forward."

I took a deep breath, squeezing her shoulders softly. Then I nodded.

"You're right. I just don't know how any of this fits together. How you and I…"

My voice trailed off as I fought to find the right words. Because there weren't any.

"We can talk about all of this later," she said. "For now, you need to focus on Anja. I'll take a car back to the condo, and we'll catch up when you get home. This is important."

"I don't know what to say." I laughed at the absurdity of it all. "I don't even know how I feel. I mean, if this is true… where do I even start?"

She smiled. "You'll figure it out, Stefan. I know how long you've been trying to find her, and obviously you two have a lot to discuss. Just take it one step at a time. You don't have to decide anything right now. Talk first, decisions later."

I wrapped her in my arms, pressing my face against her hair.

"I love you." I didn't know what else to say.

"Everything will be okay," she replied, pulling away and smoothing her hair back down.

My wife was so fucking understanding, it killed me. It also made me desperate to keep her from walking out that door. She was the only solid thing I could count on right now.

"Stay," I said. "You don't have to run back to the condo. This isn't just about me."

"It's better if I go," she said, shaking her head. "Whatever history you two have between you, it's got nothing to do with me. And I need a little time for myself, too. Okay?"

"Okay."

I searched her eyes. Her expression was guarded but resolute. My wife, the rock. Stronger than anyone ever gave her credit for. As she tilted her head back to look up at me, her diamond earrings caught the light. I'd given them to her on the way to my father's place, to represent how we were a pair, how we belonged together. I hoped she'd still give me a chance to prove that.

Leaning forward, I dropped a soft kiss on her lips, trying to communicate how I felt. Letting her walk away didn't feel like the right move. Not by a long shot. But I had to let her go. Give her some space. And I knew she was right about me needing to stay here and talk to Anja.

After walking Tori out of the building and seeing her safely into the backseat of my private car, I headed back up to my father's penthouse, lost in thought.

In spite of all the years that had passed, or perhaps because of them, my heart had ached seeing Anja's face again. She reminded me of so many things, but mostly of the person I had been when I was seventeen and in love for the first time. Far from innocent, yet innocent about the world. Maybe that's what my heart ached for. For the person I was back then. I'd had my whole life ahead of me, full of possibilities.

I'd been optimistic. Happy.

Instead of angry and jaded, obsessed with revenge and with my plan to take down my father and his vile corporation. A plan that I still had every intention of following through with. No matter what happened with Anja and the boy, I would not be stopped. I just wished Tori hadn't been dragged into it. Into all of this. My father was a monster.

Tori had put on a brave face, but I knew she had to be hurting. I had no idea if I'd be able to repair what my father had just broken.

I stormed out of the elevator and back toward the door of the penthouse. When I walked inside, though, I slowed my stride. It was true that I was dying for answers, but I was also battling the urge to kick down the library door and throttle the man responsible for all of this.

He'd told me he had arranged Anja's disappearance the first time around—deporting her right when it would hurt me the most. Now it seemed he'd brought her back just when he knew it would hurt me again. When he knew my marriage to Tori had been on the rocks. The bastard.

But he'd underestimated me. I might have chased Anja for years, but she was now more a fond memory to me than anything else. I cared about her, and I'd do right by my child, but my relationship with Tori was solid. I wasn't going to walk away and I sure as hell wasn't going to let her go. I'd never stop fighting for her.

As I walked up to the library door, I took a deep breath, steeling myself for the conversation ahead. After years of dead ends and cold trails, the mystery surrounding Anja's disappearance was about to come to light. I could hardly believe it. Even if my father's intentions had been malignant, I was grateful I'd be getting the truth.

Anja had a shitload of explaining to do, and I was finally going to get my answers.

STEFAN

CHAPTER 2

When I was seventeen, Anja and I had been in love. Or at least, that's what I'd believed. I had trusted her with my hopes and fears for the future, and shared stories about my past—my mother and how much I missed her, the difficult childhood I'd had after she'd died and left us Zoric children to be raised by a series of nannies and the occasional bit of attention from our emotionally closed-off, workaholic father. Anja always listened. Always cared. She was almost maternal at times, nothing like any woman I'd ever dated. Mature beyond her twenty-three years.

I had thought every time we had sex it was like making a promise to one another.

I was young back then. Naïve enough to think we were perfectly matched, that we were equals, that we'd be together forever and that nothing would ever come between us. It was almost laughable now, how little I'd understood her position—caught between her modeling career dreams, the sex work my father had been forcing on her, her desperation for US citizenship, how heavy the familial responsibilities on her shoulders were, and the way she'd had to send almost every cent she made back to Romania to care for her family there.

I'd believed that marrying her would solve each and every one of those problems. Instead, my hasty marriage proposal had made things worse. But if my father had admittedly gotten Anja deported, where had she gone? None of my investigations in Romania had turned up anything. How had she kept herself in hiding all these years —with a child? And why? All this time I had assumed she'd been hiding from my father, but now that she was here, I couldn't help thinking: what if the person she'd been hiding from was me?

None of it made sense. She had to have known I would have raised the child with her. Stood by her. Would have cared for her and protected her no matter what.

I didn't know what to think. My heart and my life were with Tori now. I had no regrets, and our marriage—our partnership—had made me realize how undeveloped my relationship with Anja had truly been. But I still had so many questions. And no matter what, I had to find a way forward. If not for Anja and me, for the child we had created—because I'd never turn my back on him the way my own father had turned his back on me and my siblings.

But when I turned the knob and went back into the library, Anja was gone. And so was the boy.

Instead, only my father stood there, a dark and looming presence in his typical ensemble of head-to-toe charcoal, lighting one of his disgusting cigars. He looked up as I entered, the expression on his face just as smug as it had been when Tori and I had first walked into the room, into his clusterfuck of a trap.

"What the fuck is going on here?" I demanded. "What kind of game are you trying to play?"

I was sick and tired of his machinations. As far as I was concerned, they ended now.

"No game," he said, pausing to puff the cigar.

"Bullshit," I ground out, narrowing my eyes at him.

He lifted his hands as if in surrender. "I just want what's best for you, Stefan."

I scoffed. He used to say this same thing when doling out punishment to us as children.

"I want what's best for the whole Zoric family," he went on. "I always have."

That I could believe. As far as my father was concerned, the family—his legacy—was what needed to be protected at all costs. But his motives in this were murky.

"You honestly think it's 'best for the family' to suddenly bring back my ex-girlfriend and her kid—our kid—out of nowhere?" I yelled. "How exactly is that 'best' for anyone?"

My father, unperturbed, walked over to the bar to fix himself a whiskey, shrugging his meaty shoulders as he poured. "I may have made a mistake back when you were seventeen, acted rashly in my haste to deal with...a problem. But I'm rectifying it now. Can't you see that?"

It was obvious he was lying—he had his reasons for calling Anja here, and they had nothing to do with the greater good of the family, or realizing he'd made a mistake. The fact was, my father never admitted to 'mistakes.' His motto was, 'I don't make mistakes—I make choices.' If he was standing here in front of me humbly acknowledging that he'd done something wrong, it was clearly just another form of manipulation. How stupid did he think I was?

"Where is she now?" I asked, pacing in front of a bookcase.

My father smiled, which only stoked my anger. "She's just putting the boy to sleep in their room, but she'll be back to speak with you soon. I told her to meet you here in the library, so have a seat and relax. I'm sure you're both anxious to catch up."

Have a seat and relax? Was he out of his fucking mind? "I'll stand."

That just made him laugh. "Contrary as always. Typical Stefan."

I still couldn't believe what I was hearing. Anja had a *room*? In my father's penthouse? Since when? How long had she been here? And why was he embracing the situation like this?

Biting back my questions, I walked to the window and stared out at the city skyline, lit up against the dark. Throttling my father would solve nothing, I reasoned. I had to play the long game. Let him have his small victories. His end was near, and if everything went according to plan, he'd never know what hit him.

Turning back toward him, I said, "Fine. You win." I knew those were probably his favorite words to hear. Then I sat in a chair and put my hands on my knees. I wanted him to revel in his position of power. Lull him into a sense of full control—and complacency.

"'Atta boy. Knowing when to quit fighting is half the battle." Grinning, he stubbed out his cigar and took a long drink of his whiskey. The ice cubes clinked as he swirled the glass. "Of course, I never quit. But the ability to assess the might of your adversary is a vital skill to have."

"Sure, Dad." I looked up at him and gestured to the door, letting my frustration color my tone. "Just go, so I can talk to her alone."

"Of course, son." He held up his drink in a triumphant

toast. "And I suggest you fix yourself a drink. I have a feeling you'll need it."

With another chuckle, he strolled out of the library, closing the door behind him.

Without anything else to do but wait, I took advantage of the whiskey—though it tasted bitter to me, and did nothing to assuage either my anxiety or my irritation at my father.

By the time Anja reappeared, my anger was a hot fire burning in my chest. I wasn't just pissed at my father, but at her too. Obviously she hadn't been kidnapped or killed. She'd had free will in her disappearance, and in staying hidden. Had it never crossed her mind to reach out? Especially considering we had a *son*? Whatever her reasons were, she owed me an explanation.

"Hello," Anja said, padding over to my chair and sitting on the couch across from me.

She'd put on yoga pants and a black T-shirt, but neither the clothes nor the years had changed her into anything less than the beautiful woman she'd always been. How easily I'd once been deceived into believing that her beauty was more than skin deep. Now I knew better.

"Where did you go?" I blurted, ignoring any attempt at manners or formality.

She looked confused. "I was putting Max to bed. Your father said—"

"No, where did you go all those *years ago*?" I clarified. "And why did you keep your—our son—a secret?" The words felt strange in my mouth, the idea of fatherhood still foreign. "Do you have any idea how fucking hard I looked for you? The time and resources I exhausted?"

I was practically yelling at that point, and she flinched. I didn't care. I had intended to ask one question at a time, to patiently listen to each response, but once I got started the words had poured out of me, one after another, filled with anger and bitterness. There was no explanation I could imagine that would justify the way she'd hidden herself and our child for all this time, without even a single call or email to let me know what the hell had happened.

Anja just looked at me, her cool blue-green eyes assessing me, appearing completely unmoved. The same way she'd always responded to any flares of temper I'd exhibited.

"His name is Max?" I added, starting to deflate a little in the face of her silence.

"*Maxim Andreus Fischer,*" Anja responded, crossing her arms and sitting up straighter. "And how dare you sit there and yell at me. I was a kid back then, Stefan. And so were you. I was pregnant and scared and I didn't know where to turn. What was I supposed to do, just—"

"So you ran away?" I stood, too wound up again to remain seated. "That was your solution? God, Anja, I was in love with you!"

The room felt hot, and I loosened my tie and took another pull from my drink.

"I loved you too," she said quietly. "With all my heart."

I shook my head. I didn't know how to feel about that statement. It sounded like bullshit. This whole evening was bullshit. "You loved me so much you disappeared from my life, carrying our kid," I repeated sarcastically. "Yeah. That makes a whole lot of sense."

"You don't believe me?" she asked. "You think I played you all along?"

She was searching my eyes, pleading for my forgiveness, a single tear slipping down her cheek. Years ago, that would have had me running to her side, taking her face in my hands and wiping the tear away. Asking her what I could do to make things right.

It wouldn't work on me now.

"I don't know. I honestly don't know what to believe," I said. "Running scared, yes, I can understand. But having a kid you never told me about, evading me for almost ten years, and then showing up out of nowhere like this? The pieces don't fit."

Anja got up and walked over to me, then took the whiskey out of my hand and drank down all that was left. She winced at the taste but her gaze when it met mine was fierce.

"I didn't want to ruin your life, Stefan, and everything that was in front of you. College, your father's business, your big dreams. You would have lost it all if you stayed with me, if you had to be a father and support a family. You were barely eighteen. I did what I did for *you*."

The pain of knowing she'd run from me in order to give me a chance to succeed in life made me sick.

"We would have figured it out," I said bitterly.

She laughed. "Really? An out-of-work model and an eighteen-year-old kid? What, you'd just let your father disown you and go to business school on a scholarship? Let me sit at home all day in a shitty apartment and be a full-time mother while you worked on your MBA?"

"I mean, I don't know..." I said.

"And then what?" she went on, leaning closer as her own anger rose. "You'd get your first job, maybe forty thousand a year, and I'd stay home with a toddler while we struggled to pay for groceries and diapers and health insurance? You think that would have been a good life?"

She wasn't wrong. The first jobs I'd had were with KZ Modeling, and they'd paid well, but without my father's help I would've had to start at the bottom somewhere, pay my dues with long hours and low pay. We wouldn't have been able to afford daycare or a nanny. And Anja was independent. She'd have been the baby's sole caregiver, with no life of her own.

"It would have fallen apart, Stefan," she said. "We would have ended up hating each other. You'd be staying with me out of obligation and I'd resent you for being gone all the time."

As much as I loathed to admit it, what she was saying did make a kind of sense. But that didn't make her actions right. I went over to the bar to refill the glass, then handed it back to her. She sank back onto the couch and took a long drink.

"I thought you were dead," I told her.

"I'm sorry," she said. "I just—"

"I don't want *apologies*," I interrupted harshly. "I want *answers*."

Anja looked startled. She said, "Okay," so softly I could barely hear her and then cleared her throat. "The thing is...I was trapped in the world of KZM. The modeling, and the... other work. I'd been trying to figure out how to leave for a while. Get out of the business for good. But there was never a way out. So when I found out I was pregnant...it was my one chance. I went to your father to tell him, figuring he'd fire me on the spot. But he helped me get away. Start fresh."

"He gave you money," I said flatly. "To disappear."

She nodded her confirmation. "The choice was mine, though. I *wanted* to go. I never told him the baby was yours but...I thought he knew, and that was why he let me go. To hide it. And then the way he's supported us over the years— I figured it was because Max is his grandson."

The way Anja was talking now, unspooling the facts

one at a time, it was almost like listening to a robot. I wondered how many times she'd imagined telling me the truth like this, if she was operating on autopilot now, or if maybe she was just disassociating from the difficulty of the moment between us and refusing to let her emotions leak through.

I took the glass back from her and gulped down the burning liquid.

"He didn't just give you money to leave?" I asked, her words still echoing in my mind. "He kept on paying you to stay away, to hide from me?"

"It wasn't like that." Anja looked down. "He sent monthly payments, enough for us to live on, but he supported me in other ways. Before I left Chicago he helped me get a new US identity. Social security number, birth certificate, new name, everything I needed to start over. I was glad for the change. The privacy. Nobody would ever know I was Anja Borjan the model."

I nodded, finally lowering myself into the chair across from her. "So all this time I've been searching the world for you, and you've been here in the US. Not dead. Not kidnapped. Not suffering at all." I forced myself to keep my voice calm. "And my father knew about the—knew about Max—the entire time. For eight years. Nobody thought I needed this information."

We locked eyes, and I could see the tears glistening in hers.

She'd been right here all along. Probably right under my nose. Knowing my father, he would have kept her as close as possible, so he could keep an eye on her and Max.

I clenched my hands into fists. He'd known about the kid—that I was a father—right from the beginning, and he'd never said a word. If I hadn't hated him already, this would have pushed me over the edge. And now that I knew he and Anja had worked together to conspire against me, it was hard to believe anything my former flame was saying.

"I know it wasn't right to keep the pregnancy a secret," Anja admitted. "But you were in school."

"What about later? I wasn't in school for a decade," I shot back. "In fact, once I'd started working, I would have been even better able to take care of you. Both of you."

Anja shook her head. "I knew you got a job with KZM right out of your MBA program—your father told me all about it—and you were building a life, a career. The last thing you needed was a baby to take care of. But finding out you worked for your father? That was one more reason to stay away." She shot me a glare, getting just as worked up as I was. "Do you seriously think I'd go back to you, when you were tied up with all the corruption and the lies? How could you? I would never want to raise a child with someone like that—"

"But you were happy enough to take the company handouts, weren't you?" I said, cutting her off.

"That's not fair!" she yelled. "I did what I had to do for my kid. And I'd do it all again if I had to. He was safe with me, and cared for, and I was able to provide him everything he needed. I love my son, and I won't apologize for anything I've had to do to support him."

It was ironic. The whole reason I'd gone to work for my father—the reason I'd thrown myself into the business in the first place—was because of her. Because I needed the resources my father had, the money, the connections, in order to *find* her. And now she was telling me it was part of the reason she'd kept herself hidden from me.

I wished I could tell Anja all about how I planned to dismantle the trafficking ring once I was in control. But I didn't trust her. Especially now that I knew how much she owed my father.

"Fine," I said, rubbing my temples. "I don't agree with any of this, but I won't say I don't respect your choices. It's obvious you made some very hard decisions. And I'm sure you've been...a wonderful mother." It was true. She'd always had that warm, maternal quality. I'd seen it, experienced it firsthand myself. "But I still don't understand. Why did you come back now?"

Anja got up from the couch and knelt in front of me. She took my hand, looking up at me again with that pleading expression. My jaw was clenched, and I met her gaze coldly. I couldn't deny the heat that stirred between us, regardless of all these years that had passed, but even if I wasn't in love with Tori, and committed to my marriage, I still wouldn't ever touch Anja again. She'd betrayed me in the worst possible ways. I wasn't sure I could ever forgive her.

"I have felt guilty about what I did every single day for the past eight years," she said. "I just couldn't do it anymore. Couldn't let you go on any longer not knowing about me, or your son." She took a breath, her eyes searching the room as if it would give her the right words. "Raising Max as a single mother is the hardest thing I've ever done. But also the best thing, and the thing I'm most proud of. I know you're angry, and that's okay. Just don't be angry at Max."

"Fuck." I pulled my hand away from her and got up, pacing to the window again.

Had she expected me to just fall at her feet, grateful that she was back, asking no questions, accepting her and her child without hesitation?

Everyone around me was manipulating me. I hated the way Anja had chosen to handle everything, from the pregnancy to the disappearance to the way she'd decided to just show up now out of the blue. And I hated the way my father was involved—had always been involved. Taking joy in pulling all my strings, like I was nothing more than a puppet for him to play with.

He wasn't standing in front of me right now, though. Anja was. I spun around, furious.

"What the hell am I supposed to do about this kid?" I said. "I can't just magically be a father without any notice. Does he know who I am? Does he know anything about me? Did you spend the last seven years telling him his father was a bad man? Or that I'm dead?"

Anja blinked back tears and shook her head. "I've always told him I didn't know who his father was. He's accepted it. But I understand how you must be feeling and I —I'm not going to tell Max anything until you decide what you want to do. If you want a role in your son's life."

My son.

No matter how many times I said the words to myself, I couldn't get them to make sense.

I stalked toward her, and she stood, not shrinking back. My temper was new to her, but she'd never been afraid of me and she apparently wasn't going to start now. "I will never forgive you for this," I said. "You've taken everything from me."

Even as I said the words, I knew they weren't true. My father was the one who'd robbed me of my relationship, of fatherhood, of a parallel life that I couldn't even begin to imagine. But I had Tori now—and I loved her more than anything. The life we would build together, however it turned out, was the life I wanted. In the end, I wouldn't have traded it—or her—for the world.

"I need to think," I told Anja, suddenly exhausted.

"Please do. I'll wait for you to make your choice, so just...take all the time you need," she said, stepping back. "Your father has my number."

"Of course he does," I scoffed, disgusted. Then I headed for the door.

"Stefan—"

"Yeah."

When she didn't immediately reply, I turned around to look at her. She took a long, slow breath and moved as close to me as she dared. For a moment she was quiet, but the second she placed a hand over her heart, I knew whatever she was about to say was the truth. The gesture was familiar to me, and I steeled myself for the reveal of another devastating piece of information.

But I wasn't prepared for what came out of her mouth as she stared into my eyes.

"For what it's worth," she finally said, "I still love you. I always have."

TORI

CHAPTER 3

My stepmother Michelle came into my life when I was four years old. I could still remember meeting her for the first time. Though I was the kind of child that loved every new person I met, probably due to the fact that I was left in the care of others so frequently, my initial reaction was one of suspicion. Who was this beautiful woman on our doorstep? Why was my father smiling so much at her? This new 'friend' of his was glamorous, in heels and lipstick. She was nothing like the older nannies or teenage babysitters he usually introduced me to.

The plan was to take Michelle out to lunch that day, but my father had to take a quick, urgent call from a congressman, so he asked her to help me find my shoes so we could leave as soon as possible. Upstairs in my toy-strewn bedroom, Michelle noticed my dolls and bears arranged in a circle on the floor, a variety of plastic food set out for each of them.

"Is this a tea party?" she'd asked in her gentle southern drawl.

"Nope," I answered, rolling my eyes. "It's a campfire. They're having hot dogs for dinner and telling scary stories."

"How nice," Michelle said politely, unearthing my little pink sandals from a pile under the bed and passing them to me. "And I'll just bet there will be s'mores for dessert."

"Some more what?" I asked, still wary but letting her help me with the buckles.

"S'mores is a snack," Michelle explained. "You make them with graham crackers and chocolate and toasted marshmallows, like a sandwich. Haven't you ever had them?"

When I told her I hadn't, she insisted we rectify the situation immediately. Then she somehow convinced my father to run out to the store for graham crackers while she helped me look for sticks in the backyard so we could toast marshmallows over the stove.

Our big date turned into the three of us having s'mores on the back porch while Michelle told us about a disastrous camping trip she'd gone on with her very unprepared sorority sisters back in college. I hadn't seen my dad laugh like that ever, and I decided that Michelle could keep coming around for visits. We had been friends ever since. I'd even helped my father pick out the engagement ring that he proposed to her with some months later.

All this was to say, the word 'stepmother' carried no negative connotations for me. But I had no idea what was going through Stefan's mind right now. I would never stand in the way of him getting to know his son and being a father —the very idea of interfering went against who I was as a person and what I'd experienced myself in my relationship with my own stepmother—but what if this new life of Stefan's wasn't compatible with our marriage?

Lots of couples had blended families, though, and I would be thrilled to be a stepmom myself. I imagined what kind of parents Stefan and I would be together. Kind, warm, loving. Fun. I could even teach the kid how to make s'mores, if Anja hadn't already. Build blanket forts in the den on weekends and take him mini-golfing or to the Shedd Aquarium here in the city.

But maybe my fantasy version of our future family, with Anja as a friend and Max as our shared child, was just that —a fantasy. Maybe it was stupid to assume it would be so simple.

My thoughts reeled dizzyingly as I curled up in a tiny ball in the backseat of the Town Car. The whole way home from Konstantin's penthouse, I struggled with this new reality. Thoughts of calling Michelle or texting my friend Grace went through my mind, but I didn't know what I'd say, how I'd even begin to explain what was happening—and I honestly didn't think there was anything they could say to me that would be comforting. Instead I spent the entire ride back to the condo replaying the scene in my father-in-law's library over and over again. The whole thing had a distant, unreal quality to it.

I just couldn't believe this was happening. That Anja was back.

I don't know why it was such a shock. Ever since Stefan had told me about his relationship with Anja and her deportation and disappearance, I'd assumed she was out there somewhere. I'd been aware that for the last eight years Stefan had made it his mission in life to find her, and I'd been open to the possibility that she might someday be a part of our lives. But I'd never dreamed it would be like this. Never dreamed that Stefan—my husband—had a child.

I looked out the window of the Town Car at the bright lights of Chicago whirling by. It made my eyes hurt.

Anja had a son. Stefan's son.

I'd barely gotten a look at the boy, but even at a glance, his eyes had stood out as familiar to me. They were green, with a hint of blue. The perfect mix between Anja's stormy color and Stefan's clear green. He also had Stefan's dark brown hair and full lips. I knew in my gut that Anja wasn't lying about who he was. About who he belonged to. Stefan had fathered a child with the woman he loved. The hard truth of the situation made it hard for me to breathe.

For a moment, I felt so dizzy that I had to grab onto the arm rest to stabilize myself. But there would be nothing to steady me against the fact that Stefan had another family now. It didn't matter that he hadn't known about the boy before, because I knew nothing would ever be the same for him—for us—now that Anja had shown up with their child.

It changed everything.

I couldn't even fathom what Stefan was going through as he talked with Anja back at his dad's place. What he was thinking, how he was feeling. I'd seen the blank look in his eyes at first, the complete shock. Then the way his body language had projected his anger toward his father, and the obvious emotional pain when he looked at Anja and squeezed my hand.

Anja Borjan. She was even more beautiful than Stefan had made her out to be. Of course I knew exactly what kind of women KZ Modeling hired, but I'd still been startled by the way her eyes looked like deep oceans, how perfect her shining dark hair was, her long legs. How could I compete with someone who looked like that? And Stefan had been so in love with her. At seventeen, his first love would have felt like his entire world. I'd know; I was eighteen when Stefan and I had met for the first time, eighteen when I'd realized I was hopelessly, undeniably in love with him. I was still eighteen, and the overwhelming heartache I'd experienced in the last few months had taught me more than I'd ever imagined about what first love could feel like.

So. It would be naïve of me to ignore the possibility that Stefan might want to get back together with her. Years had passed, but there was no way their feelings for each other were completely gone. Especially now that Stefan knew he and Anja had a child together. What if seeing her in person made him realize he was still carrying a torch for her? What if there wasn't any room for me in his life at all anymore?

The worst part was, things between Stefan and I had just found their way. Had just stabilized. This huge bombshell could destroy all that. Who knew what he would say when he came home. He had kissed me before I left, but what if that had been a goodbye kiss?

I touched my fingers to my lips as if I could hold onto his touch. As if I could capture it forever.

The car finally pulled up outside our building and somehow I managed to stumble through the lobby, into the elevator, and down the hall to our condo. I stepped out of my shoes in the entryway, shrugged off my coat, and then wandered into our bedroom, my mind in a haze.

Looking at myself in the full-length mirror, I couldn't believe how put-together I still appeared. I was broken, but you'd never know it judging by the outside. I'd gotten so good at pretending to be brave and strong, burying my true feelings, but none of it was real—it was just my years of training kicking in, creating a hard shell around me. My hair was still perfect, my black dress pressed, my new earrings from Stefan sparkling. But what good was keeping up appearances, when it was all a lie? When everything inside you was falling apart?

After pulling the bobby pins out of my hair, I unzipped my dress and hung it back up in the closet, then unhooked my earrings and left them on the dresser. Everything was coming apart. I didn't know what to do with myself.

In the shower I stood under the spray of hot water, my tears finally flowing, but my crying was silent. I still felt numb. This wasn't about fighting for Stefan, or fighting for our marriage. It was about giving him the time and space he needed to make his own choices about his life—his child's life—which had nothing to do with me. The last thing I wanted to do was stand in his way. All I could do was wait. I'd never felt so helpless.

I could so easily picture Stefan being a father. I saw him laughing and smiling, the little boy hoisted up on his shoulders. Or playing catch with his son in a backyard with a jungle gym or a treehouse, maybe with a dog running around, Anja looking on with love in her eyes.

That was the image that haunted me most. Because the way Anja gazed at Stefan left no doubt in my mind. She still loved him. It was obvious. What would she do to get him back? I knew what I would do: Anything. Did I stand a chance against her? She'd had his heart first; what woman could compete with a man's first love? Especially when that first love had been cruelly taken away from him, but was suddenly back in the picture. Back with his child.

Stefan and his son and Anja. The three of them made the picture-perfect family. They'd all look beautiful together. Like they belonged together. I didn't fit in that picture.

Images rose up unbidden, torturing me: Stefan and Anja raising their son, standing with their arms around each other, watching the boy with looks of admiration and joy on their faces. Stefan taking Anja in his arms and kissing her, cupping her face gently the way he'd done to me. Touching her stomach, whispering in her ear, sharing his hopes of having a second child with her. I imagined them trying for that child, their naked bodies fitting together perfectly as they made love on a lazy Sunday morning. Stefan's hands roaming over Anja's lithe body, his lips trailing kisses down her throat, her breasts, him fucking her until she screamed his name with that sexy Eastern European accent, her body arching up off the bed with the pure bliss I knew he was capable of giving a woman. And she'd please him, too. Unlike me, she was experienced. Worldly. She would know how to satisfy Stefan in ways I couldn't.

Sinking to the shower floor, I covered my eyes and cried out, finally giving voice to my pain. My body shook with sobs and I wished Stefan was here to hold me. But he wasn't. And there was no one I could turn to.

When the water ran cool, I stepped out, wrapped myself in a towel, and headed to the guest room. I couldn't bear to sleep in our bed, not after what had happened tonight. Not after my imagination had so vividly played out all the possible ways Stefan would make love to Anja. I could so easily see her in that bed, in my place. Head tilted back, eyes closed, her full lips parted in ecstasy. Her long legs wrapped tight around his torso as he thrusted into her with deep and reassuring strokes, making up for all the years they'd spent apart, his hands gliding through her dark hair, their bodies in perfect harmony. Stefan might not even want to sleep next to me while he was going through all of this. I told myself I'd sleep better in the guest bed, too.

I put on my pajamas and crawled under the crisp, cool sheets. It was just like it had been before, with the two of us in separate rooms, living separate lives. Stefan had a whole new reality spreading out in front of him. A new family. A son. And his first love, safe and sound and back in his arms where she belonged after all these years.

I thought I was done crying, but the moment my head hit the pillow and I imagined my life without Stefan, imagined him choosing Anja, choosing a life with her and their son, the tears came again. I was completely, utterly alone. My cries echoed off the empty walls of the guest room, and as I felt myself drifting off to sleep I tried to convince myself that it was for the best. That what Stefan really needed right now was his space.

Maybe our marriage was already over.

TORI

CHAPTER 4

I slowly came awake to the sound of the bedroom door closing, the soft hush of clothes hitting the floor, the shift of the bed as Stefan slid in beside me. It took me a moment to remember where I was, the guest room still dark and the shadows unfamiliar to me.

My first instinct was to wriggle back toward him, but I stopped myself. I wasn't sure what to do. Being close to Stefan, feeling connected to him, opening my legs wide for him and riding his cock, yes, I wanted all of that, and badly—but I had no idea where I stood now, no idea what had passed between him and Anja back at Konstantin's apartment. Giving in to what my body craved without any thought of the consequences would be a mistake. It was possible I'd already lost Stefan, and didn't even know it yet.

Before I could ponder things any further, though, I felt him snuggling his warm, naked body into my back. Letting out a sigh, I realized that resisting him would be nearly impossible.

He pulled my hair gently over my shoulder and started kissing the back of my neck, his lips firm and his breath hot against the sensitive skin at my nape. I could smell the alcohol coming off of him, but I couldn't bring myself to push him away. The truth was, I didn't want him to stop. I needed him, emotionally and physically. And god, he was giving me the most delicious chills. Closing my eyes, I bent my head to give him better access to my neck and let myself revel in the sensations, desire curling tightly in my lower belly.

His strong hands circled my waist, pulling me even closer to him. Through the thin fabric of my pajama pants, I could feel his cock, pressing hard and needy against my ass.

"Tori," he murmured, grinding into my backside. "I need you."

My heart seemed to squeeze in my chest. I didn't know if his words were true. It was obvious that he wanted me, and desperately, but I didn't know if it was the booze talking, or pure animal lust, or if Stefan genuinely loved me and needed to be with me in this moment.

I was torn. There was no denying that my body had already begun to respond to his touches, but I didn't want sex to confuse the situation. Was this the right thing for us to do considering everything that was going on with Anja and the boy, and our marriage quite possibly in jeopardy? On the other hand, I loved him. I always would. Every part of me cried out for him.

Stefan's hands roamed my body, sliding up under my tank top to cup my breasts. Then his fingers tweaked my nipples just the way I liked, the way that made me so hot I couldn't see straight, so hot that all rational thought fled my mind. I squirmed in the bed, grinding my ass back into him. He knew exactly what he was doing to me.

There was no holding back the soft moan that escaped my lips as he pinched and stroked both of my nipples at the same time, sending bursts of pleasure and pain through me, waves of hot need going directly to my clit. It felt so good, it was hard to imagine stopping. My hips were grinding faster under the sheets, meeting and encouraging the thrusts of his bare cock against my ass. I was desperate for him, for his dick, for his attention and affection.

But I didn't want to let myself be taken by him, body and soul, when I knew full well that there was still a chance he'd walk away to be with Anja and his son. When what I should be doing was building a wall between Stefan and myself, blocking off my feelings for him.

God, I could feel myself getting wetter every second that he had his hands on me.

If I was being honest, I wanted to protect myself from even more heartache—but I wanted to take care of him, too. And I could tell that he needed me, by his words and actions. That in itself was intoxicating.

I loved my husband. There was no doubt in my mind. And if our relationship was solid, was as strong as I thought, then it would withstand a blow like the one it had taken tonight. These new revelations might shake us, but they wouldn't destroy us. Wouldn't change what we had built together.

That's what I wanted to believe.

Because I needed him just as much as he needed me.

And, if I was wrong about everything—if nothing I felt in my heart about Stefan and me was actually true—then this might be the last night that we were together.

I pulled away, turning in Stefan's arms to face him. He searched my eyes, but before I could speak his lips halted my words, his tongue stroking aggressively against mine. I was hungry for him. Our mutual desperation was unstoppable as we devoured each other's mouths.

If he was drunk on his father's whiskey, I was just as drunk with my own desire, my hands wrapping around his neck as he rolled me onto my back, tugging my pants and underwear off and my top over my head.

"Stefan," I panted between kisses, "I need you, too. I need you now."

His hands slipped down, forcing my legs open, wrapping them around his hips. He rubbed the head of his cock against my swollen lips, the sensation so intense that I cried out into his mouth. He didn't let me go. Didn't give me a moment to breathe as he kissed me deeper.

I felt hot tears at the corners of my eyes, the intensity of my emotions and my desire overwhelming me. Trying to blink them away, I only succeeded in forcing them out, and Stefan immediately pulled back.

"What did I do?" he whispered. "Am I hurting you?"

Answering that was too fucking complicated. Lying was easier.

"No," I murmured. "I just...love you. I need to be with you."

Reaching for him, I pulled his mouth back down onto mine until I was lost in his kiss again. I didn't break away until I had to stop to catch my breath.

"You should have stayed with me earlier," Stefan said as his hand slid between my legs, tracing my seam. "I wanted you to stay."

I shook my head, hissing as his fingers found my clit, stroking softly.

"You needed to be with her," I said. "Alone." As he pinched my clit between his thumb and forefinger, tugging gently, I gasped. It felt good. Too good. So good it hurt.

I loved it, the pain and pleasure mixing together. It was perfect. He was perfect.

"I needed *you*," he insisted.

Tears threatened again, so I unhooked my legs from around his waist and rolled onto my side. I was afraid to speak, afraid that anything more I tried to say would be my undoing, but Stefan only came up behind me and spooned my body in his, holding me tight as he nuzzled my hair. We were positioned the same as before, his cock still raging hard as it pressed into me. Fighting this was futile. I knew exactly what I wanted.

I arched back against him with renewed urgency, wanting to feel him, wanting to be close, but knowing I'd be unable to look at my husband without tears welling up in my eyes.

His hand slid down to my pussy, where I was wet and ready. He stroked my clit again, making me moan slowly, deeply, drinking in every drop of pleasure. Then, without warning, he thrust a finger deep inside of me, forcing my hips back harder against his cock.

"Fuck," I groaned, bearing down on his finger, wanting more.

"You like that?" he asked. "You like it when I fuck you with my hands?"

"Yes," I said. "I love your hands. I want you to touch me."

He pumped his finger back and forth gently, too gently, making me cry out with need.

"You want it bad," he said, each word accompanied by a thrust of his finger, going deeper and deeper. "I can tell. You're dying for me to fuck you."

"Yes," I begged, my hips thrusting, my juices wetting his whole hand. "Please fuck me, Stefan. I can't be—" I gasped out a breath as he curled his finger to tap my G-spot. "Oh fuck, that's good. Don't stop. I can't be without you."

He repositioned us so that I was face down on the mattress and he was on top of me, his finger still fucking me. I grinded against his hand faster, fucking his finger, moaning into the sheets as the pleasure sparked through me. When he withdrew, I practically whimpered.

"I need more," I said.

"You're gonna get more," Stefan replied.

With rough hands against my hips, he pulled my ass up off the bed. I was exposed to him, tense with anticipation. He slid his hand along the curve of my ass cheek before drawing his hand back and slapping me hard, right there. I gasped at the sting against my skin, the wash of heat afterward, shocked by the way my pussy clenched in response.

"God, yes," I said. "Again."

I loved it. I wanted more.

"You like that?" he asked and spanked me again. This time I moaned, my hips bucking. He did it again and I could feel my wetness dripping down the inside of my thigh.

"Stefan," I begged, choking out the words. "I can't wait. I'm ready now."

"You want my cock?" he demanded, stroking my ass tenderly.

"Yes," I agreed. "Now."

Gripping my hip with one hand, he nudged my knees further apart with his thigh and then I felt the head of his cock against my wet slit, sliding up and down, teasing me. I sighed, already feeling the first hints of an orgasm.

"You're mine," Stefan said, his voice uncharacteristically quiet. "Only mine."

He tapped his dick with his finger as he pressed the tip of his cock right up against me, so I could feel the vibrations in my pussy. It was so good. So perfect.

Tears returned to my eyes.

"I'm yours," I said, echoing his words. "Give it to me."

"I'm not gonna go easy on you," he growled, and I felt another flush of heat spread between my thighs.

Then he slammed into me, hard and deep, claiming me as his own.

I cried out at the exquisite pleasure, at how right it felt, and for a moment we stayed like that, connected, his cock so tight and thick I could feel it throbbing inside me. I could have come like that, but then he grabbed my hair, tugging my head back, and started fucking me fast and hard. The friction was incredible, every thrust coaxing high-pitched moans from my throat. His fingers dug into my skin as he braced himself with his other hand on my hip, and I hoped he would leave a mark. That tomorrow morning, I'd have something visible on my body to remember him by.

"Fuck," I whimpered, leaning into it, my breasts bouncing hard with each thrust.

He went back to teasing me again, easing his pace until I begged him to go faster, then pumping into me so hard and quick I had to beg him to slow down. I loved every second of it. My face was pressed into a pillow, the sheets crumpled tight in my fists as each swing of his cock pushed me closer and closer to the edge.

"I love the way you feel," Stefan groaned, his hand slapping my ass again. "I love how tight your wet little pussy is around my cock."

"Yes," I panted, spreading my knees as far apart as I could, opening my body even wider to him, wanting to feel him even deeper. "Fuck me," I begged. "Fuck me hard."

"You're perfect for me." Stefan gripped my ass harder, groaning as he pounded into me. "You're mine."

His words made me even wetter, my entire body shuddering with the waves of pleasure he sent crashing through me. It still wasn't enough. I wanted more. Wanted to feel every last inch of him inside me.

"Harder," I begged, needing this, knowing it might be my last chance to give myself to him. Knowing this might be goodbye. "I need more."

Stefan pulled out and flipped me over onto my back. Then he turned on the small bedside lamp so he could rake his gaze over my naked body in the dim light, and when our eyes locked I could see the lust gleaming in his.

"You really are perfect," he said.

Climbing over me on the bed, he pushed my knees up toward my chest so I was completely split open for him. As I waited for him to slam into my pussy, I could feel my heart hammering. When he finally thrust inside me again, filling me up, I moaned along with him. We were both breathing hard, gasping for air as his long, hard cock stroked in and out of me in a blissful rhythm. I couldn't get enough.

"More," I ordered. "You feel so good."

He slipped his hand down and swept his thumb in circles over my clit, just above where his cock was fucking me, and my entire body jerked with pleasure.

"I love you, Tori," Stefan groaned as I thrusted in time with him, my body moving of its own volition, searching, seeking release. "I'll always love you. I promise."

Hearing his words, my eyes began to burn again and I tilted my hips up off the bed, forcing his cock even deeper. I didn't know if he would remember his promises tomorrow when he was fully sober, or if he would regret them. Didn't know if he'd remember how we'd made love like this. But I didn't care. All I cared about was taking as much of him as I could in this moment and holding on.

"Take me," I told him. "As hard as you can."

He did as I asked, fucking me even harder, almost

violently, his hips drumming against mine as my head hit the headboard. I lost myself in the movements of his body, in the way he took me, the feel of his cock inside of me, of his fingers against my clit. Hot sparks were twisting in my core, faster, hotter, deeper. I yelled his name, finally climaxing in an explosion of sensation and pleasure. My pussy clenched around him, my fingers digging into his shoulders as I came in waves, harder and stronger than I ever had before.

Leaning over me, Stefan kept fucking me, driving his cock into my orgasm, my body no longer my own, his body no longer his. My release began to ebb, the contractions slowing, and then just when it seemed completely impossible, the hints of another orgasm began to spread through me. I slid my hands down to Stefan's biceps, squeezing, holding on as tight as I could.

"I'm coming," I told him, tears pricking my eyes. "I'm coming again."

"I love you," he said, his voice hoarse in my ear. "I love you. Only you."

He dropped his lips onto mine as he fucked me hard, drawing out my second orgasm, making me cry out beneath him, moaning my pleasure into the quiet of the room. Then he spilled his own release deep and hot inside of me, whispering my name as he came.

TORI

CHAPTER 5

Sipping my coffee at the kitchen table, I looked out at the gorgeous view of Chicago's iconic skyline, the icy blue waters of Lake Michigan lapping at the shore, the expanse of trees and green space along Lake Shore Drive. It was the kind of cold, clear day that reminded you that winter could be beautiful too.

If it wasn't a Monday, I would have just burrowed under the covers and tried to read in bed all day, but I had classes to attend. On top of that, Stefan was still asleep in the guest room, and I planned to avoid talking to him until he was ready to tell me what he'd decided to do about Anja and the boy. So here I was, drinking coffee by myself, feeling completely at a loss.

Waking up in my husband's arms that morning had almost killed me. I'd told myself that the sex last night could be a goodbye, but in the light of day I realized I wasn't ready for goodbye. Not at all. I didn't want to be apart from him, either. But I forced myself up and out of bed, leaving him to his probable hangover, knowing that once I left him, I'd have to give him—and myself—some breathing room.

At least I was the one controlling my distance from Stefan. As much as I knew he'd need his space, I didn't think I'd be able to handle hearing the words come out of his mouth—I figured it was better to just keep myself away, let him take some time to process all the things he was dealing with.

If I was honest, though, I had to admit that part of me was avoiding him on purpose. I was hiding. I was afraid of what he'd say about Anja and his son if I confronted him right now. Maybe if he took a few days or even weeks to think it all over, he'd realize there were plenty of ways to work out the logistics of his new family life without ending our marriage. The last thing I wanted was for him to feel pressured, like he had to rush to make any big decisions.

I set my empty cup in the sink and padded down the hall to the master bedroom to get ready for school. It would be best to let him sleep. Get out of the condo before he woke up.

School wouldn't be much of an escape, though. I'd have to put on a happy face for my friends and teachers, focus all my energy on paying attention in class instead of wallowing over Stefan, and hope that my inner turmoil wouldn't affect any of my lessons.

My shower was quick, but it was impossible to ignore the bruises on my ass, and how sore I still was from the hard, intense sex we'd had. It made me ache for Stefan all over again.

Last night had been amazing, and I regretted nothing... but he'd obviously been at least somewhat drunk and likely not thinking straight, given the shock and the alcohol combined. I was sure he'd wake up today with his priorities sorted out, and I knew I might not be at the top of that list anymore—or even on that list at all. He'd been searching for

Anja for years, after all. And that didn't even account for the reality of their son.

Remembering the adorable, dark-haired boy with my husband's eyes, my stomach twisted. Stefan had a son now. Things were going to be completely different, and it would be stupid to pretend otherwise.

As I put on my makeup, I couldn't help obsessing over every little thing Stefan had said to me the night before. He'd said that he loved me, only me, and that he always would. He'd promised. He'd said I was his and that I was perfect for him. But he'd been drunk, too, and under an incredible amount of stress. Maybe the heat of the moment had pulled those words from his lips. It would be foolish to hold on to them, to hope that they were true.

Even though he was sleeping in the next room, he already felt miles away. It was torture.

I blinked back tears, dabbing at my now-wet mascara with a tissue, knowing I had to get my mind off the situation before I completely fell apart and couldn't make it to class. That wasn't an option. I had a test in Latin today, and finals were rapidly approaching so every point counted. Even one missed class could compromise my grades, and as pathetic as it sounded, my linguistics program was all I had to keep me going right now.

Latin vocabulary usually always put me in a good mood —how the words came out of your mouth reminiscent of the magic spells from Harry Potter, the way they so often sounded familiar since Latin formed the roots of many modern languages. But I struggled to find that joy today as I pulled out my school binder and ran down the vocab list in my notes.

Abduco, the root of abduct, meaning to detach or withdraw, to lead or take away.

Blanditia, the root of blandishments, meaning attractions, charm, allurement.

Contamino, the root of contaminate, meaning to pollute or infect.

It wasn't the distraction I'd hoped for. Everything reminded me of Stefan. The way he'd withdraw from me, leaving me bereft of his charm, our marriage contaminated by the truths Anja had hidden away for so long. I might lose everything.

Could I count on Stefan's words from last night? Would he even remember what we'd shared? Or worse—would he remember, and regret it?

Turning the page, I saw Gavin's square, blocky handwriting instead of my own neat cursive. These were the notes I'd borrowed from him when I had been either too lost in heartbreak over Stefan or too head over heels for him to focus in class.

Gavin Chase, younger brother of Frank Chase, agent with the Department of Defense. Looking at Gavin's pages reminded me that he was now a part of this whole mess as well. That what was happening right now with the Zoric family was bigger than my marriage, bigger than just Stefan and I—and always had been, even before we knew about Anja and her son.

Regardless of our personal issues, I was still committed to helping my husband take down KZ Modeling and its sex trafficking ring from the inside. With Gavin and Frank's help.

As I slid into a pair of jeans and a thick-knit cashmere sweater, I marveled at how worried I'd been about meeting Konstantin for dinner last night. How Stefan and I had spent hours going over what I should say to his father in order to convince him that I would be loyal to the Zoric family. All that practicing, all those words. For nothing. Konstantin had barely looked at me last night, let alone asked me to make some declaration of allegiance to him.

Did my loyalty even matter now? Had my father-in-law completely dismissed me the moment Anja came back into the picture? Did he see her as my neat and easy replacement?

I couldn't think about it. I'd just have to focus on getting through this one day at a time.

Heading into the closet I shared with Stefan, I pulled out my favorite brown boots and tugged them on. Then I hoisted my backpack over my shoulder and walked into the hall.

Just in time to catch Stefan coming out of the guest room.

So much for slipping off to school before he woke up.

"Where are you going in such a hurry?" he asked, his voice sounding a little hoarse, whether from the lingering effects of sleep or from the alcohol he'd drowned himself in last night, I wasn't sure.

"It's Monday," I reminded him. "I have class all day. Remember?"

Looking at him was difficult. He was in last night's wrinkled clothes, his shirt not even tucked in. His feet were bare and his hair was a mess. And yet, to me, he looked perfect.

I wanted to drop my bag at my feet and run into his arms. I wanted him to take me to bed. To hold me. To tell me again that he loved me. But I couldn't. I had to get out of here.

Before I could turn away, Stefan reached for my arm. "Don't you think we should talk first?" he asked. "Why were you sleeping in the spare room last night?"

My throat felt tight, but I refused to cry in front of him.

"Can we talk about this later?" I said, pulling away. "I'm going to be late."

A look of confusion crossed his face, or maybe it was just his hangover. "Are you mad at me?" He ran a hand through his hair.

"Of course not," I said, flashing a fake smile.

And it was true. I wasn't mad at all. I was just trying to keep myself together so I wouldn't be destroyed when he told me he was leaving me. Which was something I absolutely couldn't deal with at the moment.

I looked at my phone, pretending I had a notification. "My Uber's downstairs," I lied. "I'm not mad, really. See you tonight. I'll probably be home late."

With that, I kissed him on the cheek, spun on my heel, and practically bolted out of the condo.

STEFAN

CHAPTER 6

All I could think about was how quickly my life had imploded in the last twelve hours.

Tori was blowing me off right when I needed her most, Anja had shown up out of nowhere, I had a son that I'd never met, and my father was still an asshole. Add to that how precarious my plan to take down KZ Modeling was, and it was almost too much to handle.

I was at a loss over my wife. The way she was acting so distant today had me worried. Obviously she had to be feeling some shock and upset over the whole Anja and Max situation—who wouldn't? I was upset too—but it almost seemed like Tori was trying to punish me for it, and I wasn't sure why. Especially considering how close we'd been in bed, just hours ago.

Had I done something wrong? The events at the penthouse last night had been a total mindfuck, but Tori was the one who'd insisted that I stay at my father's place with Anja. I had wanted Tori to stay, but she'd refused. What should I have done? Put off talking to Anja and gone home with my wife, instead of leaving her to sit in our empty condo and go to bed alone in the guest room? Should I have pushed harder to keep her at my side, so she'd have been with me during the discussion with Anja? Tori had been so adamant. Maybe I should've fought her.

I went into the kitchen and poured myself some of the coffee Tori had made, gulping it down black and lukewarm, and then stuck a slice of bread in the toaster oven. My mouth was dry, my head pounding. I was beyond hungover from the whiskey and from skipping both lunch and dinner the day prior. I'd been so focused on prepping Tori for the big Sunday night dinner at my father's that I hadn't bothered taking care of myself. And now I was paying for it.

As I forced down the dry toast, I went over the events of last night. I could still remember every moment in detail, from the confrontation with Anja to arriving home and finding the bedroom empty. For one, long, horrible moment, I had thought that Tori had left me.

Not that I would have blamed her. The whole thing was a fucking mess. Anja. Max. My father. Who wouldn't want to get as far away from that nightmare as possible?

I'd found her easily enough in the guest bedroom, her body curled up almost self-defensively under the pile of covers. My heart ached at the sight, at the realization that she'd hidden herself away from me. And then the way she'd acted this morning. It was killing me.

I wanted Tori at my side. I needed her to help me through this, to be my wife and partner. Somehow, though, it seemed like I had fucked everything up. Being a husband was new to me. Being a good husband was even newer. How was I supposed to know how to act, what to say? My own father had never provided much of an example on that front. I was doing my best.

Speaking of which—how the hell was I supposed to

know how to be a dad? That was the newest role of all. I could barely stand to think about it. Knowing that I owed it to Max to step up after all these years helped, though. In a way, it took the decision right out of my hands. Of course I'd be there for him. However I could. I just didn't know where to start.

I had barely gotten a good look at the boy before he was taken away to bed, but I'd seen his green eyes. Zoric eyes. They'd looked like a perfect mix of mine and Anja's blue-green.

Coming home to Tori, my mind blown, I'd stripped off my clothes and crawled into the guest bed, automatically reaching for her. I'd wanted her so much, needed to be inside her with a primal need that I'd never felt before. It hadn't taken much to wake her, had taken even less to seduce her. Tori had always been easy for me to read, so I'd made it a point to learn everything that turned her on. I knew she liked it when I took charge, when I dominated her, and I was always more than happy to comply. Her body had been warm and welcoming under my hands, and I'd fucked her until she was panting and begging beneath me.

The tight clench of her pussy as she came had been nearly enough to set me off as well, but I'd managed to hold on for a bit longer, wanting to savor the feel of her body against mine. I'd wanted to possess her, to fill her up, to claim her completely. And she'd wanted that, too. I could tell by the way her body reacted to mine, how quickly she came again on my cock.

I'd fucked her hard, but she had liked it, had begged for it. I'd given her everything she'd asked for, whispering words of love and desire the whole time. I'd meant it all, even if the alcohol had loosened my tongue more than I had expected.

None of it had been a lie. I loved her. I needed her. I wanted to believe she felt the same.

My head had ached when I woke up that morning, but finding the bed empty I'd dressed quickly. When I'd stepped out of the guest room, I found her standing in the hallway, frozen, looking like she'd been caught sneaking out. And then she'd proceeded to evade me.

She'd denied her odd behavior when I'd called her out on it, but I saw right through the act. Her eyes were too wide, her smile too bright and quick. Even her voice had sounded off, higher pitched and cheerier than its usual timbre. She'd left in a hurry.

I didn't understand. She was being distant—first insisting she leave me alone with Anja at my dad's, then coming home and sleeping the guest room, and then trying to sneak out this morning while I was sleeping. What was she playing at? Why wasn't she being honest with me?

It had taken all of my strength to stay upright while I questioned her. Now that she was gone, I slumped in my chair. I was exhausted. Everything ached. After finishing my breakfast, I took a few ibuprofen and got in the shower, hoping the hot water would help me think.

As I stood under the spray, I realized that I couldn't put off my paternal duties any longer than I already had—and since Tori had said she would be gone until later tonight, I might as well tackle the kid issue right away. Decision made, I started feeling better already.

I toweled off and got dressed, putting on my usual uniform of a perfectly tailored suit, Italian shoes, sleek designer watch, and a slim silk tie. When I looked in the mirror, I saw what I needed to see: someone who had their shit together. Someone formidable. Someone who wasn't going to be pushed around.

Then I grabbed my cell phone and dialed my father.

"I'm not going to make it into the office today," I told him, keeping my voice calm and collected. "Figured I should take some time off and get to know the kid."

He couldn't know how thrown I'd been by all of this, or that I was worried about my marriage or Tori or anything else. I had to appear unflustered. Untouchable.

"You have my blessing," my father said. I could hear the glee in his tone, could tell he was gloating over all his vile plans coming together, whatever they were. "Take all the time you need, Stefan. Nothing's more important than family."

After asking for Anja's number, I'd gotten off the phone, hating him even more.

As I dialed her number, I found myself pacing in the living room, unable to sit still. I wasn't nervous about talking to her—I was nervous about seeing my kid. She wouldn't deny me that, based on the conversation we'd had last night, but I had no idea how I was supposed to act around Max, or if he'd even accept me as his mother's 'friend.' Springing the whole dad thing on him today wasn't part of my plan, but I was hoping to at least start building some kind of relationship with him. Anja and I could discuss the logistics of it later, once I had a better idea of what I was capable of offering, and if the boy seemed open to seeing more of me.

"Hello?" she answered.

"Anja. It's Stefan," I said.

"Hey. I'm glad you called," she said, sounding relieved.

Hearing her voice, I realized I was still angry at her. Even though most of my fury was rightfully directed at my father for instigating and enabling the whole disappearance, I still couldn't help feeling frustrated and betrayed over the fact that Anja had been fully capable of reaching out to me for the last eight plus years—had had every opportunity to contact me and tell me that we had a son—but instead chose to remain silent and hidden.

And I still didn't know if I could trust her.

It was then that I realized I didn't know what name to use. She'd mentioned that my father had helped her get a whole new identity; surely she wouldn't go by Anja anymore.

"What name do you use now?" I asked. "Should I call you something else?"

She laughed. "My friends call me Annette. But Anja is good. It's nice to hear it again."

"Okay. So. The reason I'm calling is because I've given it some thought, and I feel like we should spend some time together," I began.

"Yes of course," she said eagerly. "Max too?"

"Max is the only reason we have to spend any time together," I said. "And if he was over eighteen, I would be calling him, not you."

I wasn't trying to be harsh, but I wanted to be clear with her from the beginning. This wasn't about her and me. This wasn't about what we'd had or even about the declaration of love she had dropped at my feet last night. This was about Max. This was about our son.

"Okay," Anja said, but some of the happiness had gone out of her voice. "I understand."

"I took the day off," I went on. "Pick a place we can go. Somewhere Max would like."

"Somewhere Max would like," Anja repeated slowly, taking a moment to think. "Why don't we go to the zoo? He loves animals. Those are his favorite channels on TV, too."

I filed away this information in my mind for later, committed to learning everything I could about my son. It would also help me break the ice when I saw him. Part of me wanted to beg Anja for a full run-down, to take notes on all his likes and dislikes, to get whatever information I could that would make it easier to build a relationship with the kid. But I also wanted to learn about him on my own. Do the hard work myself. Let Max tell me what he liked, and show me who he was. Children were more complicated than people gave them credit for, but I was willing to take the time to figure him out. Hopefully he'd feel the same about me.

"I'll send a car over to pick you up at my dad's place," I told her. "My driver will wait at the curb. Meet me at the front gates." I hung up before she could say anything else.

Maybe it was cold, maybe it was cruel, but Anja's feelings weren't my priority right now.

Tori's were. Unfortunately, she'd left that morning without giving me a clear understanding of what she needed or wanted from me. I had no idea what to do. But as I'd learned in the past, when it came to Tori, she valued honesty and openness. I could manage that.

Quickly I texted her, telling her what I was doing with my day.

Took off work—going to the zoo to get to know Max better. Anja will accompany us. Let me know if this is a problem. I don't want you to be uncomfortable with any of this.

I waited for a response. And waited.

Nothing.

I knew she was in class, but I couldn't wait all day. I also couldn't imagine she'd have a problem with my plans, and I hated the idea of canceling on my kid last minute. I kept an eye on my cell until I had to walk out the door to meet Anja and Max, but Tori never replied.

STEFAN

CHAPTER 7

The hardest thing about trying to figure out this whole dad thing was that my own had never provided much of an example. Growing up motherless in my father's house, I'd learned early on that his responsibilities included putting a roof over his kids' heads and meals on the table—any needs we had beyond that were best met by anyone else but him. Looking back, I couldn't help wondering what my childhood would have been like if I'd had the kind of dad who was around more, who took me to Cubs games or encouraged me to join the Boy Scouts or even just showed up once in a while for school plays or feigned interest in my model planes. I'd grown up so fast and buried my feelings for so long that I was only now starting to realize how much it had affected me. But it wouldn't do any good to dwell on it. It was time to step up.

"Welcome to the Brookfield Zoo," the employee at the ticket counter said, his voice crackling through the speaker in the glass divider.

"Three tickets, please," I said. "One—no, two adult—and one child admission."

I slid my card across the counter and the employee swiped it, slid it back to me, and smiled as the tickets printed out.

"Have a great day with your family," he said, passing me the tickets along with a map.

For a moment I froze, the word practically knocking the wind out of me. *My family.*

"Sir?" he said. "You need something else?"

"Uh, no. Thank you. I'm great," I said, shuffling away.

Family. I had a family now. Tori was my family, and obviously so were the Zorics, both immediate and extended. But this kid made me the head of my own little clan—Max was the first of my bloodline. It was wild.

Map and tickets in hand, I went back and stood at the front gates of the zoo, waiting for Anja and Max. I saw families of all kinds, nannies pushing babies in strollers, older folks with their grandkids, a few school groups all lined up in their bright colored coats. I felt out of place in my suit and tie. Everyone else was dressed casually, and even though the day was warm for November, I saw a variety of mismatched hats, scarves, and gloves. Still, this was who I was. Professional, put-together, buttoned-up.

Thinking better of it, I took off my tie and slipped it into my coat pocket. The last thing I wanted to do was intimidate my kid.

I checked my watch and tried not to start pacing, tried not to get cold feet.

People talked about maternal instincts, but you didn't often hear about paternal ones. Was I cut out for fatherhood? I just wasn't sure. All I could do was give it my best shot.

Pulling out my phone, I was about to call Anja and see where they were, but when I looked up I saw her and Max walking toward me through the parking lot. She looked classy and sleek in head-to-toe black and big sunglasses, her hair pulled back in a ponytail, and Max was wearing a red puffer jacket and matching hat, his dark hair curling out from the bottom.

When they came up to me, Anja stepped to the side and said, "Max, I want you to meet Stefan. He's Mommy's old friend. A man who's always been important to me."

Her words were like a knife to the gut. Suddenly I felt like I was the one who'd given up on her, who hadn't been around when she needed me most. I should have found her. Should have fought harder to get her back. But if I had, I wouldn't have Tori now. And I couldn't imagine my life without her. I hoped to god I wasn't losing her. That this wasn't all a mistake.

"Hello," I said, resisting the urge to kneel, trying not to tower over the boy.

Max looked up at me, studying my face curiously for a moment, and then grinned shyly, revealing a missing front tooth. "Hi. I'm Max."

Then he stuck out a small hand for me to shake. I was completely undone.

"Good to meet you, Max," I said, shaking his hand firmly but gently.

Up close I could see how much he resembled Anja—he had her same wide-set eyes and high cheekbones, the same exact shape of the ears. Like most young kids, he also had round cheeks and a snub nose, his with a spray of freckles across it. Objectively speaking, he really was adorable.

"I got us tickets already," I said pulling them out, "so why don't we head inside and check out some of these animals? Max, you want to look at the map?"

"Sure," he said, taking it from me and studying it. "Hey, look, there's a swamp in here!"

"Wow," Anja said. "You're gonna get to see some big alligators."

"Uh huh," he said, flashing that shy grin again.

"You're into alligators?" I asked him.

He nodded. "Yup. Did you know that their ancestors were *dinosaurs?*" he informed me solemnly.

"That makes sense," I said, scrambling to keep our conversation going. "You, uh, you like dinosaurs?"

"Of course," Max said. "Come on."

With that, he charged into the zoo.

Inside, Anja kept a hand on Max's shoulder to guide him while he pored over the map, and I kept a little distance. I had no idea what I was doing—kid stuff was new to me. Even hanging out with my siblings when we were little, it never felt like I was doing much besides taking their lead. Pushing toy cars or plastic dragons around on the carpet with Emzee or riding bikes with Luka. Reading books out loud to them once I started school and got a library card.

"Do you like dinosaurs?" Max asked, looking at me over his shoulder.

"Yeah," I said. "I mean, I used to."

That seemed to relax him in a big way, and I saw him nodding to himself as he fell in step beside me.

"So what's your favorite? My mom's is the pterodactyl because it can fly."

Anja shot me a little smile, as if apologizing. But it didn't bother me. The more he was able to open up, the more I'd learn about him, and the easier it'd be to engage. I could only imagine how awkward the day would be if the conversation was all on me.

"Probably a T. rex," I said. "King of the dinos."

Max nodded. "Yeah, but not the biggest. Gigantosaurus was bigger."

"Giga*noto*saurus," Anja corrected.

"That's what I said," Max huffed. "Spinosaurus was bigger, too. That's my favorite 'cause they could swim. They had these spikes all over their back to keep off predators."

I had to smile. My kid was an encyclopedia. He definitely didn't get that from me.

"The Swamp!" he announced, pointing at the building with its triangular rooftop and triple-arched entryway. "We made it."

Heading into the building, we were immediately hit with a fug of warm, humid air, and the sound of running water. There were cypress trees and ferns and palms, the light filtered as if we really were walking through a swamp. It was a whole ecosystem. Max loved it.

After that initial walk through the swamp building, we rode the carousel and went into the butterfly enclosure, per Anja's request. The day seemed to get easier, with Max getting less shy with each new experience, excited to talk to me about every new animal we saw. We took a break to have a pizza lunch, followed by Dippin' Dots—Max insisted, despite the cool weather, telling Anja, "It's not for me, it's for my friend. We can share!"—and my chest felt tight as I realized Max's 'friend' was me.

As we strolled around the Reptiles and Birds building, taking in the Komodo dragons, iguanas, and lizards, I couldn't help feeling proud of the kid Max had turned out to be. Anja deserved a lot of credit for raising him so well.

Despite everything, I felt myself softening toward her. A little. Even though I didn't agree with what she had done and why she had chosen to keep her location and Max a secret from me for all these years, I could understand—given my involvement with KZM—why she had. I could also imagine that even with my father's money and support, it hadn't been easy to raise Max on her own.

That didn't mean anything was going to happen between the two of us, though.

"Re-tic-u-lated python," Max read out loud. "It's the world's longest snake. Cool!"

I looked into the enclosure alongside him and smiled. "That is pretty cool. Why do you think he's got that pattern on him?"

"It's for camouflage," he said. "A lot of animals have it. It's like a disguise."

Anja and I watched proudly as Max went from one tank to the next, reading the plaques next to the enclosures to us. Occasionally I'd help him spot scaly animals that were hiding out in corners or under rocks, away from prying eyes. He was having a blast.

Max was so sweet, so genuinely good, and so curious about everything around him. Nothing like me as a kid. Losing my mom when I was six had made me turn inward, and I'd been fairly closed-off emotionally, and resistant to authority figures. I was so glad Max wasn't like that. In fact, the more I thought about it, the more he reminded me of Tori. He had the same bright intelligence, inquisitive nature, and kind heart.

Then again, everything reminded me of Tori. No matter what I did or where I was, my thoughts always seemed to return to her.

Not for the first time that day, I wished she was here with us. That she was the woman at my side. She'd know exactly what to say, how to act around a kid like Max. In fact, she'd probably be great at it. I checked my phone again, hoping for a response, hoping for any indication that she had gotten my message. Nothing.

"Hey, buddy—you wanna go see the Big Cats?" Max was saying, interrupting my thoughts. He held up the map, now scrunched and limp in his fist, and pointed. "There's lions."

He was calling me his buddy. "Sure," I said.

"Let's go!" he exclaimed, taking my hand and dragging me along.

I looked back at Anja and she just shrugged and smiled, trailing us in her heels. It was obvious by the way she interacted with Max that she loved him. That she'd do anything for him.

"You two go ahead," she said. "I'll catch up."

As we left the reptiles and birds behind, I realized that Anja had been especially quiet all day, even deferring to me if Max asked her a question about the exhibits. She was letting me get to know him, one-on-one. I appreciated that.

Walking hand-in-hand with my kid, it was hard not to dwell on all the lost time. His entire life, I'd been a stranger to him—hell, I still was—when I could have been there for him. Could have been his father. A real father.

My heart twisted. I'd never thought much about being a parent or having a family, but spending the day with Max was forcing me to think about what I wanted. And that was to have a solid relationship with my son—and any future kids I might have. But what did Tori want?

"Looks like you found the lions," I told Max as we stopped in front of the enclosure.

A pride of females lounged, some blinking in our direction, others stretched out for a nap. The male was further off, perched on a rock.

"In the wild," I said, "the females do all the hunting. They're fierce."

"My mom's like that too," Max said seriously.

Anja came up behind us then, and Max stretched out his free hand to grab hers. With our kid in the middle, holding onto both of us, and the content smiles on all our faces, we probably looked like the picture of a happy, perfect family to anyone who was walking by. No one would guess that this was my first formal outing with my child, that he still didn't know I was his father, and that his mother had been hiding from me for almost the last decade.

Still, it didn't matter what anyone else thought. I knew the true score.

I glanced down at Max. "You want to check out the tigers?"

"Yeah!"

The rapid click of a camera sounded from my right and my head snapped instantly in that direction. A young man was casually turning away, tucking something into the black bag at his hip. A camera? It had sounded like he was taking pictures, but this was a zoo and there were plenty of people taking photos all around us with their phones or digital cameras.

Max had already run off toward the tigers, and Anja was chasing him down. I followed after them, trying to ignore the uneasy feeling in my chest.

This wouldn't be the first time someone had tried to photograph me while I was out in public. I wasn't famous, per se, but I was definitely recognizable due to the high profile of KZ Modeling. The agency was never far from the public eye, and that meant occasionally getting recognized or having people attempt stealthy cell phone pictures that would sometimes end up on the gossip sites. Usually Luka (drunk and disorderly) or Emzee (glammed up for an event or an art show) was the target, though, not me. The worst was when the photos showed up on the internet immediately. I was a private person, and it always felt so invasive.

Thank god I'd texted Tori earlier about my plans. I'd hate for her to see any images of Anja and Max and I today and get the wrong idea.

I checked my phone again, but there was still no response from her. I tried not to read into it too much, but given her behavior that morning, I couldn't help wondering if she was ignoring me on purpose. If our marriage had crossed a line last night, and there was no going back.

TORI

CHAPTER 8

I dropped the vocab test off on my Latin professor's desk as I headed out the classroom door, hoping my years of high school Latin would be enough to carry me through. My mind had been miles away during the test.

The truth was, school had been an absolute daze all day. I couldn't focus, couldn't stop thinking about Stefan. My marriage. My stepson. I had to talk to Stefan, as soon as possible. Putting it off had been a poor choice on my part. There was no way I'd be able to focus on my classes or anything else if I kept avoiding the conversation we had to have. Better to just do it now. Rip off the Band-Aid.

You have to be strong, I told myself. *You can do this.*

Knowing he'd be at work didn't make me feel any better. He might not even pick up my call. Maybe I should just ask him to come home early from work so we could sit down and have dinner together, just the two of us, and figure out where things stood.

But as I dug around frantically in my bag, I realized my phone wasn't in there. It had been in my hand on my way out the door that morning, but...no. I'd set it down on the entry table in order to put on my coat and scarf, and then I'd grabbed my keys and backpack but not my cell. Being in such a hurry to get out of the condo had made me careless.

Well, then. Tonight. I'd call him the second I got home.

Getting through my last class of the day seemed even more agonizing now that I knew I had no way to reach out to Stefan. I wondered what he was thinking. Had he already chosen between me and Anja? Was his mind made up? Had last night been his way of saying goodbye?

I knew I had to brace myself for that possibility.

The minutes seemed to inch by and I found that I was paying more attention to the clock on the wall than the sign language exercises we were supposed to be doing in groups of three. The other students were kind in correcting me, but I found it impossible to stay on track. What was wrong with me? Getting this linguistics degree had always been my dream, and here I was in one of the country's most prestigious programs, supported by a brilliant and committed faculty, and I was fucking it up. Maybe Stefan leaving would be for the best. Maybe then I'd be forced to focus on my education and my career, like I had always intended.

But that thought didn't make me feel any better.

After my ASL professor dismissed the class, I was planning to hail a cab and go straight to the condo. But as I was walking out of the classroom, I heard a familiar gabble of voices at the end of the hall. Looking up, I saw a bunch of students I recognized standing in a little cluster. Everyone was talking, laughing, and gesturing animatedly.

Had something happened? Was it something to do with the program? Something I needed to know about? Walking closer, I picked out my friends Audrey, Lila, and Diane all huddled around Audrey's cell phone, absorbed by whatever was on the screen.

Impatient to know what all the fuss was about, I came up behind them and peeked over Audrey's black leather-clad shoulder.

My stomach dropped at what I saw.

Pulled up on the screen was a celebrity gossip site called *The Dirt*, featuring a photo of Stefan in a sharp suit, Anja looking sophisticated and gorgeous in a black ensemble, and the little boy I'd seen at Konstantin's last night, wearing a red down jacket. They were standing together next to a lion enclosure at a zoo. The boy smiled up at Stefan, and they were holding hands. His other hand was tucked into Anja's, and the former KZ model was looking adoringly at both my husband and their son. They were all glowing and happy, the perfect family. A family that didn't include me. The caption read, "NEWLYWED KZM SUCCESSOR STEPPING OUT ALREADY?"

So it was true. I'd lost Stefan.

I couldn't tear my eyes away from how the kid was holding Stefan's hand. He seemed so blissfully happy to be with both of his parents. How the hell could I stand in the way of that?

The realization gutted me, and I rasped out a shocked breath. It was loud enough that my friends turned and noticed me and immediately went silent.

My cheeks were burning, my pulse pounding, and I desperately wished I'd never walked over to the group. I wished I'd never seen the picture, either, but I especially wished I hadn't seen it surrounded by a crowd of my friends and classmates. Now everyone was staring at me, their expressions a mixture of pity and sympathy. I didn't want either.

"I'm so sorry, Tori," Audrey said gently, tucking her phone into her pocket.

"About what?" I said, forcing a smile onto my face. "You think that *National Enquirer* type crap has anything to do with reality? She's an old friend of the family. She and her kid are just in town for the week."

"Oh," Audrey said, but I could tell she didn't believe me by the way she was exchanging a sympathetic look with the others. "So your husband is just...taking them out sightseeing?"

"Yeah. Just keeping them entertained. They've been friends for like ten years," I said, trying to make my voice sound bored and casual. "You know how those gossips sites are—always trying to make drama out of nothing."

"That makes total sense," Diane said, coming to my rescue as usual. "She looks like one of KZM's models. Is that how they met?"

"That's exactly it," I said. "They go way back. She's retired now."

"Of *course*," Lila said, sounding sincere. "People just love gossip."

"Yeah," Audrey agreed. "Scandal sells. I mean, and just because you have *history* with someone, it doesn't mean you're automatically getting back together every time you go out."

Ah. Was it that obvious, judging by a single photo, that Stefan and Anja had been an item? Or was it just blatantly apparent that they were still attracted to each other?

Lila went on, "I'm sure he's totally over her. I mean, he's married to you now, right?"

"Right..." Except I didn't know how much longer we might be married for.

My chest felt tight, and it was getting hard to breathe. I could feel a full-blown panic attack coming on.

"What's going on here?" a familiar voice interrupted.

Gavin stepped into the center of the circle, breaking up our little group, and my tunnel vision instantly cleared. I had never been more glad to see him.

"Catch you later, Tori," Lila said, scooting off arm in arm with Audrey. "Don't let the fake news get you down."

"Call me if you need anything," Diane said, hanging back just long enough to give me a tight side-hug and leave a cloud of patchouli lingering in her wake.

The rest of the other students all seemed to scatter as well, and then Gavin and I were alone in the hallway. The moment the coast was clear, I dropped the smile I had been forcing.

"What's wrong?" Gavin asked, drawing me toward a quiet corner nook and squeezing my shoulder gently.

My friends seemed to buy my cover story, but I couldn't fake it for him, too—and I knew I didn't have to. If anyone would understand, it would be Gavin. Stepping closer, I pressed my forehead against his chest, letting him hold me as I took several deep breaths. There was nothing I could do to erase the image of Stefan and Anja and their son. Every time I closed my eyes I saw the three of them, smiling and happy together.

"Are you okay? Did something happen with KZ?" Gavin asked in a whisper, stroking my back. "Talk to me. Is something going down?"

I leaned back, grateful that I wasn't crying. "Yes and no. Last night we went to see him. We were supposed to have dinner and talk. But when we got to his place—there was no talk. Konstantin found Stefan's old girlfriend and brought her there," I said.

Gavin frowned, looking confused. "Okay," he said slowly. "So what happened?"

"She had her son with her," I continued. "He's...Stefan's son."

His eyes went wide. "Holy shit."

I took another deep breath. "Stefan has been searching for her for years. She disappeared when he was seventeen, but he had no idea that she was pregnant. That he had a son."

As I recounted everything that had happened in the past day or so, Gavin listened silently, his face full of concern but nonjudgmental. I detailed everything, from Konstantin springing Anja and her son on me and Stefan, to the conversation they'd had last night that I hadn't been around to witness, all the way up to the paparazzi photo that was now showing up on the gossip sites that seemed to show Stefan stepping out on me. The only part I left out was the emotional, sexually charged night I'd spent with my husband. Even if Gavin was over his crush on me, he still wasn't the person to confide in about that particular aspect of my life.

When I was done, he walked me to the coffee kiosk and bought me a chamomile tea. Then he led me outside and sat me down on a nearby bench where we wouldn't be disturbed. He took a breath and then reached for my free hand.

"Can I be honest with you, Tori?" he asked, squeezing my hand between his.

I nodded, sipping the hot drink, not sure if I really wanted to hear what he had to say.

"You know I've never been the biggest fan of your husband," he began.

"Yeah. I know," I said, laughing wryly.

"And selfishly, part of me hopes that things don't work out, just so I can finally have a chance with you." He cleared his throat and looked me in the eyes. "But I gotta say, when I talked to him myself, it was obvious that he cares about you very much."

My heart leapt.

"So, as your friend, my advice is to just talk to him." He said this almost grudgingly.

"Really?" I managed. Gavin's words were reassuring, and unbelievably touching. He was a true friend—one who really cared about me, even if it meant we'd never be anything more.

He nodded. "He's always acted like a man who was crazy about you. One who would do anything to make you happy. I don't think it's over between you two. Not by a long shot."

"Thank you," I told him.

I felt a little better, but I was still so overwhelmed. Tears burned the corners of my eyes and my bottom lip trembled.

"Hey." Gavin gave me a sympathetic look and opened his arms to me. "Come here."

Setting my tea down, I leaned into his embrace and let my tears fall as his arms wrapped around me.

"You're okay," he soothed. "It's going to be okay."

I knew there might be witnesses around, or even photos of this scene between me and Gavin—photos that might get back to Konstantin later—but I didn't care. It was safe to assume that even with Anja back in the picture, my father-in-law was still having me watched, but I wasn't going to build my life around the man's opinion of me or the way I lived my life.

Still, there was a twinge of guilt about what Stefan might think. After all, Bruce was out there somewhere watching over me. He was never far off, and sometimes I'd even bring my new bodyguard a coffee in between my classes. There was a definite possibility that he'd send pictures to my husband right away, that Stefan was already looking at them now.

But I didn't care.

As petty as it seemed, after seeing him with Anja and their son, I couldn't help feeling like he deserved to be hurt, too. That was, if my actions still had the power to affect him that way.

If he still cared about me at all.

TORI

CHAPTER 9

Stefan was waiting for me when I got back to the condo. I don't know if I was more shocked by the fact that he was home so early, or that he seemed to be in such a great mood as he sat on the couch. The smile he flashed glancing up at me was almost painfully joyful. He looked younger, too, the recent stress and familiar worry lines suddenly gone from his face.

Obviously spending a perfect day with Anja and their son had had an impact on him.

"We should talk," he said, full of energy.

"Yeah," I agreed, my guard instantly up. "We should."

I set my bag on the floor and dropped myself into a chair across from him, bracing for the worst. What I really wanted was to go to the guest room and hide under the covers with my hands over my ears, but now wasn't the time to act like a little kid afraid of nightmare monsters; it was time to face the facts.

Besides, I'd thought of nothing but worst-case scenarios all day, and after seeing the paparazzi photo on *The Dirt*, I felt like whatever Stefan had to say to me was already firmly decided. He was going to tell me he was leaving me for Anja and his new family. I could feel it. There was no point in putting off this discussion any longer.

"So here's the thing," he began softly, leaning toward me.

"I already know," I said, cutting him off as I fought back tears. I couldn't stand to sit here and let this play out in slow motion. The last thing I wanted was for him to stretch out the agony. "I know about you and Anja."

Hearing him actually say the words, or beat around the bush in some well-meaning attempt to let me down gently, would have destroyed me. Maybe I could preserve some dignity by cutting him off at the pass.

A look of confusion crossed his face. "What about me and Anja? What are you talking about?"

I cleared my throat and regained control of myself. "I saw the picture of you on *The Dirt*—one of the gossip websites," I said calmly, trying to remove any hint of accusation from my tone. "All three of you, actually. At the zoo today."

Stefan frowned and pulled out his phone, tapping at the screen for a moment before breaking out into a huge grin.

"Yeah, that's us." He turned his phone toward me. "It's a great photo. I think it really captured the day."

Refusing to look, I blurted, "A day I had no idea you were planning! How do you think I felt when I saw that?" Anger flickered in my chest at how callous he was acting. "I had to cover in front of my friends! Pretend I already knew you were out on the town having the best time in the world with another woman and her son—*your son*," I quickly corrected.

"Didn't you get my text?" he asked, seeming genuinely puzzled.

"No..." I said cautiously. "I left my cell home by mistake when I was rushing around this morning." What kind of text could he have sent?

Holding his cell out to me, Stefan said, "Just look at the message. Please."

I took it from him and read what he'd sent: *Took off work—going to the zoo to get to know Max better. Anja will accompany us. Let me know if this is a problem. I don't want you to be uncomfortable with any of this. 9:37 AM*

Shaking my head, I handed the phone back. So he really hadn't been trying to hide anything about his day with Anja —or Max, rather. In fact, he'd given me fair warning and tried to make sure it wouldn't upset me. He'd been open and honest, just like I'd wanted.

I felt myself relax a little. The text did nothing to change the fact that the three of them looked like the perfect, happy family together, but at least it seemed like he hadn't sat me down just now to break up with me. Not tonight, anyway.

"Will you sit with me, please?" he asked, gesturing to the couch.

Nodding, I rose from the chair and settled in beside him. "So how was it?" I asked. "With Max?"

"It was...such a good day," Stefan said, almost in wonder.

He seemed oblivious to the turmoil I was feeling inside, but I set aside my emotions and leaned closer to listen. This wasn't about me. This was about Stefan and his kid. Supporting their relationship wasn't the problem; I just wish I knew where I fit into my husband's new life.

"That's great," I said, and meant it. "I'm glad you're getting a chance to know him."

Stefan briefly filled me in on the conversation he'd had

with Anja last night, saying she'd confessed to using her pregnancy as a bargaining chip with Konstantin, as a way to leave KZ Modeling and start a new life—not in Europe, but right here in the States. My father-in-law had been more than happy to oblige, in return for Anja's silence and cooperation in her own disappearance. In the process, he'd been able to ensure that Stefan followed in his footsteps and stayed on the path to joining forces with KZM. Sounded like a win for everyone involved. Except my husband.

"I'm sorry she hid all of this from you," I said. "Max, especially. And for such a long time. You've been through so much."

He shrugged. "In the end, it doesn't matter. The important thing is that she brought my kid back to me. Everything between me and Anja died a long time ago, but Max—he's everything. You know how smart he is? He can name every kind of dinosaur. He gave me a lecture about the functions of camouflage!"

I couldn't help smiling. It was obvious that Stefan was smitten with his kid. "He sounds pretty brilliant," I said, meaning it. "I bet he's a lot of fun to be around."

"To be honest, I didn't know if I was ready to be a father. Especially considering the way I was raised..."

He let his words trail off, staring into the distance, probably replaying the day he'd had. I took his hand, squeezing it gently. My heart went out to him. To the child he'd once been and the man he'd grown into today. "Oh, Stefan. That's not what defines you. When it comes to being a parent, you get to make all your own choices. And I know they'd be good ones."

Fatherhood would suit him. I'd already pictured it, envisioned how he would be with his kids. Strict, but loving. He would support them, encourage them to be their best selves.

Do everything in his power to care for them and keep them safe and protected.

"I think I'm really ready," he finally said, his gaze searching mine, a look of determination in his eyes. "I want to do right by my kid. Be a good dad."

"You're going to be great at it," I told him. And I meant it. It was endearing to hear him talk about the time he'd spent with Max, though the fact that I'd had nothing to do with Stefan's new role was bittersweet. It made me ache that I hadn't been a part of it. "I would've loved to have seen you with him today," I added.

Stefan nodded. "I wish you'd been there, too. But it was probably better that you weren't. Even Anja hung back all day, so the kid and I could have our one-on-one time."

His words hurt, but at least he was being honest. Logically, I knew I would have just gotten in the way. But the reality of our situation stung.

"So what now?" I asked. "When will you see him again? This is just step one, right?"

"Right. So Anja wants us to get together tomorrow night, so we can all have dinner with my dad." He shot me a look, as if trying to gauge my reaction.

"Okay…I guess I can handle that." Dinner with Konstantin was far from the top of my list of favorite activities, but I'd manage. I could tell Stefan was still hesitating. "What else?"

He squeezed my hand as he spoke. "She said it might be too many new people if you were there too. But I told her that you're my wife and I want you there with me. That we're a package deal."

"Great. I'll definitely be there, then," I said brightly, forcing a smile.

Anja's suggestion seemed cruel, but I had to admit it

made sense. Max was a child, caught in the middle of a lot of confusing things. The last thing he needed was another new face added into the mix.

"You have nothing to worry about," Stefan said. "Anja's just being overprotective."

"I mean, I can see her point," I said. "It's a lot of strangers for a kid to be meeting all at once."

"Max will be fine," Stefan said breezily. "He's a little shy at first, but he warms up fast. Just ask him what his favorite dinosaur is, and you guys will be best friends in no time."

His reassuring smile did little to assuage the anxiety I was trying to hide. Because despite my husband's efforts to keep me included, I knew I'd still be the third wheel. I could feel it more and more as this whole thing developed. There just wasn't a place for me.

Even *The Dirt* seemed to think Stefan looked better with his shiny new insta-family. And he'd really been in love with Anja once upon a time—she'd been his first love. He'd cared enough for her all these years to continue searching for her, chasing after her. And now he finally had her back. Along with an adorable child. What else did he need?

Stefan and I, on the other hand, had been thrown together for business reasons. Ours was a marriage of convenience—one that wasn't convenient anymore. Though Stefan might not have realized it yet, Anja obviously did. And Konstantin was the one who'd made all these moves to get me out of the picture. I didn't fit. I was the outsider. I always had been.

I knew what I had to do.

STEFAN

CHAPTER 10

It was Tuesday night, and I was late for dinner. Getting out of the office had taken longer than I'd anticipated, thanks to all the catch-up work I had to do after playing hooky yesterday. And it had started raining just after dark—really coming down, pelting everything with hard, ice cold torrents of water—so traffic across town had been infuriatingly slow, the visibility poor.

Shaking the rain off my coat in the elevator up to my father's top floor penthouse, I couldn't help wishing Tori was at my side. But she'd insisted on coming straight from UChicago and meeting me here. I'd tried to tell her we'd both be more comfortable if we showed up at my dad's together, but her argument was that it would look better if at least one of us was on time. I couldn't fight her on that. Punctuality was something my father valued highly, and considering the way things had been going lately, Tori needed all the brownie points she could get with him.

This dinner was already a lot to ask of her. I could only imagine how hard all of this was on Tori. Truthfully, I wasn't exactly looking forward to it either. While I was eager to spend more time with Max, that enthusiasm didn't extend to seeing my father and Anja.

I was doing my best to forgive her, to convince myself that the choices she'd made all those years ago had been driven by her fear of my father's power and her love for Max. My father, on the other hand, deserved no mercy from me. Unfortunately, there was too much at stake to risk alienating him in any way. So for the time being, I had to pretend that everything was fine. That I still planned to take over KZM and run it exactly the same way he always had.

Stepping off the elevator and heading down the hall, I checked my phone, hoping for a text from Tori telling me that things were going fine. Nothing. It was hardly a surprise. She'd been quiet lately, probably because she was processing a lot. We both were. There were going to be a lot of changes in our lives now that Max was in the picture. I wasn't exactly sure how we were going to make it work, but I knew that we had to. For Max's sake.

I rang the doorbell and one of my father's domestic employees let me in and took my coat. A huge clap of thunder cracked outside, and I couldn't help feeling like it was an omen.

My father, Anja, and Max were all waiting around the dining room table. The room was lit with candles and the soft glow of the chandelier overhead, the best china and crystal laid out. There were even cloth napkins folded into little origami triangles at each place setting, like at a formal meal. I couldn't remember the last time my father had hosted something this extravagant in his home, and that was saying a lot. He was the kind of person who loved to show off.

"Where's Tori?" I asked, pulling out the chair next to Max.

"Not here," my father said airily.

"Really? I thought she was—"

"Hello, Stefan," Anja cut in. "How was work?"

"Hi, Stefan," Max said quietly, echoing his mother. "Did you see the light-ling before?"

I gave Anja a half-nod and then sat down and grinned at my son. "I sure did," I said. "It was pretty cool. Thunder's kinda loud, though. You hanging in there okay?"

"Yeah," he said, but from the looks of it the poor kid seemed overwhelmed. My father could be intimidating enough, but the set-up was a lot to take in as well.

Max was sitting up unnaturally straight in his chair, hands tightly clasped in front of him, eyes wide as they roamed the room full of antiques and the formal table settings. I understood how he felt. It was hard not to be nervous around my father's things. You could tell at a glance just how expensive and priceless everything was. And if you broke something, god help you. My father was quick to punish.

Not that I'd ever let my father do anything like that to Max—or any other children I might have. Nor would I do that to my own kids. I'd never repeat his parenting mistakes.

"You're late," my father said, standing from his seat at the head of the table. He gestured for me to move chairs so I'd be next to Anja, but I didn't budge.

"I was getting caught up on a few projects," I said. Then I looked at Max. "Sorry it took so long," I told him. "You guys should have started without me."

No doubt the kid had to be hungry. It was obvious from the near-empty bread basket and bowl of olive pits on the table that they'd been sitting there picking at the appetizers for a while.

"We'll eat now," my father said, his words a command.

The domestic worker standing near the doorway nodded and then scurried off to the kitchen.

I frowned. "We should wait for Tori. I don't know what's kept her; she should have been here already," I said, but then noticed there wasn't another place setting. "Where's her seat?"

My father just ignored me, leaning back as a bowl of soup was set in front of him.

"We can set her up when she arrives," Anja said, reaching across the table and gently putting her hand on my arm. "If she shows."

"She'll be here. Probably just got caught in traffic. People here can't drive in the rain."

Pulling my arm back, I looked over and narrowed my eyes at my father. It was no secret to my wife that he was a complete asshole, but even still, I knew that Tori would be hurt if she arrived and there wasn't a place setting for her. Not that she'd be surprised. But I couldn't ask them to wait any longer, that much was obvious. Max was practically inhaling his soup and had taken the last piece of bread as well.

Excusing myself and slipping out into the hallway for a moment, I slid my phone out of my pocket and checked my missed calls and texts. There was nothing from Tori. When I called her, it rang through to voicemail.

"Hey, hope everything's okay. Call me back when you get this, or text me," I said in my message. "Either way, let me know what's up. Dinner's started, but we'll be here. Love you."

Hanging up, I paced the hallway. I expected her to call me right back. But a few minutes went by, and she didn't. Worried, I sent her a quick text.

I'm here at KZ's. You on your way? Shoot me an ETA when you get a sec.

I sent it off, waiting to make sure it was marked as delivered, but it didn't change to "read." Still anxious, especially with the torrential downpour that was flooding the streets out there, I waited a few more minutes. But I knew I had to return to the table.

"Don't you think you're being rude?" my father asked as I sat down, when he noticed I was looking at my phone. "This is supposed to be family time."

"Forgive me for being worried that the woman I love is missing," I told him coldly. "It feels a little too familiar."

My father just laughed, as if I was making a great joke. It was a challenge to keep my hands from clenching into fists as I tried to eat my soup.

For a moment I considered calling Bruce, but I didn't want to resort to that. I'd hired the bodyguard to keep Tori safe, and I felt guilty about the idea of using him as a babysitter or my personal spy like I'd done with Dmitri in the past. I'd worked hard to build trust with my wife, and I didn't want to compromise that. Plus, it was safe to assume she might be running late from a study group or that she was hiding out from the rain or else caught in traffic. Bruce would have called if there was anything to worry about. So I'd just have to wait.

Staying focused on Max as the main course was brought out, I managed to dodge the awkwardness of Anja's attempts at small talk and my father's blatant and vocal disregard of my concern over Tori. It was uncomfortable, to say the least. But nothing could ease my worry. I had to keep telling myself she'd just bailed out at the last minute, that the pressures of playing house with my ex and my kid, along with my overbearing father, had seemed like too much to handle.

"Anja hasn't aged a day," my father was saying, as I tuned back into the conversation. "Most women, it's all downhill after they have kids. They go soft, start to sag. Get lazy about taking care of themselves."

"Dad," I cut in, disgusted by his chauvinism. Anja's smile was tight and thin, but it was her eyes that gave her away. She was looking at him like she wanted to stab him with her fork.

"Not this one, though!" my father went on, ignoring me. "Just look at her, Stefan. You really lucked out. No wonder the kid turned out so good looking, am I right?"

"Yeah," I said, hoping he'd move on. I didn't want to be rude in front of Max, but I also didn't want to give my father or Anja any ideas. Especially since my father kept acting as if she was my wife. As if Tori could be replaced just because she wasn't here for dinner.

Instead, he just leaned over and pointed at her with his knife. "Don't you think she's even more beautiful than when you two were young?"

"She looks very strong and capable," I said pointedly, refusing to play his game.

My father just grinned and reached out to mess up Max's hair in an affectionate way that almost made my jaw drop. "Hey kid, you want to tell me more about those aardvarks?" he asked.

"*Pangolins*," my son corrected him.

"Still buzzing over your trip to the zoo yesterday?" I said. Max was the only person I wanted to talk to.

He flashed me a huge grin. "Yeah!"

"Max was telling me all about it over breakfast this morning," my father butted in. "We talked about every exhibit he saw. I heard you got to walk through a whole rainforest."

"Did you now?" I couldn't help glaring at him, but he just smiled indulgently at Max, avoiding my gaze. Apparently, he was going to play the role of doting grandfather this evening.

As if we were all some big happy family.

But that definitely wasn't how I saw it. Tori was my family and she wasn't here. My father could act like a kind, attentive grandparent all he wanted, but I knew the truth. He was up to something.

As dinner progressed, my anxiety gradually shifted to relief that Tori hadn't made it. It would have killed her to see the way my father was acting. Though I did nothing to encourage it, he was talking like Anja and I were a married couple, and that we'd be staying that way indefinitely. He was also treating Max as if he'd already fully bonded with him as his first grandson. The hypocrisy stoked my rage toward the man, who'd barely spared me a second glance when I was that age.

"Your son is going to be very handsome," my dad told me and Anja. "Especially with such good-looking parents."

"He'll be smart too, if he takes after his father," Anja added with a smile.

My father grinned. "Beauty on one side, intelligence on the other. He's lucky to have the two of you."

Pie and ice cream had just been brought out, and I was glad that Max was devouring his with gusto and thankfully oblivious to the tension simmering between the adults at the table.

What the hell was my father doing? Had he forgotten that he'd been the one to take Anja away in the first place—or at least make me believe that she was gone for good? He'd mocked my feelings for her when I was a teenager and now he was acting like the last eight years hadn't even happened. I drank more wine and kept quiet, surreptitiously checking my phone again.

Why wasn't Tori calling me back? Had she left her phone at home again? No, that couldn't be it. She knew she was supposed to meet me here tonight—knew I had wanted her here with me. She'd even insisted on heading here directly from school. Where was she?

Finally Max's face was so covered in ice cream that Anja excused both of them so she could get him in the bath and put him to bed. After they left, I rounded on my father.

"What do you think you're doing?" I demanded. "Stop acting like Anja and Max are my family. *Tori* is my family. She is my wife. Not Anja. I'll make room for Max, but Anja and I aren't getting back together."

My father laughed. "Don't be melodramatic," he said. "I'm merely interested in welcoming the newest member of the Zoric family line. You're reading into it too much."

I wasn't. "Regardless of the fact that Anja gave birth to your grandson," I told him firmly, "Tori is the person I made vows to. Not Anja."

Shrugging, as though he wasn't convinced, he said, "Whatever you say, Stefan. Although I do find it interesting that she couldn't be bothered to show up tonight."

He shot me a smug smile. It was maddening. And the worst part was, he was right.

Storming out of the dining room, I pulled out my phone and ducked into the bathroom to call Bruce. My father's words had sent my anxiety over the edge, and I'd finally hit my breaking point. It wasn't like Tori to make plans and then not show up. We'd moved past that stage in our relationship—to a place of mutual trust and understanding. Or at least, I thought we had.

"Bruce," I said tensely when the man picked up. "You have eyes on Tori?"

He paused and my heart plummeted to my feet.

"You serious?" he finally said. "I dropped her off at your father's place hours ago. I knew she was meeting you so I watched to see she got into the building okay. Then I drove down the street for a coffee and came right back to wait for you guys. Same way I always do."

I clenched my jaw. My father was dead.

"She's not here," I told him. "Stand by until you hear from me."

Without waiting for Bruce to apologize or explain, I hung up and stormed back to the dining room. I knew it wasn't his fault. He had done exactly what I had ordered him to do.

My father on the other hand had been too calm, too smug during dinner. Smirking every time I glanced at my phone, gazing at me pointedly as he complimented Anja or talked to Max.

This was all his doing. I knew it.

As I rounded the doorway, I saw he was pouring himself another drink.

"What did you do to her?" I demanded, panic rising inside of me. "Where is Tori?"

I'd been through this before with Anja, but this was different. This was my wife.

"I didn't do anything," he said, taking a sip of his drink. "Perhaps she just...took a look around and realized there wasn't room for her in your life anymore." He nodded to himself with a look of satisfaction. "Smart girl. Maybe I should have given her more credit."

He was lucky I'd spent years learning how to temper my anger at him. But part of me couldn't deny that his words had a ring of truth to them. I wanted to believe he was lying, and I'd learned long ago to never trust my father's words at face value—but what he was saying made sense. If my father hadn't done anything to her, though, then where the hell was she?

"I'm going home," I said.

Bruce gave me a ride back to the condo. My mind was racing with frantic thoughts, none of them good. I grilled him again about what had gone down earlier, and he confirmed again that he'd definitely seen Tori enter my father's building. All I could think was that maybe she'd gotten cold feet on her way up to the penthouse floor and had decided she couldn't stand to go through with the dinner. Maybe she'd simply changed her mind, gone home, and fallen asleep.

I tried her phone again and again, alternately texting and calling. No answer.

When we got to the condo, I got out of the car and told Bruce to go check all of Tori's usual spots while I went up to the apartment. Maybe she was hiding out someplace at school or at that Middle Eastern coffee shop where she liked to study. It was possible she felt bad about bailing on dinner and didn't want to talk to me about it yet. I wouldn't be mad at her over it.

But the second I stepped through the front door, I could tell the condo was empty. All the lights were off, the place was cold instead of Tori's preferred tropical temperature of 78 degrees, and her coat and shoes weren't in their usual spots. As I walked down the hallway to look in the bedrooms, my footsteps echoing on the tile, I got a bad feeling that I wouldn't find her.

My gut instincts were dead on.

The guest room was devoid of her things—but so was our bedroom. Her side of the closet was stripped bare, the bathroom vanity was cleared of all her toiletries and prescriptions, and every one of her dresser drawers was completely hollowed out. As empty as the hole suddenly gaping in my chest.

My father was right.

Tori had left me.

STEFAN

CHAPTER 11

When you wake up alone every day, you don't even think about it. Your routine is locked in place; you get up, shower, have breakfast, go to work, live your life. But when you've slept next to someone every night for weeks or months—or years, even—it's nothing short of devastating to roll over in the morning and find nothing waiting there but the cold, empty bed instead of the body of your lover, warm and inviting.

I tried to avoid the whole thing by spending the night on the couch. The last time Tori had "moved out" and into the guest room, I'd slept like shit in our bed. But it was no use. In fact, I probably slept worse this time around. Because she wasn't just down the hall.

She was gone.

Every part of me was exhausted the next morning. Physically, mentally, emotionally. I'd spent hours last night pacing the living room with my phone in one hand and a black coffee in the other, running through my contacts one by one as I tried to find my wife. From Tori's dad to my brother Luca and my sister Emzee, all of Tori's girlfriends, even my former nemesis Gavin Chase. I'd reached out to everyone. Nobody knew where she was. I'd had to leave messages for both Tori's father and Gavin, but I was just covering my bases at that point.

It seemed unlikely that she'd gone back to the senator's mansion. Tori hadn't spoken to her father since the day she'd stormed into his office begging for his help in bringing KZ Modeling's sex trafficking activities to justice. I'd had to stand there and watch silently as he both admitted his complicity and flat out refused to help—and she'd told him he wasn't her father anymore. So it was hard, if not impossible, to imagine her running back to her childhood home with her tail between her legs.

I also doubted she was with Gavin. Initially he'd seemed the most likely person she'd go stay with, but Bruce had been posted outside Gavin's apartment since last night and his surveillance report thus far hadn't turned up anything out of the ordinary. Tori was also smart enough to know that Gavin's would be the first place I'd look.

After instructing Bruce to keep an eye out on the UChicago campus, I brewed a fresh pot of coffee, choked down some toast, and sat at the kitchen table with my head in my hands. Tori wouldn't skip town this close to finals, would she? Her education was everything to her. I couldn't imagine her dropping out of school. In fact, getting her degree was the whole reason she'd agreed to our marriage in the first place. And the tuition was already paid for. She'd have to show up in class eventually. At least, that's what I told myself. It was my only consolation.

But I couldn't help the panic edging into my thoughts. This was exactly like what had happened with Anja all those years ago. One day I was in love, and the next? The woman I loved had disappeared. Gone without a trace. I dialed her cell for the tenth time, but to no avail.

As much as I loathed to do so, I finally admitted to myself that it was time to call my father. It was getting more and more difficult to believe that he wasn't involved.

When I confronted him, though, he just laughed at me.

"She really is quite clever," he cackled. "Knows when she's no longer wanted, and removes herself from the equation before anyone else could! That's called self-preservation, kid. I'll bet she learned it from her old man. You should try it yourself sometime."

If he had been standing in front of me, I wouldn't have been able to control myself. I would have knocked him to the floor. Instead, I hung up on him and took several deep breaths. This was no time to let my temper get the better of me. I had to focus on Tori.

Checking my watch, I realized Tori's first class of the day was letting out in less than thirty minutes. Bruce was posted outside the building on campus, and hadn't confirmed seeing her enter, but I was going to stand right outside that classroom door and wait for her. She couldn't hide out in a lecture hall all day.

Guilt tore me up on the ride over to UChicago. As worried as I was about Tori, the last thing I wanted to do was infringe on her privacy. But she wasn't picking up her phone, and I had no idea where she was or if she was safe. I just had to know she was okay. I wouldn't force myself on her. In fact, if she didn't want to talk to me, I'd let her walk away. Maybe seeing me in person would give her second thoughts about leaving, though.

The whole thing had felt so abrupt, so unexpected. When I'd seen Tori last she'd seemed shaken by the whole Anja and Max situation, but understanding as well. I'd felt grateful to have a wife who realized that what I was going through was complicated and confusing.

Now, it seemed like maybe I'd read her reaction all wrong.

One minute she was here and we were committed to navigating this hurdle together; the next moment, she was gone.

I had already gone through a life-altering loss like this before, with Anja. I couldn't do it again with Tori. Especially since things were different now. The love I'd felt for Anja when I was seventeen—practically a kid—was nothing compared to how I felt for Tori. She understood me like no one else did. I had believed we were building a life together. That we were a team.

Yet the only thing she had left behind were the diamond earrings. A symbol of the fact that we were meant to be together.

I'd seen them in the bedroom before I left for UChicago, so I had slipped them into my pocket. My fingers were wrapped around them now, even as my driver was pulling up to the curb at East 59th Street.

"Find a parking spot nearby," I told him as I stepped out of the car and into the cold air. "I'll call when I need you."

"You got it, boss," he said before driving off.

Heading across the quad, my Italian loafers slipping a little in the mud, I saw Bruce and gave him a nod. He was posted exactly halfway between the Harper Library, Tori's favorite study haunt, and Stuart Hall, where her first class of the day was held. I'd told him to keep an eye on all the doors and call me if he saw her.

If she didn't walk out of that lecture hall when class got out in ten minutes, maybe I could speak to one of her school friends and try to find out if someone—anyone—had finally heard from my wife. Or if they had any more suggestions or theories on where she might have gone.

I wasn't entirely comfortable violating her privacy like this, but she had to know me well enough to realize that since I hadn't heard from her, I'd be doing everything I could to find her. If she wanted to be left alone, she could have easily called or texted me to say so.

As I paced in the hall outside the classroom, my entire body was practically vibrating with anxiety and stress. Admittedly, some anger as well. Of all people, Tori should know exactly what Anja's disappearance had done to me. How it had affected me. Changed me.

Why would she put me through the same thing again?

Even though my father had insisted he wasn't involved, that he'd said nothing to her, I could easily imagine him poisoning her thoughts. Telling Tori she was better off leaving, that I was divorcing her to be with Anja. Maybe even offering her money. If I ever found out that was the case, I'd make him sorry. Sorrier than he'd be when I put his ass behind bars for trafficking.

The thought of me choosing Anja over Tori, of course, was absurd. Tori was my wife, my family—the woman I had chosen to spend my life with. Come hell or high water, or ex-girlfriends, or even children I never knew I'd had. We'd find a way through.

If I could just find Tori, I would tell her that. I would convince her to come home.

Time was crawling. With a few minutes still to wait, I answered a few work emails and cancelled a meeting. I'd already called out for the day. It was only my second non-medical absence—besides my honeymoon—in the entire time that I had been working at KZ Modeling as an adult. I knew my father would find out, and question my loyalty to the company, but right now my priority was Tori. He could fire me for all I cared.

Finally, class was over and students began streaming out the door and into the hall. I watched, my heart pounding, my eyes focused on every face. Tori never emerged. When the flow of students stopped, I checked the room to make sure it was empty. No Tori. I hurried after the few students who were still meandering away at a slow, lingering pace.

One of them looked a little older than Tori, in a black leather jacket and heavy black motorcycle boots. She looked vaguely familiar. I was pretty sure I'd seen her on the night I had found my underaged wife at a strip club about to do some shots.

"Excuse me," I called out, causing her to stop and wave at her friends to go on.

She turned toward me, her eyes down as she typed something on her phone. When she lifted her head, I could tell immediately that she knew who I was—either that she recognized me from the tabloids, or from my relationship with Tori.

"You're Stefan," she said in a vague New York accent, narrowing her heavily-lined eyes.

"I am," I confirmed, and gave her a polite smile. "I think we've met before. You're friends with my wife, aren't you? Tori Zoric?"

She gave me a hesitant look. "Maybe," she said cautiously. "We have some classes together. What brings you here?"

"Well, that's what I need some help with."

I gave her my most charming smile—the one that could melt the panties off even the iciest of ice queens. And I could see it working. The sassy New Yorker's smile became a little more friendly, and she lowered her phone and tucked it into her pocket.

"I was going to surprise my wife and take her out for lunch," I went on, then gestured toward the classroom behind us. "She's usually in that class with you, right?"

"Yeah, usually," the woman said, tucking a strand of hair behind her ear and giving me a more attentive once-over. "But not today. I haven't seen her since Monday afternoon. Actually, she was...never mind."

"She was what?" I prodded.

Shrugging, she glanced away, suddenly very focused on her nails. Evading me, obviously. Trying to cover for Tori. Or covering up something, at any rate.

Thinking back, Monday was when I'd taken Max to the zoo. I'd gone home and talked to Tori, told her about my day, invited her to the family dinner at my father's on Tuesday. She'd agreed. Everything had seemed fine between us. Strained, but there'd been no red flags.

"Did she seem...upset?" I asked, trying again.

The woman went quiet all of a sudden. "I should go. I'm gonna be late for my next class."

"Wait. Please. I won't tell her you said anything," I assured her. "The thing is—I think she's pissed at me, and you know how she gets all distant when she's upset about something."

"Yeah. That's exactly Tori," she agreed. "Look, do you want to walk with me? It's the Social Sciences building, so I have a few minutes. I'm Audrey, by the way."

I nodded, and we started walking. "I just want to figure this out. Make it right."

"I get it." Audrey adjusted her scarf as we stepped outside, took a few moments to think, and then finally said, "Okay, so. She seemed kind of weird about that picture of you and the brunette that went up online, in *The Dirt*? She told us that you guys were old friends, but—"

"We are," I interrupted. "There's nothing else going on. Tori and I discussed it already."

"Cool then," Audrey said. "The thing is, the last time I saw her—on Monday—she was with Gavin."

"Gavin Chase?" I said, keeping my voice steady despite the fact that my gut was twisting.

"Yeah," Audrey said, looking apologetic. "They were sitting on that bench over there." She pointed across the quad. "She seemed distraught, honestly. He was sort of... holding her."

I saw red. But I was also crushed. How could I have been so stupid? Of course Gavin had been there for Tori in her time of need. I hadn't even seen how upset she was, but Gavin had.

My anguish must have been obvious, because Audrey reached out and patted my arm.

"Sorry, man," she said. "This is me, though. I gotta go." She gestured at the building.

"Thanks for your help," I choked out.

"No problem. Hope you guys work it out," she said, and then walked away.

For a second I just stood there, frozen. Gavin. Fucking. Chase.

I pulled out my phone and called the asshole. He didn't answer and my rage grew. I never should have trusted him. In my gut, I'd known that allying with him might be something I regretted. That getting him involved in my life and my attempt to take down KZM from the inside had been a calculated risk—one that now made me feel like I'd made a deal with the devil.

Beyond enraged, I walked back to the quad outside of

Stuart and confronted Bruce. "Did you see Tori in the arms of Gavin Chase on Monday?" I demanded.

He paused and I clenched my jaw, already knowing what his answer would be.

"You told me to keep her safe," Bruce finally responded. "And you told me Gavin Chase was someone we could trust —someone who would keep her safe, too. You didn't tell me to report on what she did with the man."

It was true. I'd said all of those things to Bruce, thinking I could trust Gavin. No, that wasn't true. I'd never fully trusted him. But I *had* trusted Tori. I'd believed her when she'd said there was nothing going on. That Gavin was interested, but the feelings weren't mutual.

"If you want me to report on her activities in the future, say the word. But the job as I understood it was to ensure Tori's safety," Bruce reminded me.

"And you've done a great job of that, haven't you?" I lashed out.

Bruce cleared his throat. "As much as you may not want to hear this," he said, "in my professional opinion, Tori's probably exactly where she wants to be. Nothing about this says abduction to me. Professionally speaking. I apologize if I'm overstepping here."

He spread his hands and took a step back. Though Bruce hadn't touched me, I felt like I'd gotten the wind knocked out of me. His words were a confirmation of exactly what I had feared.

I'd thought I could trust her. I'd thought I could believe her.

The first time I'd confronted her about Gavin, she'd made excuses. Had reasons for why they were caught kissing in a public space. Gavin had been the one to make the move, she'd said. She'd rebuffed him immediately after.

But now?

Now I didn't know who or what to believe. Not when she had been caught in Gavin's arms again, just before disappearing. They obviously had a relationship.

And it was because of me. I was the one who'd enabled them to get together. By arranging for Tori to pass information along to Gavin. I never should have used him as an intermediator. Never should have depended on the relationship between Gavin and Tori to get back at my father.

I was furious at Bruce for keeping this crucial and damning information from me. Furious at my father for doing everything he could to meddle in my personal life and chase my wife away. And Anja—she'd returned at the worst possible time, after years of keeping my son away from me. I was glad to have Max in my life, but Anja had wrecked my marriage. I was also livid over the way Gavin and Tori had deceived me. Infuriated by their lies, by Tori's cheating.

But mostly, I was furious at myself.

I had all but pushed Tori straight into Gavin's arms. It was my fault I hadn't been able to hold onto the best thing in my life.

I should have realized it was too good to be true from the beginning.

I never should have allowed myself to fall in love with Tori. Never should have allowed myself to be open and vulnerable with someone; should have learned my lesson the first time, with Anja. When you loved someone, they always left you. Giving someone your heart meant that they had the power to break it. And I was fucking broken.

From now on, though, I was done with that.

For good this time.

Fuck love, I thought to myself. And fuck Tori.

TORI

CHAPTER 12

I hated being back at my father's house. It was like being a kid again, staying in my old room, all of my clothes and toiletries from Stefan's house still packed up in suitcases that I didn't even want to open. The whole place felt too small for me—*Springfield* felt too small for me—like I had outgrown my old life and now I was being forced back in.

But I had been the one to come here. And I had no other choice.

I didn't know where else to go. I didn't know what else to do.

After speaking with Gavin on Monday, I'd hoped that my gut instincts about Anja and Stefan were wrong. That despite the sudden arrival of my husband's old flame and new child, he'd still want to be with me. That no matter the obstacles in our path, we'd find a way to work it out. Together.

Every single one of those hopes had been crushed that night, though. After listening to Stefan talk about his perfect day with Anja and Max and how excited he was to step up and be a father to his kid, and still haunted by the paparazzi photos of the three of them as one big, happy family, I'd known immediately what I needed to do.

I couldn't stay with Stefan. I couldn't stand in the way of him having the family he wanted and I couldn't wait for him to realize that and break my heart into a million pieces. It was clear to me that my father-in-law had somehow brought Anja and Max back to Stefan in an effort to replace me.

There was nothing I could do about it.

So I'd pretended that everything was fine. On Tuesday I'd had Bruce drop me off at my father-in-law's for the family dinner I'd agreed to, and I'd even gone inside so that Bruce wouldn't realize anything was amiss—and then I had walked through the lobby and snuck out the back entrance before anyone could see me, got an Uber, and headed back to Stefan's condo.

It hadn't taken long to pack everything, even though I'd done it through my tears. Knowing it was the right thing to do didn't make it any easier. Finally, I'd called another Uber and had them take me and my things all the way to Springfield, and I hadn't looked back.

Leaving UChicago was almost as upsetting as leaving my marriage. Yet I knew there was no point in continuing to attend my classes. Stefan wasn't going to keep paying my tuition once he divorced me, of that I was certain, and I knew my father sure as hell wouldn't step in to help me either. We'd been over the school thing before. He'd even denied me a temporary loan.

The only thing worse than leaving Stefan was the thought of what my father would say when I showed up on his doorstep.

Thankfully, when I knocked on the door, it was

Michelle who'd greeted me. She'd taken one look at me, standing there in the cold rain, and said, "Well, whatever is the matter, darlin'?"

When I started crying again, she'd wrapped an arm around me and said no more.

My father wasn't even home, it turned out; he was in DC for a work trip. I was grateful for that at least. We hadn't spoken since the huge fight about KZM at his office, when I'd told him he wasn't my father anymore. And while I knew he wouldn't turn me out on the street in my time of need, I also knew he'd be pissed that I'd left my marriage. He'd demand to know what had happened. Would want to fix it. I couldn't bear the thought of explaining Anja and Max to my father, telling him why the deal he'd made with Konstantin Zoric was ending.

In fact, I still wasn't sure I wanted to speak to my father ever again.

I'd had dinner with Michelle the night I arrived, and I'd tried not to stare at her across the table, but I couldn't help searching her face whenever she was distracted, looking for hints that she knew the truth behind my father's connection with KZM and their shady underground businesses. But all I saw was a woman who'd done her best to raise me, who loved me like her own. A trophy wife who'd tried to prepare me for a life of ease and relative luxury, just like hers.

I didn't want to believe she knew the truth behind what my father did. Behind the money he raised to run his campaigns.

"Do you want to talk about it?" she'd asked, over a meal of all my favorite comfort foods: buttery mashed potatoes, fried chicken, glazed carrots. I hadn't been able to eat a bite.

"I can't," I'd managed, right before excusing myself to go cry in the bathroom again.

Michelle had agreed when I requested that she and the house staff not answer any calls from Stefan. A clean break seemed like the best way to go. I hadn't even brought my phone with me when I left, tucking it in a bottom drawer of the desk in the guest room after arranging for a car. Stefan would have just tried to track me with it anyway. Though I was regretting it now that I was so isolated. I'd have to get a new phone soon, if only to text Grace and call myself Ubers when necessary.

My stepmother hadn't asked too many questions just yet, but I knew that she wouldn't remain silent forever. And though I was fairly certain she hadn't told my father I was home, he'd be back soon enough. At some point I'd have to admit why I was back and what I planned to do.

Just the thought of my husband made my heart ache.

Forcing myself out of bed on Wednesday, I resolved to hit the pause button on my grief and figure out my next steps. Even if those steps were more grieving. I just couldn't sit around waiting for someone else to figure out my life for me. Looking back, that was exactly what had gotten me into this mess in the first place. It was time to take action. Make some choices.

My first choice was a hot shower, my second was jeans and a sweater, and my third was to go find coffee. Giving myself plenty of credit for getting so far before noon, despite feeling like my world had shattered, I headed downstairs. The kitchen was empty, which was a relief.

I didn't want any company.

On the counter sat a bright pink box stamped with the name of my favorite bakery. Michelle knew well my weakness for pastries. It was sweet of her to try and care for me, and she was clearly also giving me space and not pushing me right now, which I appreciated. I grabbed a flaky croissant, but gave up once I'd had a few bites. Everything tasted like ash in my mouth.

After reheating what was left in the coffee pot from that morning and adding a liberal amount of vanilla creamer, I curled up in the window seat that looked out into the backyard and stared out at the rose garden that was rapidly dying in the face of the approaching winter.

A surge of guilt ran through me for running away like this, but I knew that in the end, Stefan would understand. He'd see that I had left out of love for him—that I wanted him to be happy. Maybe I should have left him a note, but I knew that if I'd told him where I was going, he would have come to Springfield immediately to talk me out of it. He would have probably done everything in his power to convince me that he still loved me and I would have believed him.

Because I would have wanted to believe it.

And I knew that Stefan would have wanted to believe it too.

I also knew that it would have just prolonged the inevitable. That eventually, Stefan would realize that he belonged with Anja—and his son. Their son. It was only right.

As I sipped my warmed-over coffee, I tried to re-envision my future. Maybe, if I was divorced and single again, and officially over eighteen, I could apply for federal financial aid. Get approved for a loan to cover my tuition and the cost of student housing. My girlfriends lived in the dorms, ate in the student cafeteria, worked part-time jobs. I could do that, too. I might have to take the rest of the school year off and reapply for admission again next fall, but I'd manage. It would be hard—and I would be alone—but I would survive. I'd be on a path.

The main house phone rang, startling me from my thoughts. I cringed, wondering if it was Stefan again. I'd seen his number on the caller ID multiple times since I'd disappeared last night, but nobody had picked up his calls, per my request. But this time it wasn't Stefan's name on the digital screen—it was *Zoric, Mara*. My sister-in-law Emzee.

Part of me knew it would be best to ignore the call like I had Stefan's, but I couldn't resist. I wanted to talk to Emzee. I needed her. She was the closest thing to a sister I'd ever had. And I knew I could trust her to keep my location a secret.

"Hi, Emzee," I said, hearing the guilt in my own voice as I answered.

"Tori?" My sister-in-law sounded frantic. "You're in Springfield? Are you okay? What happened?"

"I'm fine," I told her, my eyes already tearing up at the concern in her voice. "I've been at my dad's since last night. I'm really okay."

"Well, but when are you coming home?" she asked. "Why did you leave?"

I took a steadying breath and walked back to the window seat, sinking into it with a sigh. "I'm not going back. And I need you to promise me you won't tell Stefan we talked."

"Wait, what?" Emzee sputtered. "Why? He's freaking out."

"This is the best thing for everyone," I told her. "You have to believe me. I just—"

"Not good enough," she said, cutting me off. "You and my brother are a match made in heaven. I've never seen him this happy before. He thinks you hung the moon! And you guys are crazy about each other, I've witnessed it with my own eyes. So you better start talking. *Now*."

Emzee was talking a mile a minute. It took me a second to process everything she'd said before I was able to respond.

"Listen," I told her gently. "Remember how you told me Stefan was a different person when he was younger—back in high school—and then suddenly everything changed?"

"Yeah..." Emzee said cautiously.

"Well, the reason he was so different was because he was in love with a woman named Anja. But then Anja disappeared and never came back," I informed her. I heard Emzee's shocked intake of breath. "And three days ago...she showed up on your father's doorstep."

"Are you fucking kidding me right now?" she hissed.

I told Emzee the rest of the story, though I left out Anja's involvement in the sex trafficking ring. All I told her was that Anja had been an up-and-coming KZM model who'd disappeared without a trace just days after Stefan had proposed, and that he'd spent the last eight years searching the ends of the earth for her.

"There's more," I said, taking a breath. "She—she and Stefan. They have a kid."

"What?!"

"He didn't know Anja was pregnant when she disappeared," I told her. "So it was a huge surprise when she came back with this seven-year-old, but Max—that's the kid's name—is really smart, and really sweet, and Stefan's basically already in love with him. I know he wants to do the right thing and be a father to him."

"Okay," Emzee said slowly. "I get that this is all kinds of crazy. But I still don't understand why you're hiding out at your dad's house. I thought you loved Stefan. Don't you want to work things out? He was only seventeen when all this went down. How can you hold it against him now?"

"He doesn't want me!" I said, feeling the pain rise up sharp and swift again, like a knife in my chest. "He wants *Anja*. He's always wanted her."

"That can't be true," Emzee said. "That was a million years ago. Things have changed. *He's* changed."

"They have a child together," I said, closing my eyes and pressing my forehead against the cool glass of the window. "I'm not going to stand in the way of that. They're a family now."

"That's not fair," Emzee snapped.

"It will be easier for everyone if I leave now," I insisted, my voice hitching as my tears started to fall. "Before he has to ask me to go."

"But Tori," she said, starting to cry along with me, "You can't make this decision for him. And you're *wrong*. You haven't seen Stefan—he's frantic with worry. *He loves you.* He wants you back, with him."

I wanted to believe her. I wanted to imagine that he would choose me if it came down to it. But not one thing about this situation pointed to a happy ending where Stefan and I would ride off into the sunset together. This might have been the cowardly way to go, but it was also the safer way. The only way I was getting out of this with my heart intact.

"I need to do this my way," I told Emzee, hoping she would understand.

"No. You need to talk to him," she said. "If you just listened to what he has to say, he'd tell you that he's in love with you. That he wants you. Not anybody else."

"Just let it go," I begged. "Let this be goodbye."

"Damn it." Emzee was sniffling, trying to get it together. "Fine. Do it your way. But don't leave my brother hanging. You at least have to tell him where you are and why you left," she said. "You owe him that. And don't think for a second that you're breaking up with me, too."

"We'll still be friends," I said, meaning it. "This doesn't change anything between us."

Still, I wished I hadn't answered the phone. I should have known my headstrong, feisty sister-in-law wouldn't let me off so easily. But I also knew that she was right. It wasn't fair to walk out on Stefan, and our marriage, without a word. He deserved at least a call from me.

I just wasn't read to do it. Not yet.

"So will you call him?" Emzee pushed. "Please?"

"Give me a few days," I said. "I need some time to get myself together and think. I'm sure Stefan does too. He needs to figure things out with Anja and Max. Okay?"

"Okay," she finally said. "A couple days. But that's it. If you don't talk to him by the weekend, I will. I'll tell him everything. Believe me, though, he'd rather hear it from you."

"I know," I whispered. "I'm sorry."

"I don't need you to be sorry," Emzee said. "I need you to be honest."

We said our 'I love you's and hung up, but unlike our usual calls, I walked away feeling even more upset.

I had a ticking clock now, but I didn't know if it would give me enough time to learn how to be strong.

STEFAN

CHAPTER 13

By Friday morning I had come to accept what Bruce had tried to tell me: that wherever Tori was, she was safe—but that she didn't want to be found. Not by me and apparently not by anyone else, either. Taking into account that the last time Tori's friend Audrey had seen Tori she'd been in Gavin's arms, and the fact that Gavin wasn't answering or returning any of my calls, it seemed almost certain that my wife had moved in with her conniving, back-stabbing little study buddy. It didn't mean I accepted her leaving me, though.

I had to try to get her back. Take a final stand. I had no idea how to do that, but I'd find a way. There was nothing I wouldn't do for Tori. She had to know that.

In the meantime, I had to take the situation day by day. The Tori I knew had integrity above all else, so I convinced myself she'd reach out when she was ready, come clean about her betrayal, give me a chance to talk to her...but until then, I was losing my mind.

Focusing at work all week had been an exercise in futility. Most of my days had been spent pacing the halls of the

KZM offices, staring blankly at the paperwork piling up on my desk, or canceling the meetings and lunches on my calendar. My father was livid. I didn't give a damn. I knew I needed to do my job, knew I was moping, but it was impossible to force myself to push paper when I was caught between my missing wife and my father's criminal empire.

Regardless of the turmoil in my personal life, I needed to get my shit together. Get back to figuring out how to bring KZM down. I couldn't count on my Gavin Chase connection anymore. It still infuriated me that he was too cowardly to pick up his phone when I called, didn't even have the decency to text me and let me know Tori was safe. I had thought we'd reached an understanding—a place of mutual respect and cooperation, if not friendliness. But now he was ghosting me, when he had to know that all I wanted was to talk to Tori one last time.

Even showering was like a waking nightmare now. Standing under the scalding water, all I could think about was the first time I'd watched my wife come, while fingering herself in a hotel shower during our honeymoon in Vienna. Her head tilted back, her mouth open as she gasped and moaned. Or the time I'd eaten her out right here, sucking on her sweet clit while my hand fucked her to an explosive orgasm, drops of water rolling down her full, perfect breasts. The images were too vivid, impossible to ignore, my arousal almost physically painful. I handled it quickly, joylessly, the memory of her body in my hands torturing me the whole time.

After getting dressed, frying an egg for breakfast, and trying to convince myself to go to work, I gave up and dialed my private car. Desperate for a distraction, I told my driver to take me to my father's penthouse. The only other person I wanted to see right now was Max.

If there was one thing that could take my mind off of things, help me step away from the emptiness and heartache, push me to at least go through the motions of being okay, it was my son. Just seeing Max's face made me light up. The kid could talk about dinosaurs like nobody's business, and he was at just the right age to be full of questions about absolutely everything. Maybe I could take him to a movie or the aquarium downtown. Hell, we could even order in a pizza and sit around playing videogames if that's what he wanted. I'd let him decide.

I hated that I had to go to my father's place to see Max, and I wasn't looking forward to being in such close quarters with Anja again, but I'd grit my teeth and bear it for my kid's sake.

Arriving at the penthouse, a member of the house staff let me in.

"Good morning, Mr. Zoric," he said.

"Is Max here?" I asked. "I was hoping to take the kid out for the day."

He frowned. "The boy and his mother aren't in at the moment."

My stomach dropped. "Do you have any idea what time they'll be back?"

"No. I'm sorry," he said apologetically. "I can make a call if you like—"

"That's okay," I interrupted. "I'll call myself. Don't worry about it. Thanks anyway."

I turned to leave, but heard my father calling out from his study. I should have left, just pretended I didn't hear him, but against my better judgement I went down the hall.

"Max and Anja aren't here," he told me as I leaned against the doorway.

"I gathered," I said. "Where are they?"

"Downtown," he said, not elaborating.

He was seated in a tufted leather chair in the dark room, looking like a Bond villain in a sharp, well-cut charcoal suit with a glass of something reddish orange and thick—probably a bloody Mary, from the looks of it—in his hand.

It was just after ten in the morning. Hard not to believe he'd been lying in wait for me to come and visit Max and Anja.

"A little early for a drink," I commented. "Not going into work today?"

"I could ask you the same," he said with a smug grin, taking a long sip from his glass.

Annoyingly, my father didn't become addled or distracted when he drank. Just more focused. More cruel.

"What are they doing downtown?" I prodded. "And when will they be back?"

Maybe my best bet was to just call Anja and arrange to meet them wherever they were.

He shrugged. "No idea. I sent them out with my AmEx, to get some things for the little one's room. I told Anja to buy whatever he wants. Money is no object where Max is concerned."

I got a chill hearing my father call Max "the little one." It was too intimate. Too personal. It also reminded me that he'd been aware of Max all these years and had purposely kept him from me. That hurt far worse than the knowledge that he had essentially paid off Anja to stay in hiding the whole time.

"How long are they planning to stay with you?" I asked, growing uneasy.

After taking a leisurely slug of the bloody Mary, my father said, "As long as they want."

Fuck. The fact that he was trying to make Max's room

here more comfortable—likely in an effort to entice the kid and Anja to stick around more permanently—was sending up a million red flags in my mind. I hated that my son was under my father's roof at all, even temporarily. It was a miracle I hadn't ended up as twisted as he was after growing up under his influence, but I sure as hell wasn't going to risk letting Max go through the same hell that I had.

I couldn't let Max get tangled in his web, or allow him to be influenced by my father.

But what could I do? I would have been happy to remodel the spare room at my condo for the kid, but I didn't want to live with Anja. Plus, Max still had no clue I was his dad. As far as he knew, I was just a friend of his mom's. Offering to take Max in would have to wait.

I just didn't understand why my father was suddenly so devoted to Anja and my son. The man could easily have put them up in a hotel nearby, so why had he arranged to keep them here at his place? He'd known about Max for *eight years* and then out of nowhere he decides he needs to get involved in the boy's life? It made no sense. There was no reason for Anja and Max to still be here unless my father wanted something from them. Wanted to use them.

That my father was playing happy grandfather with Max was deeply suspicious.

It also made my anger boil up inside of me. I had been so angry at Anja for keeping Max a secret from me, but it was as much my father's fault as hers. Because of his secrets and manipulations, I'd never gotten a chance to know my son until now.

"He's a good kid," my father mused, looking thoughtfully at his drink. "Smart, resilient, personable. No doubt he'll be Zoric royalty someday. A nice addition to the family."

His words were enough to put me over the edge.

"*A nice addition?*" I snapped. "This isn't like adding a fucking room onto a house! He's *my son*. And the reason I never had a chance to be a part of his life until now is because *you* took Anja away from me in the first place."

I couldn't stop myself from pacing the room, the rage rolling off of me. My father just watched me and laughed.

"Do you still believe that's what happened?" he said. "It was her decision! I never coerced her. In fact, I tried to talk her out of it."

"Bullshit," I cut in.

"Don't pin this on me." He slammed his glass down. "You think it wasn't obvious to me that the child would do better being raised by both parents? That's what I told her! But Anja wanted out. So I helped her do that, in exchange for being able to keep tabs on my grandson. She was more than happy to take the money and run, trust me. It's what she wanted all along."

I didn't believe him, didn't know what to believe anymore, but it was hard to ignore the pain that came along with his words. After all, I seemed to be a man who women had consistently chosen to run away from.

"You almost sound like you buy into your own lies," I told him bitterly. "I guess that happens when you never tell the truth."

"The truth is always relative." He got up to pour himself another drink. "But you need to let go of the past, Stefan. It doesn't matter what happened all those years ago! What matters is that Anja is here now, with Max." He smiled, lifting his glass in a toast. "Can't we just take a moment and agree this is tremendous?"

"My son is seven years old," I said, grinding out the

words. "And the first time I saw his face, or even knew of his existence, was six days ago."

"I told Anja not to buy any new furniture," my father said breezily, putting the cap back on the bottle of vodka and heading back to his chair. "Since I'm sure you're going to set up something at your house for both of them soon enough."

That stopped me in my tracks.

"Both of them? I'm not bringing Anja into our home." I still thought of the condo as Tori's, too, even though she'd been gone for days now.

"You will," he said. "It's only a matter of time, now that you have a son to raise."

I felt my fury rise even higher. There was no way I'd be inviting Anja to live in the home I shared with my wife, even if my wife had left me for someone else.

"Anja and I are not getting back together," I told my father, my words firm. "Regardless of what you—or she—might be thinking otherwise."

He just shrugged. "You'll come around," he said. "As soon as you're over that bitch wife of yours."

I was standing over him before I even realized I'd crossed the room. "Don't ever talk about her that way again," I said, my voice steely, my rage barely contained.

My father gave me a look that was both patronizing and pitying.

"How can you stand there and defend her?" he asked, putting his feet up. "She left you. Walked right out the door without a second thought. The sooner you move on, the better."

It was all too familiar. The ache in my chest, the sour feeling in my gut, my father's nonchalance, the fury I was battling in his presence. This was exactly like the last time he had chased a woman away from me, and all at once I felt like I was seventeen again. Helpless and trapped. Even though I knew that Tori had left me for Gavin, and had probably been thinking about it for a while, I couldn't help blaming my father. If he hadn't brought Anja back, Tori wouldn't have needed to seek comfort in Gavin's arms. She'd have had no reason to doubt my commitment to her and to our marriage. My wife would still be with me.

As I stormed out of the penthouse and took the long elevator ride back down to the lobby, I seethed over the way this whole thing had been playing out. Every step of the way, my father had been pulling all the strings. Holding all the cards. Regardless of his deflection and his lies, it was obvious that he'd planned his every move. After all, it was the Zoric way.

But two could play this game.

It was time to do something about my father, once and for all.

STEFAN

CHAPTER 14

Now that Max was in the picture, and considering everything my father was doing to control—and ultimately destroy—my life, I was more intent than ever on turning KZ Modeling into a legitimate business and getting my father out of the way. I would destroy the seedy underbelly he'd created to fund the agency's operations and then expand the branches of the company that were successful in their own right, giving them room to grow organically.

After all, KZM had made a name for itself by representing the fashion industry's most sought-after faces, models with both striking features and strong presence. We'd sign even more.

Our top-notch talent scouts knew the business inside and out, so I'd hire more of those as well. Give everyone incentives for signing fresh faces or for renewing contracts with models that were already doing great work for the agency.

I'd also pick up the pace on my end, even if that meant taking even more calls and meetings in order to forge new relationships with designers, fragrance companies, my contacts in the cosmetics industry—whatever was needed to secure KZM's future. And I'd make sure the clients we already had were happy, too. Maybe I'd have my assistant send them all champagne baskets or artisanal chocolate. Whatever it took, I'd woo them and keep them wooed.

The confrontation with my father at his penthouse had been exactly what I needed. Exactly the motivation necessary to force me to get my ass back in gear.

And if Tori came back—no, *when* she came back—she'd be proud that I had followed through with my plans to dismantle the trafficking ring, expose my father's corruption, and bring all the responsible parties to justice. She'd see that I'd accomplished something important. Righted some of my father's wrongs. Done something genuinely good to change the world.

My father was going down.

In the meantime, it was hard not to stress about the fact that my father was plotting to keep Max and Anja in his home like his own personal human pets, obviously in order to control them. Everything he did, from providing them with money and a place to stay, to feeding them three meals a day and allowing them to go on these lavish spending sprees, was a way to make them completely dependent on him. To manipulate them. And to manipulate me, *through* them. We'd all be under his thumb. Nothing my father did came without strings.

So it was critical that I acted as quickly and discreetly as possible—before he was in a position to use Max against me. I knew he wouldn't think twice about treating my son like a bargaining chip, and if Max was threatened, my hands would be tied. I couldn't let that happen.

It was time to reach out to Gavin's brother, Frank Chase, directly.

Knowing my father might have someone watching me, and that any attempts to contact the feds meant I was at risk of exposing both myself and the agency's involvement, I had my driver drop me off at Union Station, where I tucked myself into one of the few remaining payphone booths left in the city of Chicago. Then I made my call.

After giving Frank the fake name we'd agreed I should use over the phone, I said, "Tell me what your agency has to have in hand so you can take this man down. Because I'm ready to move, and it has to be soon."

He'd sounded surprised to hear from me, but he only hesitated briefly before saying, "What's changed? Something we should know about?"

"There are some new players involved," I said. "People close to me, people who could get hurt. One of them is a child, and this man...he knows the kid is a weak spot for me. I don't want to have to walk away, get uncooperative, you understand?"

"I understand," Frank said.

"So what do you need?" I prodded. "Let's move on this."

"To be honest, we're in a good place," he said, his voice detached and business-like. "We've almost got everything set up to be able to make our arrests."

It was a surprise, but I was glad to hear it. My father's brutal reign was almost over.

"Okay, so how soon are we talking?" I asked.

"These things take time," Frank said. "Everything has to be by the books, the evidence has to be rock solid, we can't risk a mistrial over a technicality, yadda yadda."

"You're telling me I'm supposed to just sit here and

wait?" The fucking feds. It was infuriating. I didn't have time for this shit.

"Everything's under control. You gotta be patient," he said calmly.

"I've been nothing but patient," I shot back. "I put my ass on the line for you guys and every day that goes by is another day for him to plan a way out of this. I'm ready for things to start happening."

"Soon," Frank promised, unperturbed by my outburst. "Is that all?"

Tori's name was on the tip of my tongue. I wanted to ask him about her, ask if she was safe—because he had to know that my wife was shacking up with his little brother by now. But I said nothing. I wasn't supposed to know where she was, and I wanted to give her the space she needed, even if that space was in Gavin's apartment. I'd honor what Tori wanted. For now.

"That's all," I said, and hung up.

～

WHEN I GOT HOME, I found that my misery was about to have company. Because Gavin Chase was waiting for me in the lobby.

It took all my strength not to punch him in his face.

"What the fuck are you doing here?" I said, causing the uniformed woman at the security desk to raise an eyebrow and lift the phone. "We're good," I told her. "No need to call the cops."

Turning back to Gavin, I folded my arms and waited for his answer.

As much as I hated him, he didn't seem the type to gloat. And looking closer, I realized his expression wasn't one of smug victory. In fact, he looked worried. There were dark circles under his eyes, and he seemed uncharacteristically...slumped. A lot like me, come to think of it.

"Where's Tori?" he demanded, obviously on edge. "You got her locked up in your apartment?"

"What, you can't keep track of her either?" I shot back, bitterness seeping in. "Not my problem, now that she ran off to be with you."

His face went slack. "What?"

"Yeah, I know all about it," I said. "The last time anyone saw her, she was with you. So it was pretty fucking obvious she ran straight into your arms the second she walked out on me."

"Wait, what are you talking about?" Gavin said, narrowing his eyes. "She didn't run off to be with me. She's been gone all week. I haven't seen her since Monday."

I ran my hands through my hair in frustration. "Are you lying to me right now? I've been calling you for days and you never picked up. Never returned a single one of my messages. What the hell are you trying to pull?"

Gavin's eyes were wide. He took a step back, shaking his head.

"I blocked your number," he said, pulling out his phone. "My brother thought it would be better if we didn't have any direct contact. Look."

He showed me the screen that listed all his blocked contacts. My number was right on the top of the list. No wonder he hadn't gotten any of my frantic phone calls or messages.

My stomach dropped, my pulse kicking into overdrive.

"So you really haven't seen Tori?" I asked.

"I swear to god I haven't," he said.

I sank down onto the lobby bench, Gavin standing

warily over me. For a moment, I had no words. With sudden, gut-wrenching clarity, I realized that I should have looked harder for her. That I never should have stopped looking. I had let Tori down. I couldn't believe I'd given up on her so easily.

"Maybe she went home," Gavin suggested.

"I tried her Springfield number," I said, already pulling my phone out.

I scrolled through my contacts and tried calling Senator's Lindsey's house line again. Predictably, there was no answer. I knew Mitch was in DC for work, but I hadn't tried him directly. Once I was sure that Tori had left me for Gavin, I'd given up on trying to reach her friends and family.

This time I dialed his cell. He picked up after the third ring, sounding distracted and annoyed.

"Stefan," he said flatly. "What is it?"

"Is Tori at your house in Springfield?" I asked.

Gavin leaned forward, and I tilted the phone in his direction so he could hear the senator's reply.

"She's your wife," Mitch said with an obnoxious laugh. "I thought it was your job to keep a leash on her now."

I hated him, but forced myself to take a deep breath before I responded. Even Gavin was clenching his jaw, having overheard the senator's booming voice.

"We had some words and she took off," I said, keeping the details vague. "I'm trying to track her down."

"She isn't there as far as I know," Mitch said, "but why don't you try the house? The staff will answer. Or maybe she's with one of her school friends. Either way, I'm sure she'll turn up soon."

He hung up on me and Gavin and I stared at my phone. How could this man be so dismissive when his daughter, his only child, was missing? She wasn't with her school friends, and no, the staff at the senator's mansion would not answer. I had been calling the Springfield house day and night, but no one had ever picked up. Which was strange if you thought about it, since it was their job to answer calls and take messages for the senator and his family.

"Fuck."

"What?" Gavin asked anxiously.

"I'm an idiot."

Gavin put his hands up. "You said it, not me. Where is she?"

"She's gotta be at home," I said. "I've called that line more times than I can count, and the staff hasn't picked up a single one of my calls. They're avoiding me. On purpose."

"You think she's there, then?"

I nodded. "Has to be. I'm gonna head out. If I leave now, I can probably make it in under four hours."

"Wait. Can you—can you have her text me?" Gavin asked. "Just so I know she's okay."

"Sure, man," I said, holding out my hand. We shook on it. "Thanks for showing up."

"No problem," he said. Maybe he wasn't such an asshole after all.

We went our separate ways and I headed to the underground parking garage to get my BMW. The M5 had over 600 horsepower and went from zero to sixty in three seconds. This wasn't the time to call a chauffeur. I needed to get to my wife as soon as possible. I needed to see her now. Even if that meant breaking a few traffic laws in the process.

Just as I was about to pull out of the garage, ready to ignore every speed limit sign in the state of Illinois, my phone rang. I glanced at the screen on the dash and saw that it was Emzee calling. I put her on speaker and sped away from the condo, my tires screeching as I peeled out.

"Not a good time," I told her.

"It's about Tori," she said, and I eased up on the gas pedal.

"I know where she is," I said. "I'm on my way now. Make it quick."

Emzee let out a huge sigh. "Good," she said. "I'm glad. Did she call you?"

"No." I cut somebody off, waving as I sped by. "But I'm going to get her anyway."

"Okay. Never mind then," she said. "I'll let you drive."

"Emzee," I ordered, using my best big brother voice. "Spit it out."

She let out a huff of air. "I'm not supposed to be telling you this, but I know why she left. And it's not because she doesn't love you."

"Keep talking."

As zoomed toward I-55, I listened to my sister explain why Tori had walked out on me. There was no doubt in my mind that I could still fix this.

I was going to get my wife back.

TORI

CHAPTER 15

"Just hang in there, lady," Grace said. "I know everything sucks right now, but it won't be like this forever. And whatever you decide to do, I'm here for you. I'm here for all of it."

I was sprawled out on my bed, staring up at the ceiling, with the cordless house phone tucked between my shoulder and my ear. Surrounding me were clumps of used tissues and a bunch of little tin foil wrappers from the bag of bite-size dark chocolates Michelle had dropped off outside my bedroom door along with a stack of romance novels. Comfort, delivered.

"Thanks," I said, wiping away a stray tear. "But I don't even know where to start."

"I don't want to sound like an obnoxious Instagram yogi or anything, but you can start by being kind to yourself," she suggested gently. "And stop thinking you have to figure it all out in three days. My breakups were always hell, remember? Ryan Evans, junior year?"

"Oh god, I remember," I said. "That was bad. You cut off all your hair, flashed the entire football team at a pep rally, and cried through first period Latin every morning for weeks."

"It was a rough time," she said defensively.

"And then, the last day of school before Christmas break, you shoved an entire pound of thin sliced limburger cheese through the slot in his locker so it would rot in there over the holidays."

"Tori!" she gasped in mock horror. "You said you'd never speak of it again!"

"That was pretty diabolical," I mused.

"Well if you feel like a little revenge-cheesing is in order, let me know."

I laughed. It was probably the first time I'd felt my mood lift since I'd left Chicago.

"Anyway," Grace went on, "I gotta run to a marketing thingy for my handbags, but let me know when you're ready for wine and cookie dough and Jane Austen movie night, okay? Just say the word. Ooh, and p.s., I'm sending you one of my purses! You're going to love it."

We said goodbye and I went out into the hallway to hang the phone back up on its cradle. Talking to Grace had been good—great, actually—but it was mostly just a temporary distraction from the disaster that my life had turned into.

The deadline Emzee had given me for coming clean to Stefan was tomorrow, but I had no idea what to say to him when I called. If I had thought that a few days would give me time to sort things out in my head or help me become braver, I had been sadly mistaken.

If anything, I felt even more confused and worried than ever about what I was supposed to do. My heart ached for my husband, but my mind kept telling me that leaving him was the best thing to do in the long run. That he belonged with Anja. And his son. That if I stuck around, at best I'd be a third wheel. At worst, I'd have to watch my husband fall back in love with the first woman he'd ever cared for.

Still, I resolved to call him first thing in the morning. Emzee was right, I owed him an explanation. Especially considering all the upheaval he was going through in his life right now.

I'd strap on my emotional bulletproof vest, pick up that phone, and tell him I understood that he loved Anja, and that he needed to try and make it work with her, try to be a family with her and their son. But even thinking the words sent me off on another crying jag. It felt like my heart had been ripped out of my chest. I wondered if I would always feel this way.

Exiling myself inside for the past few days had only made me feel worse. More isolated, more trapped. I had to get out of the house. Rifling through my closet, I found some old running shoes, workout clothes, and a thick, down-filled Lululemon vest. After pulling on a knit hat and gloves, I went out for a run.

Technically, it was more of a jog-and-walk. I stretched for a few minutes and then took off, following the same route through the neighborhood that I used to sprint in high school. I quickly realized that my fitness level wasn't what it used to be back when I was forced to run laps regularly in gym class. Still, I leaned into the familiar burn in my lungs, the ache in my muscles, the hard slap of my shoes against the sidewalk. It was probably forty degrees outside, but by the time I got back to the house I was sweating and had unzipped my vest.

"Why are you so out of breath?" Michelle asked, all dolled up and about to walk out the front door with her purse over her arm.

"Running," I panted. "Went for a jog."

My stepmother wrinkled her nose. "If you want to work out, darlin', just use the home gym. It's freezing out there. You'll catch your death of cold."

"Thanks," I said, not wanting to explain further. "I'll do that next time."

I stopped in the kitchen to chug a glass of water and then headed upstairs, my whole body vibrating with the exertion. But although I'd gotten my blood flowing, the agony of losing Stefan still remained just as strong. There was no running from the breakdown of my marriage.

Exhausted physically and mentally, I went back up to my bedroom, stripped off my clothes, and then shut myself in my bathroom for a good, long soak. I didn't even wait for the water to fill the tub all the way before I climbed in, curling tight around myself and letting the hot water and bath salts do their work.

Once the water was a few inches from the lip of the bathtub, I turned off the taps and let myself sink into it. Grace was right; I needed to be kind to myself. There was no way I was going to have all the answers.

But I just couldn't imagine my life without Stefan. He was the one I wanted to be with. The one I wanted to grow old with.

Leaning back, I let my tears fall. There was no point trying to fight them.

A few minutes later, I was all cried out. The heaviness in my chest had eased a little, and my muscles had relaxed in the steamy water. It felt good. I was about to get out of the tub when I heard a commotion downstairs. Someone banging on the front door, an exchange of voices. Had Michelle forgotten something? Was my father unexpectedly home early? I settled back in the tub, wrapped my arms around my knees, and tilted my head to listen.

There were footsteps on the stairs, and a moment later my bathroom door burst open.

It was Stefan, hair disheveled, out of breath, the picture of concern and anxiety.

"Tori."

"Stefan—"

But he was already kneeling beside the tub, pulling me into his arms, heedless of the hot water and bubbles that were soaking his nice suit and spilling onto the floor.

"What are you doing here?" I said, letting him hold me. "Why did you come?"

We were sitting on the plush bath mat, my body naked and slick in Stefan's embrace. It was almost like he was trying to wrap his entire body around me, and I leaned into him, inhaling the comforting scent of his cologne, not caring that I was probably ruining his shirt and his tie.

"Because you ran away from me, and I fucking need you." His voice was angry and desperate. "Anywhere you go, I'll follow. I love you."

"But—" I started.

"Listen to me," he said, easing his grip to look me in the eyes. "We might have been thrown together unwittingly for political reasons, just our fathers' pawns in an arranged marriage, but I made those vows to you—not to Anja. You're the one I want to be with."

"How can you say that?" I murmured. "You married me before you even knew she was still alive. Now that she's back, there's not even a choice."

"You're right," he said. "There isn't a choice. There never was. Because between the two of you, *I choose you*. Nobody else. I don't even need to think about it."

"You haven't given it a chance," I insisted. "She's the mother of your child. What if you're giving up the best part of your life for me? The chance to be a family?"

"*You* are my family, Tori. And I will always stay true to you, because I can't imagine living a life without you," he went on.

"I...I feel the same," I admitted. "I don't want to live without you. I want us to build a life. Together."

"Good. Because I made my vows already, and I'm standing by them." Searching my gaze, he took a deep breath. "Are you going to keep your vows too, for better or worse, and love me through thick and thin, 'til death do us part?"

"Yes," I said. "Of course I am."

Stefan held me even tighter, kissing my forehead, my cheeks, my neck, my shoulders, giving me goosebumps and sending a shock of hot tension straight between my legs.

"But what about Anja?" I asked, refusing to let myself be distracted. "You love her. She was your first...everything. You've been looking for her for all these years. How can you just walk away from that?"

He eased back and exhaled slowly.

"I wanted to know what happened to her, Tori. I needed closure. That was it. I haven't loved her for years. We're not the same people we used to be—I don't even know her anymore."

"You could know her," I argued. "You haven't even tried."

"I know *you*." He was breathing hard, worked up into a frenzy, and he slid a hand up to cup my cheek just like he always did. "I *love* you. So stop fighting me. Stop fighting *this*."

"I love you, too," I said, pulling him closer for a kiss.

His mouth closed over mine, hot and needy, and I wrapped my arms around his neck and let myself get lost in the hard press of lips, the desperate slide of our tongues. Even though I was wet and cold from the bath, my entire body suddenly felt warm and safe, secure in the unwavering steadfastness of my husband's love.

"Don't ever leave me like that again," he whispered between kisses, his voice hoarse. "Promise me."

"I promise," I whispered back.

I couldn't believe he was here, right here in front of me, saying all these things, kissing me so hard I was gasping for air. It was an outcome better than I ever could have imagined.

And if it was a dream, I never wanted to wake up.

STEFAN

CHAPTER 16

At some point between convincing Tori that I loved her, and her promising to never leave me again, my cock had started responding to the fact that my wife was wet and naked, her supple curves pressed against me. Now I was hard and straining against my pants. She was all I could think about.

Reaching over the edge of the tub, I tested the water.

"It's still hot," I said.

She smiled in my arms. "You want to get in?"

"I want *you* to get in. I like the way you look when you're all wet."

"Oh *really*," she purred.

"Really."

As she looked into my eyes I stroked her cheek, tucking a strand of hair behind her ear. Then I kissed her. Making my intentions clear, I thrust deep into her mouth with my tongue. Her grip grew tighter against my biceps, and throaty little moans escaped her. She reached down to trace the outline of my cock through my pants, and I couldn't help but groan. Our attraction was electric and undeniable. I was desperate to touch her. Taste her. Show her exactly what she meant to me by completely losing myself inside her.

"Get in there," I ordered, forcing myself to break away. "You're shivering."

Tori stood and turned around, giving me a million-dollar view of her perfect ass as she stepped back into the bath. Then she took her time sinking down into the hot water, letting out another soft moan as it enveloped her again. "Feels good," she murmured. "Nice and steamy."

"You're teasing me," I growled, shrugging out of my damp blazer and tugging off my tie.

"Mm-hmm," she agreed, locking her eyes on mine.

She reached her hands behind her head, arching her back as she stretched, just to show off. I let my eyes linger over her full breasts, the way her taut nipples peeked out from the dissolving bubbles, the droplets of water clinging to her skin like tiny diamonds. Then she traced a finger down her neck, between her tits, slipping under the water where I could only imagine it dipping inside the hot, slick walls of her pussy.

"You sure you don't want to get in here with me?" she asked, looking into my eyes as she stroked herself. Licking her lips, a pink flush spread across her cheeks. I was momentarily stopped from undressing myself by the sight of her hand tucked between her thighs, the slow rocking of her hips under the water. Using her other hand, she twisted her nipple hard enough to draw another moan from her parted lips, the sound of it going straight to my cock.

"You're being very naughty," I rasped, so turned on I could barely think. "I'm gonna have to punish you."

I saw understanding spark in her gaze, along with desire. That was my girl. That was my Tori. Whose sensual appetite could not be denied.

Stepping next to the tub, my cock was just above her eye level. Seeing the hard evidence of my arousal, a pleased grin curved her beautiful lips.

"Come here," I said, tugging off my shoes and socks.

She abandoned her toying and leaned forward to wrap her hands over the edge of the bathtub—an old-fashioned clawfoot that was more than big enough for two people.

"Take off my belt," I ordered as I unbuttoned my wet shirt.

Tori obeyed without hesitation, licking her lips again. The sight made me even harder.

"And your pants?" she asked breathlessly, fingers poised over the zipper, her thumb stroking me through the fabric again.

"Take those off, too," I said, tossing my shirt on the floor. "Take off everything."

Her nails dragged down my hips as she finished undressing me, my cock springing free.

I was standing naked and hard before her, and she was on her knees in the tub, steam still curling up from the water, her tits glistening and wet. "Now suck," I commanded.

Her eyes bright with pleasure, she wrapped her warm hand tight around me. Then she gave me one slow stroke before opening her mouth and taking me inside it.

"Good girl," I groaned, shivering a little at the hot pressure of her lips and tongue. "Now make it nice and wet. Just like I taught you."

"Mm hmm," she agreed.

She moved her head back and forth, sucking softly as she circled my cock with her tongue, moaning her pleasure. Being inside her mouth felt so right. Like coming home.

"That's right," I breathed.

I placed my hand on the back of Tori's head, guiding her pace, setting the rhythm I knew both of us liked. Slow and deep at first, letting her adjust to it. Then faster. Rougher. My cock fucked her mouth, teasing her, reminding her of how it would be when I was pumping inside her pussy, strong and sure, giving her exactly what she craved.

"Take me deeper," I said.

She relaxed her throat as I thrust even farther inside her mouth, closing my eyes against the perfect sensation of heat and wetness. The way she was sucking me off so good, it took all my willpower not to come right away—but I wasn't going to let her off that easy.

"Enough," I finally said.

I pulled away and she let out a whimper of disappointment, but it disappeared the second I got into the tub with her. It was big enough for two people, but still cozy, water sloshing out onto the tiled floor, but I didn't care. I was done holding back.

"Get over here," I told her. "Straddle me."

She did as I ordered, her knees on either side of my hips as her tits rose in front of me, at the perfect height for exactly what I wanted to do to them. To her.

"You're perfect for me," I murmured, rubbing my lips gently over her taut nipples. "And I'm going to fuck you until you remember how perfect we are together. Until you can feel exactly how much I love you."

"Yes," she moaned as my tongue slid across her nipples, one at a time, teasing her. "I love you, too."

The words made it all the sweeter, her hips already moving with the anticipation of my cock. But I wasn't ready. Not yet. I wanted to torment her a little. Give her a small taste of the desperation I'd felt for her while she was gone.

I sucked one nipple into my mouth, twisting and tweaking the other one before I switched off, lavishing attention on the other. I used my tongue and teeth and fingers to bite, lick, tug at the softly pebbled skin. Torturing and pleasuring her at the same time. She was moaning louder, her wet hair falling in front of her face and showering both of us with water droplets. Her hips were pressed tight against mine, my hot, hard cock brushing the soft lips of her pussy.

"You want this?" I asked, reaching between us to drag my cock up and down the length of her opening.

"God yes," she whimpered. "I want it. Please."

I pushed the head of my cock just barely inside her but didn't thrust. Not yet.

"Tell me what you need," I said, drawing it out.

"I need you to fuck me, please," Tori whispered, over and over, panting against my shoulder with anticipation now. "Please, Stefan, please fuck me. Fuck me please."

It was all I could do to hold back.

"Tell me you love me," I demanded, fisting my hand in her hair and pulling her head back so I could kiss her neck. "I want to hear you say it again."

"I love you," Tori gasped as the head of my cock inched a little deeper into her. "Fuck, I love you so much."

"And who do you belong to?" I pressed, easing almost all the way back out of her, holding her sexually hostage, making her breath catch in her throat.

"You. I belong to you," she said. "I'm yours. Only yours."

We were both breathing hard now, fighting our need for each other.

"You're goddamn right," I told her, gazing into her eyes. "And I'm yours. For always."

Tori started to nod, but without warning I gripped her hips tight and thrust up into her, hard and deep, both of us groaning at the intensity of our connection.

"Now ride me," I ordered. "Ride me until you come."

She grabbed my shoulders, steadying herself, and then started grinding on me, up and down, so much faster and harder than she normally would, her thrusts increasingly frenzied as she panted her pleasure in my ear. Neither of us cared how much water was splashing onto the floor.

"Come for me, kitty cat," I coaxed. "Come on my cock."

She obeyed almost instantly, crying out her orgasm, her pussy clenching deliciously around me. She was so hot and responsive, it was all I could do to not come with her. But I'd spent my life honing my powers of self-control and it served me well in this moment, with my wife's cunt contracting around my cock—my cock which had been aching for her for days.

I held her, waiting until her body had stopped shuddering before I began to move again.

"You feel so good," she whispered.

"So do you," I said.

I loved the slide of her wet body against mine, how easy it was to drag her hips up and down, the water guiding each thrust. Tori's hands were tight on my shoulders as she recovered and began matching my strokes, riding me hard again, her wet hair flung back. Her eyes were glassy with lust, her skin flushed, and I could tell she was close to coming again.

"Say it again," I ordered, unable to get enough of her.

"I love you," she gasped, riding me harder and harder, chasing her new orgasm. "I'm yours."

"I love you," I said, pulling her mouth over mine, our fierce kiss matching the unrestrained pace of our thrusting beneath the water.

"Oh my god, Stefan," she cried out, tensing up. "I'm coming again."

She closed her eyes and arched her back against the tub, her tits displayed beautifully for me as she cried out with the power of her release. Then she leaned forward, her body going limp against my chest as she tried to catch her breath.

"We're not done," I whispered to her, my hands still tight on her hips, my cock still hard inside her.

"Good," she moaned, her lips against my ear. "Because I want more."

"You think you can handle more?" I asked, picking up my pace again, forcing her body down on my cock.

"Yes," she cried out, loving the way I was using her body. "Fuck me."

I did, pounding into her with abandon, watching her tits bounce with every stroke. Now that I'd given myself permission to let go, my orgasm came hard and fast, my release filling her up, hot and full. She shuddered against me, her own desire satiated—at least for the moment.

We lay there in the tub, the water calming and growing cooler around us. I stroked her hair, and she ran her hands along my arms.

"I want to be with you, Stefan," Tori whispered. "Always."

"You promise?" I asked, my hand slipping down her back to cup her ass.

"Yes," she sighed.

"Make a vow," I said.

She leaned back far enough to cup my face and kiss me.

"I vow to stand at your side, for life. To love you. To be honest with you."

"I vow to love you and be honest with you, too," I

repeated, smoothing her hair back. "I vow to stand with you and trust you."

"I vow to trust you," Tori repeated. "To put you before anyone else."

"You are my family," I told her. "I vow to protect you. To cherish you. To put you first."

"You're my family, too," Tori murmured, kissing me deeply. "You're mine."

I was already getting turned on again. I didn't think I would ever stop wanting her. Stop needing her.

"Water's getting cold," I said, gently pulling away and moving her off of my lap before standing and stepping out of the bathtub. Then I dried off quickly and motioned for her to stand.

When she got to her feet I wrapped a towel around her, then lifted her into my arms.

"I'm taking you to bed," I told her.

"I like that plan," she murmured, her head resting against my shoulder, almost as if she was drunk with love.

I knew how she felt. I never wanted to let go of her.

Back in Tori's room, I set her down on the bed and locked the door that opened out into the hallway. Then I climbed in beside her and kissed her deeply, tugging the towel away so my hands could have full access to her body, still warm and soft from the bath.

Her legs parted for me eagerly as I stroked downward, but that wasn't what I was after. Instead, I rolled her onto her stomach, kissing my way down the length of her spine. As I reached the curve of her ass, her body arched up toward me as if she knew what I was planning.

"So responsive," I teased.

She knew exactly what I wanted, and I was pleased to know she wanted it too.

Cupping her ass, I gave her a firm slap. She cried out with lust, the sound muffled by the pillow her face was pressed into.

"You want this?" I asked her, dragging my finger along the line dividing her cheeks.

"Yes," she groaned, her hips rising up, her legs spreading wider.

Unable to help myself, I teased her first with my finger, dragging it along the seam of her ass until she was panting softly, her breath coming faster with the growing anticipation. Then, when I knew she was ready, I slid my finger inside.

She gasped, her entire body seeming to tremble from the pleasure. I was already hard again, and more than ready to be inside her, but I wanted to savor this. Wanted to savor her. I fucked her with my finger gently before adding a second finger, stretching her even wider.

She rocked back against my hand, her fingers clutching the blankets as she moaned with delicious pleasure.

"You ready?" I asked.

"Yes," she said. "I want you so bad."

Giving her one more firm slap on the ass, I knelt on the bed and positioned myself behind her. Rubbing my cock against her wet pussy first, I teased us both for a moment. Tori was practically sobbing with need, face down, thighs wide, her perfect ass in the air.

I was ready to claim her, for now and always.

Sliding my pussy-wet cock back up to her tight asshole, I reminded her, "You're mine."

"Yes," she murmured, pushing back against me. "Always."

Carefully, slowly, I spread her ass open and eased myself inside of her. She was so hot and so tight—so goddamn tight. I didn't want to rush, didn't want to come before I had a chance to make her feel good too, so I went inch by inch. Waiting for her to adjust to the fullness and then relax each time before pushing in even deeper.

It was as if time stood still. All I was aware of was the tightness of her body around me and her soft, breathy moans as she gasped her pleasure. I could feel her clench around me each time I went deeper and I kept pushing, tantalizingly slowly, until I was fully inside of her.

"You feel perfect," I said, taking a breath, willing myself to calm down. "Too good."

We'd done this before and the pleasure had been indescribable, but somehow, now, it was even more intense. I felt incredibly close to her, as if I was possessing her completely, body and soul. She was mine in every way.

I began to thrust, slowly at first, but it was a rhythm I couldn't maintain. I needed more. Needed to go faster, harder, to fuck her ass until she came—until I came. Until we were one.

Picking up the pace, I let myself get lost in the sensation of her body and mine, fully connected, drawing pleasure from each other in the most unguarded, intimate way. I could tell she was loving it by the way she moved against me, pushing back to meet each of my thrusts, her throaty moans filling the room. I wanted only to satisfy her, to give her everything she needed.

"Fuck my ass," she murmured, over and over. It was so hot, I could feel myself being pulled toward the edge of my orgasm, starting to lose control. "It's your turn to come."

"You first," I said, fighting my climax with every thrust.

"No," Tori said, gasping out the words as I pounded into her. "You, this time. I want you to come inside me. Come inside my ass."

"Fuck," I groaned. I couldn't hold back any longer. With my hands tight on her hips, I pumped harder and harder until I began to jerk and shudder, my release barreling toward me, unstoppable now. "I love you," I told her, thrusting deeper than I'd ever been before.

"Yes," she cried out. "I love you, Stefan."

Her words triggered the most intense orgasm I'd ever felt, long and deep, and I fully let go, groaning and spilling hot cum into her, my hips moving frantically, my desire beyond my control.

"Yes," Tori moaned, and I felt her contracting around me one last time. "Yes, yes, yes."

We rode out our orgasms until our movements slowed, our breath still fast and jagged, both of us spent. I pulled out and climbed next to her, rolling her over to gather her in my arms.

Tori's face was flushed, her entire body relaxed against me. I'd never felt such desire, such satisfaction before.

"I love you," I told her.

She pressed even closer to me, kissing my chest.

"I love you too," she said. "For always."

Then she tucked her head under my chin, our bodies fitting together like two perfect puzzle pieces, and I knew that I'd never let her go again.

TORI

CHAPTER 17

The next twenty-four hours went by in a blur. After explaining to my very-relieved stepmother that we'd mended our marital rift, Stefan further informed her that he planned to take very good care of me and that we'd head back to Chicago the next day (in the process nearly charming the pants off Michelle, just as he had the first time they met). Then he took us out for a fancy dinner and slept with me in my tiny twin bed, holding me close all night long.

In the morning he made a few calls and arranged to have my clothes, my things, my life, packed back up and sent home. *Home.* Our home. It was amazing he was able to get anything done, since we both seemed to be having a hard time taking our eyes—and hands—off of each other. By the time we pulled up to the valet stand at our condominium that afternoon, my body was deliciously sore from all the intense sex, but I still couldn't get enough.

We tumbled into bed again, and once we caught our breath afterwards, Stefan told me that he wanted to make sure his family understood my place in his life. Now that we had officially pledged to have a real life together, he wanted it to start now.

"They need to see that we're a united front," Stefan said, getting up to grab his phone off the dresser. "Especially my father."

My pulse kicked up just thinking about Konstantin's strong dislike of me. "What are you planning?" I asked.

"We'll hold a dinner here for everyone," he said. "Tonight."

I sat up straighter. "Tonight? There's no time."

He waved his hand, unconcerned. "Gretna will make it happen. I'll pay her double overtime and have her bring in a few extra staff if need be."

"Okay..." I said, nodding. "What about Anja and Max? They should be here too."

My stomach dropped even as I said the words, but I tried not to show my nervousness. I didn't want Stefan to think I'd bolt over the situation with Anja again. As if he could read my mind, Stefan came back over to the bed and took my face in his hands.

"You're the one I chose," he reminded me. "And yes, I do want Anja to come tonight. But not Max. This isn't about him, it's about you and me. I need Anja to come to terms with my choices and see that I'm committed to my marriage, without worrying what Max might think."

It made me feel better to hear him say that.

"If this is what you want," I told him. "Then let's do it. Let's go all out."

Stefan made a few calls to his family and put Anja in touch with a babysitter that Gretna saved the day by recommending.

Once he hung up, we took a quick shower and then got to work. Stefan had the housekeeper come over for an emergency deep clean, and I was put in charge of making sure dinner would be ready on time, which meant conferring with Gretna about the menu and sending her to the store immediately to get all the necessary ingredients for a lavish meal for six. It was going to be me, Stefan, Anja, my father-in-law, Luka, and Emzee. Our preparations were all last minute, but thank goodness we had an amazing staff who were happy to help us pull it together. My husband's years of being a generous and fair employer were really paying off.

Out of everyone we'd invited, the only person I was excited to see was my sister-in-law. Stefan had admitted that on his way to Springfield, she'd called him to explain why I'd left Chicago. So, thanks to Emzee, he understood exactly what had happened. I would always be grateful to her for that.

As I fussed over my makeup and hair, which I put in a French twist, I tried to tell myself everything would work out with Stefan by my side. I knew the dinner on the table was going to be incredible, but no matter how much I repeated positive mantras to myself, I couldn't shake the feeling that the whole thing was going to be a nightmare. I'd never been more intimidated.

With minutes left until everyone was set to arrive, and the staff busting their butts in the living room and kitchen, I stole away to our bedroom to finally get dressed. Flipping through my hangers in the closet, I tried not to panic. I wanted to look confident, powerful, poised. Like someone who belonged with Stefan, who was equal to the Zorics—even Konstantin.

"This one," Stefan murmured in my ear, coming up behind me to reach over my shoulder.

The knee-length dress he chose was a deep shade of

burgundy, body-skimming without being tight, and made of a slightly slinky fabric that gathered in an artful knot over the left hip.

"Why burgundy?" I questioned doubtfully. I loved the dress, but it seemed a little flashy.

"Because," he said, turning me toward him. "You have absolutely no reason to hide." He kissed me, and I melted in his arms. "And besides, it looks amazing on you."

I changed quickly and put on the diamond earrings that Stefan had given me recently. He'd said they were a symbol that he and I were a pair. I could reach up and touch them if I felt unsure, and they'd serve as a reminder of his devotion to me. To our life. Our little family.

Standing in the doorway of the living room just before seven, I gave myself a moment to take it all in. Our staff had done an incredible job—managing to make the place even more luxurious and opulent than ever. It looked more like a fancy restaurant than a private home with fresh flowers everywhere, a gorgeous spread of cheese and fruit already set out, a hand-stitched linen tablecloth spread across the table, its gold threads glinting in the candlelight. There were thick candles set out on every available surface, their light giving the space a warm, homey glow. Our exquisite Haviland and Parlon dishes and silverware were set out, their dramatic combination of black and gold very much in line with my husband's aesthetic—strong and masculine, yet perfectly stylish. The condo looked impressive and smelled even better.

As nervous as I was, my mouth still watered at the sight of all the fancy European cheeses, the split figs with golden honey, the spiced almonds and green olives and prosciutto. There was even caviar and tiny pickles. And that was just the appetizer. I could have easily made a whole meal out of it.

"This looks incredible," I told Gretna as she fussed with the table settings one last time. "I feel like you're our fairy godmother. I can't thank you enough."

She only grinned and flashed me a wink, passing me a rolled-up slice of paper-thin prosciutto she'd speared with a toothpick. It tasted like heaven.

The doorbell rang and I almost jumped out of my skin. Stefan came over to take my hand, sending one of the staff to get the door. In his Armani suit, he looked good enough to eat.

"We're in control," he soothed me. "This is our home, and this dinner is on our terms."

"I know," I said, nodding, though I was well aware that my father-in-law would probably still do whatever he could to maintain the upper hand.

I wondered if Konstantin had any idea what he was up against. Stefan had always been careful around his father, doing his best to get along with the man and feigning compliance and tractability. They'd had arguments in the past, sure, but I had a feeling my father-in-law would be truly shocked to discover what his son was capable of if pushed too far.

And I was pretty sure Stefan—thanks to his father's threats to me and our marriage—had finally been pushed too far. Tonight he was going to let Konstantin know, in no uncertain terms, that we were a team and that nothing could come between us.

Suddenly a squeal pierced the air and as I turned around, a set of perfumed arms had flung themselves around me. "Emzee," I said, smiling so big my cheeks hurt.

"I'm so glad you're back!" she told me, squeezing me tight.

I hugged her back. "I'm so glad you got here first," I said.

"Don't be nervous. I'm on your team," she said, flashing a confident grin.

Besides Stefan, she was the one member of the family I loved and trusted completely.

"Ooh, I spy green olives and cornichons with my name on them. Can we sit?" she asked.

We settled down at the table with Stefan and chatted a little bit about how she was doing, my stomach clenching when the doorbell soon rang again. This time it was Luka. He walked in, looking as handsome as always, but a little rumpled and unsteady on his feet.

"Dear brother, you are clearly intoxicated," Emzee scolded, but she said it teasingly. She pushed away from the table and ran over to hug him.

His pregaming certainly didn't stop him from heading straight to the bar and pouring himself another drink, though Emzee followed and tried—unsuccessfully—to take it away.

"It's fine," Stefan said. "As long as he behaves himself."

Luka just laughed and took a seat.

I wasn't the biggest fan of my brother-in-law, but I thought I could understand why he drank like he did. If Konstantin was my father, I'd probably have a drinking problem too.

Konstantin and Anja were the last to arrive, and they came together. Part of me had almost expected Konstantin to disregard Stefan's request that Max stay home and bring the boy along anyway, if for no other reason than to assert that he, as the family patriarch, was the Zoric in charge around here. I was glad to see that he had actually honored

Stefan's wishes. Maybe it was a sign that he was interested in diplomacy after all.

Anja, as a former model, looked predictably flawless, wearing a black dress that swirled over the floor as she walked, the neckline featuring a daring slit that was cut so low it hit her sternum, but was so narrow that there was no cleavage visible.

"That dress is incredible," I told her warmly. "You look great." And I meant it. Seeing her up close again was actually a lot less stressful than I had imagined. Now that I knew where I stood with Stefan, and we had renewed our vows to each other, I had nothing to fear from her.

"So do you," Anja replied, but I noticed that her eyes slid away from me and locked on Stefan. Well, she could look all she wanted. He was still mine.

Meanwhile Konstantin was talking to Luka and Stefan, and completely ignoring me.

"Hello, Konstantin," I said, trying to take the high road.

My father-in-law waved irritably in my direction, as if my greeting was a fly to shoo.

Anja shot me a sympathetic look and my heart softened toward her a little more. Who knew what she'd been through over the past years, with only Konstantin as her resource and a son to raise all on her own? That was a fate I wouldn't wish on anyone.

With Konstantin's arrival, the mood in the condo had gotten noticeably more tense, so I suggested that we all sit down and eat. We took our seats, chatting idly over the cheese plate until the staff cleared it away and brought out the real food.

Gretna and I had chosen a menu of impeccably prepared comfort food, hoping it would make the meal more harmonious than something overly complicated, so there was beautiful Kobe steak with garlic butter, grilled lobster tails sliced on the bias, potato gratin with truffles, and a light salad made with shaved autumn vegetables. I knew for a fact that everything was cooked to perfection—thanks to the taste test that Gretna had insisted I perform—yet despite the enjoyment our guests were getting out of the meal, an anxious mood had settled over the table. As if we were all waiting for a bomb to explode.

I glanced over at Stefan. He was watching his father.

Following his eye line, I watched Konstantin talk loudly at Anja about the benefits of boarding school for children, gesturing almost violently with his steak knife. She was giving him a polite smile as she delicately ate her truffled potatoes, clearly leaning away from him. Emzee seemed okay enough, but Luka had pushed his untouched plate away and was leaning back in his chair, brooding over what appeared to be his second glass of whiskey.

The whole scene was tense and awkward, but I had no idea what to do. Interrupting Konstantin wouldn't earn me any brownie points, though I was dying to redirect the conversation to something less fraught, something we could all participate in. As I wracked my brain for safe topics, I felt Stefan's warm hand squeeze my thigh under the table. And then—

Clink clink clink—he was tapping his knife against the side of his wine glass, signaling for quiet.

The room, already fairly subdued, went silent...except for Konstantin, who was still talking to Anja. Her gaze shifted between father and son, and then she cleared her throat.

"I believe Stefan would like to speak," I said, flashing her a tiny smile.

Konstantin grumbled, but finally shut up. I was sure

he'd heard the tapping, but was trying to maintain control over the situation. Just as I had expected.

"If you'll just give me a moment to say something to everyone," Stefan said, standing. His voice was strong and sure, and he took his time making eye contact with each person at the table. "I'd like to raise a toast to our family. The Zorics. To the empire we've built."

Everyone raised their glasses, though Emzee and I exchanged slightly confused looks. This wasn't what Stefan had told me he was going to say.

"I also wanted to share how grateful I am that Anja has returned safe and sound, and with our amazing son."

"He's a great kid," Emzee murmured sweetly.

Anja brightened at their words, but then gave me a cautious look. I tried to keep my own expression neutral at this point, not knowing what was going to happen next.

Stefan nodded. "Her reappearance came as a great surprise to most of us," he said, looking pointedly at his father, who sipped his drink with a smug little smile on his face. "But now that we've all had a chance to process the news of her return—and the arrival of Max—I trust that they will both be welcomed into the family with open arms."

"Of course! They already have been," Konstantin blustered, looking thrilled, but I could tell that Stefan wasn't done yet.

"However," my husband continued, "the reason I invited you all here was to make something very clear. Something I would have stated earlier had I known there would be any possibility of confusion." He reached out and took my hand, pulling me up beside him. "Tori is my wife. I am devoted to her, and our marriage, first and foremost. I have never wavered in that." He speared his father with a look. "And I will cut off anyone who tries to tear us apart."

You could have heard a pin drop.

Everyone was staring at Stefan, myself included. I knew that he'd planned to set boundaries with his family once and for all, but I hadn't imagined he would do it so forcefully or explicitly. He had chosen me, now and forever. And had made it abundantly clear, in no uncertain terms. To Anja and all the Zorics. Even—and maybe especially—Konstantin.

Emotions washed over me and I lifted my chin, forcing back the tears that threatened.

But it was no use. My vision blurred, my chest tightened, and I murmured an "excuse me" and fled the table. The last thing I wanted was to cry in front of Anja and my father-in-law. I went into the bedroom and closed the door, utterly choked up by Stefan's announcement.

I heard footsteps in the hallway, and I turned to find Stefan rushing through the door, pulling me toward him, his face beautifully concerned at the tears spilling from my eyes.

"What did I do?" he asked. "Was that not okay? I didn't mean to upset you, Tori."

He was stroking the back of my neck, holding me tightly against his chest, and I nearly burst into fresh tears at how worried he sounded.

"I'm not upset," I said, pulling back to look up at him. "That was perfect. You were perfect. I just got overwhelmed."

"By your overpowering love for me?" he teased.

I laughed. "Actually, yes."

"I love you too," he said. He smiled, and I smiled back.

"You think you can handle going back out there, or should I cover for you?"

"I want to go back out. I just need a minute," I said. My makeup was probably a mess.

I dashed into the bathroom and dabbed at my wet lashes with a few folded tissues, giving my mascara a quick refresh before heading back out to Stefan.

"How do I look?" I asked.

"Stunning, as always," he said, and then pulled me in for a deep, slow kiss.

Together, we went back into the dining room, ready to face his family as man and wife.

STEFAN

CHAPTER 18

Back at the table, in the aftermath of my declaration, I suddenly realized how good I felt about what I'd said. Better than good, actually. A huge weight was off my shoulders. Reasserting control over my life gave me strength and validation. Power. I'd stated my loyalties resolutely and definitively; now the people closest to me could either support my decision—and my marriage—or stay the fuck out of my way. It was a win-win. Tori and I were officially done making space in our lives for anyone trying to undermine or oppose us.

Refilling Tori's wine glass, I glanced around at our guests, trying to gauge their reactions to my announcement.

My wife, of course, had been surprised and moved. It was clear by her tears and the moment we'd shared in the bedroom that I'd done right by her. Meanwhile my father had a scowl on his face as he took out his obvious displeasure on his food, shoveling it in, and my sister, the one person at the table who seemed to care for Tori almost as much as I did, was smiling broadly at the two of us as she talked animatedly about her upcoming photography work.

THE CHOICE

I grinned back at her, happy she was here, bolstered by the knowledge that Emzee was on our team—always had been and always would be.

My brother Luka was staring off into the middle distance with a tumbler of my most expensive whiskey in his hand, undeniably drunk, but that was par for the course for him these days. I watched him drain the rest of the glass and then nearly stab himself with his razor-sharp knife as he tried to cut a piece of steak on his plate. It might have been humorous if he wasn't such a mess. I made a mental note to look into rehab centers...though I knew convincing my brother to check into one would be the bigger challenge.

And finally, Anja projected an air of obvious discomfort. She was barely eating, picking at her dinner and avoiding eye contact as she forced a smile to go along with Emzee's happy chatter. If anything, she looked ashamed. I was positive now that she wasn't a villain like my father. She was just a single mom trying to do her best with a hard life, who'd gotten drawn into a situation that in many ways was beyond her control. I'd make sure, no matter what happened, that she and Max were taken care of. That they weren't my father's prisoners and playthings.

Gretna and another staff member bustled in to clear our plates and serve dessert, which consisted of poached pears and white chocolate mousse with an elaborate spun sugar decoration perched on top. As I looked closer, I realized the sugar seemed to be dusted with gold flakes.

"Bon appétit," Gretna said, bowing a little before leaving the room in her black dress and starched apron.

"Thank you, Gretna," I called out after her.

I had to stifle a smile—I never made our personal chef wear a uniform, or stick around to serve us. She was merely playing a part tonight, and clearly enjoying the chance to lay it on a little thick, although I hadn't specifically asked her to do so.

What I *had* made clear to Tori and the staff, however, was that tonight was meant to be a demonstration of wealth and power. It was the only language my father understood. I wanted him to see that I wouldn't be controlled or threatened by him. That I was confident enough in my ability to maintain my privilege that I could afford this kind of lavish spending.

Of course, my father was more than done playing second fiddle at this point. Ignoring the artfully constructed dessert, he threw his napkin down and pushed back from the table.

"We're leaving," he said, snapping his fingers at Anja.

She obeyed his order immediately, jumping to her feet and going to get her coat. I wasn't sorry to see my father go, but I couldn't stand the way he was treating Anja. Especially since he had claimed that he viewed her and Max as part of the Zoric family. How quickly her value had plummeted in my father's eyes, now that I'd reasserted my commitment to Tori.

"Thank you both so much for coming," Tori said, rising to follow them to the foyer and escort them out. I knew it was rude not to join my wife in seeing our guests off, but I'd had enough of my father's pouting. He could stew for all I cared.

The front door slammed, and Luka jumped a little in his seat.

"That went well," Emzee said sarcastically from across the table.

"As well as could be expected," I pointed out as Tori came back and sat down again.

Tori smiled at Emzee and Luka and said, "Glad you're

both still here," though I was pretty sure the comment was directed solely at my sister.

"Of course! Couldn't let any of this dessert go to waste," Emzee said, reaching over to slide Konstantin's untouched dish toward her. "This mousse is a dream."

The whole room seemed to have stopped holding its breath now that my father was gone. And Tori seemed more relaxed and glowing as well. I was so impressed with her. She'd kept her head high and managed to treat my father in a distant but polite way throughout the entire meal, despite her nerves and the fact that he'd never been kind to her. It took a lot of strength.

As Emzee dove back into her descriptions of the assignment she'd soon be shooting in the indigenous forests of South America, Luka quietly eased out of his chair and half-walked, half-stumbled to the bar in the adjoining living room.

Tori reached over and put a hand on my arm.

"He's so drunk already," she whispered. I could hear the worry in her tone.

I nodded, already rising from my seat. Even though my younger brother was an adult, I still felt responsible for him. Still felt as though I needed to take care of him, to protect him from the world. My father certainly never had. And as much as I disapproved of Luka's self-medicating and destructive behavior, I thought I understood where it came from.

"Luka," I started as I walked over to the bar, where my brother was pouring himself another very generous glass of aged Glenfiddich.

I doubted he could even taste it at this point, he was so intoxicated.

"Brother!" Luka slurred, raising his glass in my direction. "Great dinner," he said with a sneer. "Great toast. Really livened up the party."

He reeked of booze, as if he was sweating it out of his skin, to the point that I had to take a step back. Now that I was standing in front of him, I realized exactly how terrible he looked. It wasn't just that Luka was intoxicated; I'd seen plenty of that lately. His shirt was only half tucked, and buttoned incorrectly. His hair stuck up greasily in places, as if he hadn't showered properly in days. And his face had changed, with new lines fanning out from his eyes, and a pale puffiness that hadn't been there before. He looked like he hadn't slept in days.

"You look pretty peaked," I told him honestly. "Maybe you should cool it on the booze."

"Maybe you should mind your own business," he said, glaring at me. "I'm perfec'ly capable of handling my shit." He was slurring.

"Okay," I said skeptically.

I suppressed the urge to knock the glass out of his hand. Truthfully, I was torn between giving Luka a dose of tough love or treating him with more compassion. I didn't want to enable his drinking, but at the same time I knew that he had only just recently learned the truth about what our father did behind the scenes of KZ Modeling. The fact that KZM made most of its money via sex trafficking had clearly hit Luka hard. And he in turn had hit the bottle hard.

I wasn't unsympathetic—I'd been shocked as well when I found out—and I still felt a little guilty that I hadn't been able to protect my brother better. I also hated that I couldn't tell him about my current plants to ensure that our father's illegal business dealings would crash and burn. I loved Luka, and I knew he would be on my side, but at the same time I couldn't trust him not to say anything to our father. Not when he was constantly in a drunken state like this.

Still, I could at least try to help him not lose his life to alcohol.

Luka was taking a long gulp of whiskey, not realizing that he was dribbling a good portion of his drink down the front of his shirt.

"You've had enough," I told him firmly, trying to ease the glass from his hand.

Instead of giving it up, he wrestled it away from me, managing to slosh the rest of the whiskey all over the hand knotted silk rug. Realizing what he'd done, he slammed the empty glass on top of the bar.

"Who are you to boss me around, anyway?" he railed. "*Everybody* was drinking tonight, and that was just fine—how come *I'm* the one who gets the spotlight on me?"

"Everything okay in there?" Tori called out through the doorway to the dining room.

"We're great!" Luka slurred, pulling the whiskey bottle across the bar toward him.

I turned toward the doorway and motioned for Tori to stay at the table, trying to give her a reassuring smile. The last thing I wanted was for her to witness this altercation.

"*You're done*," I repeated to Luka, grabbing the bottle and locking it in the cabinet.

It didn't feel good treating him like he was a child that needed to be protected from himself, but the fact was, it wasn't so far from the truth.

"You're a real fucking drag, Stefan," Luka said.

I took a long breath, searching for the kind of words that might get through to him. "I care about you, Luka. And I know you're an adult who can make his own choices. But this has to stop. You're destroying yourself."

Luka laughed bitterly. "You're not my father," he said, and then he gave me a mean smile. "Though you are *somebody's* father now, aren't you? Kind of funny, isn't it?"

"Luka," I warned.

He ignored me. "I'm not entirely convinced, though," he said, tapping his finger against his chin. "You know, I've seen the brat myself."

"His name. Is Max," I grinded out, tamping down the first stirrings of rage.

"Sure, Max," Luka repeated, before glancing up at me and tilting his head as if he was studying me. "The thing is... he doesn't really look like you, does he?"

I didn't like where this conversation was going.

"You're drunk," I told him.

"Are you sure he's even yours?" Luka said. An uncomfortable chill went up my spine. "You might have loved that bitch, but let's not forget she was a hooker for a living."

Without realizing I'd made the choice to do so, I had Luka shoved up against the wall, my hand around his neck. Fear flashed in his eyes, but he still had the nerve to smirk at me as I stood there breathing hard and trying to calm down.

"Shut the fuck up," I seethed.

"The truth hurts, brother," he said, his voice rasping from the pressure on his neck.

Suddenly, Tori appeared in my periphery, a steaming cup of coffee in her hand. I wondered how much of the conversation she had heard.

She cleared her throat and I released my brother, stepping back. I regretted my outburst.

"Here's some coffee for you, Luka," she said, in a much kinder tone than he deserved. "Why don't you go sit with Emzee for a bit?"

I half expected Luka to argue with Tori, to start cursing

or trying to pour another drink for himself, but he took the coffee without comment, his head lowered like a chastened dog.

"Sure," he said quietly and shuffled back to the dining room, where my sister was waiting—hopefully to pour a carafe of coffee into him before sending him home.

I leaned back against the bar, feeling suddenly weary. Tori squeezed my shoulder.

"Are you okay?" she asked.

I glanced in the direction my brother had gone in. "I don't know," I said honestly.

"I heard him," Tori admitted. Her voice was low; perhaps she didn't want Emzee to hear. "He's...very drunk."

"Yeah," I responded. "Anyway. Let's go sit."

As I sipped coffee back at the table, I couldn't help brooding. I knew Luka was drunk and spouting off, but I couldn't deny that he'd succeeded in planting the seeds of doubt in my mind. And he had a point about Anja. A solid one. She'd slept with other men—that was a fact. I didn't judge her for it, but it certainly called the issue of paternity into question.

And then that first day at the zoo with Max, I remembered thinking that although he had seemed familiar, especially his expressions and quirks, he hadn't really reminded me of myself. And he didn't look anything like the younger versions of me that I'd seen in my childhood photos. Maybe the familiarity was just seeing Anja in the kid, but I wasn't sure. I'd believed her when she'd said Max was mine, but Luka's words had thrown everything into question.

I continued mulling it over as I helped Emzee escort Luka to the foyer.

"Can you make sure he gets home safe?" I asked her as he struggled with his coat.

"I'm fine," Luka mumbled, misaligning the buttons.

Emzee nodded. "Sure. In fact, I won't leave his side until he sobers up. My boyfriend's at home with Munchkin anyway, so I don't need to rush back to my apartment any time soon."

"Life saver," I told her. At least there was one person in my family I could always depend on. Then I gave Luka a hug, even though he tried to pull away. "Take care of yourself," I said.

Once Tori and I had ushered them out the door, we sank onto the living room sofa with the last of the coffee. The staff was already in the process of dismantling the décor and candles in the dining room and cleaning up the remaining dishes on the table.

As the comforting, familiar sound of Gretna's humming issued from the kitchen, I leaned my head against Tori's and went silent for a long time, lost in thought.

Finally, I turned to look at my wife.

"I'm going to ask Anja for a DNA test," I told her. "What do you think?"

She nodded. "I think that's a good idea. You need to know the truth."

STEFAN

CHAPTER 19

The lab waiting room was white and cold and sterile, the neutral abstract art on the walls only adding to the stark feeling of the place. It smelled of antiseptic and everything seemed meticulously clean. I'd done my research to find the best DNA lab in Chicago that provided expedited test results, and now I was sitting here waiting for those results that would either confirm or deny a permanent connection to the woman sitting to the left of me. Eight days had passed since I'd thrown the dinner party for my family—the night Luka had put the seed of doubt in my head about Max's true father.

When I'd confronted Anja with the possibility that Max might not be my son, she had been surprisingly quick to agree to the DNA test. We'd decided not to mention it to my father until we got the results back. It would keep things cleaner, avoid sowing further discord.

Since a cheek swab was all that was required, Anja had gone with Max to the lab last week to submit their DNA samples first, telling him it was just a doctor's appointment. Anja thought it would be less suspicious if Max didn't see me there too, so I'd gone to the lab later that day to submit my DNA. Even with the expedited testing, we still had to wait a few days for the results. So here we all were now, minus Max, holding our breath in this waiting room.

Anja was currently sitting on one side of me, her hands folded tightly in her lap, while Tori sat on my other side, her fingers entwined with mine.

I was so grateful she was here.

No matter what the results were, I needed Tori by my side. Needed to know we'd be facing this together.

It was a little awkward, the three of us, but it was better this way. Better we all got the news together. Anja was handling the whole thing with shocking grace and composure; except for some tears when I first asked for the test, she'd been supportive of the process throughout. She said it would be best to know for sure before introducing me formally to Max as his father.

Tori had been incredible all along. I knew she was anxious—I could tell from the way her knee was jumping underneath our linked hands—but she was still doing her best to be brave. She had barely stopped fidgeting since we got there, and truthfully I was just as nervous.

"How much longer, do you think?" Tori asked, in a hushed tone.

We were the only people in the waiting room, but the stillness of the place, the harsh whiteness of it all, made it seem like whispering was required.

"I'm sure it'll be soon," I murmured, stroking the back of her hand with my thumb.

Sitting around waiting was stressful, but in some ways, dealing with the Max paternity issue had been a welcome distraction from what was currently going on with the federal investigation into my father and KZ Modeling. Tori had spent the last week getting back on track at UChicago, taking the opportunity to slip the last few pieces of incriminating information to Gavin between classes, and the latest news from his brother was that a raid would happen soon.

But it couldn't come soon enough. Frank had told me to be patient, but I was not a man known for my patience. Especially when it came to getting things done. I wanted my father arrested. I wanted his company destroyed and I wanted him out of the picture.

And I wanted it now.

Glancing over at my wife, I examined her beautiful profile. There were dark circles under her eyes—she was brave and strong, but she hadn't been sleeping well. Even the combined distraction of her studies and the marathon sex at home wasn't enough to chase the worry away.

Right now she was biting her bottom lip, and I squeezed her hand. Looking over, she gave me a smile, and I was even more comforted by her presence and support.

That was another reason I was eager for the feds to put my father behind bars. I knew that he was furious that his attempt to drive me and Tori apart had failed, and despite my family dinner speech, I still wasn't convinced he wouldn't do something awful in order to get what he wanted. He was a man who didn't like to be told no, and it was impossible to not worry about Tori whenever she left my sight. Days during the week were a nightmare. I found myself texting her constantly just to make sure she was okay, and at class where she was supposed to be.

"Do you have any of that gum?" Anja asked, leaning over me to talk to Tori.

"I think so!" Tori lit up and started digging around inside her bag.

The most surprising thing had been the way that Anja

and Tori had found a way to bond during this whole process. With a little squeal of triumph, Tori pulled out a fat pack of the pink and green watermelon-mint bubblegum that both of them were equally obsessed with.

"That stuff is foul," I said. "Watermelon and mint do not go together."

"Then why is it so hard to find?" Tori pointed out, passing the pack to Anja.

"Because nobody wants it," I said.

Anja laughed.

"It's because *everybody* wants it, so they can't keep it in stock anywhere," Tori argued.

Soon enough I was enveloped in the scent of the gum, while Anja and Tori chewed away happily on either side of me. I feigned disgust, but I didn't actually mind. If anything, I was amused. It was just like Tori to make friends with Anja. The two of them could have been enemies, but instead, whenever the three of us were together, Anja and Tori often got so chatty that I found myself leaving the room and letting them get caught up talking about books and ethnic food and random old movies I'd never heard of.

"I finally watched *Spirits of the Dead* last night, after Max went to bed," Anja told Tori.

"And?" Tori prodded, on the edge of her seat.

"Very good. Just like you said."

"Yeah," Tori said. "It's hard to do a bad adaptation of Edgar Allan Poe."

The two of them had been texting non-stop about a French director named Roger Vadim. I'd only heard of him because he directed *Barbarella*, but apparently, he'd done tons of movies that both Tori and Anja loved, though Tori seemed to know a little more about them.

"The last segment was the freakiest," Anja said. "The severed head?"

Tori shivered. "I know. Terence Stamp is totally haunting. You should watch *Pretty Maids All in a Row* next," she suggested. "It's the one he did after *Barbarella*. With Rock Hudson."

"Rock Hudson, is he the one from all the Doris Day movies?" Anja asked.

Tori grinned. "That's him. It's a weird movie but I think you'll like it."

"They're all weird. That's the best part," Anja said eagerly.

"Sounds like a good distraction," I said, inadvertently reminding us why we were there.

A quiet hush fell over the three of us as the reality of the situation sank back in. In the distance I heard the clip clop of shoes against the tile floor. The door to the back offices swung open and our heads snapped up as a nurse said, "We're ready for you," and gestured for us to follow her.

"I guess this is it," I said, standing.

Tori took a deep, shuddering breath, and I kept a firm hold of her hand. My heart was pounding in my chest as we followed the nurse, Anja walking behind us. I had no idea what to expect. I wasn't even sure I knew what I wanted anymore.

For all these years, Anja had been a dream; a ghost from my past that I was constantly chasing. Then, just when I'd started to think it was time to give up on finding out what had happened to her, she had returned—bringing the possibility of a child, of a *family*, into my life. I'd realized that I didn't hate the idea of being of father, more confident than ever that I would not repeat the same mistakes my own father had made...but was I ready to be the father of a seven-year-old child who I barely knew? Who I'd never had a chance to bond with?

The nurse stopped outside an office and gestured for us to go inside.

"The doctor is in," she said with a smile. "Don't worry, her bark is worse than her bite."

We took our seats across from a doctor sitting at a desk. She was young, with a shock of unruly dark curls, and wearing a serious expression that didn't seem to match the hair. It was hard to gauge any information from her expression, though. A file was open on the desk.

I strained to see what was written on the pages spread before her, but I was too far away. The writing was too small, and it was upside down anyway.

"Ms. Fischer," she said, using Anja's legal pseudonym, "Mr. Zoric. And Mrs. Zoric." She nodded at all of us gravely. "I have your DNA results here. As you know, we run all our tests twice, and we now have a conclusive answer for you regarding the paternity of—" she glanced down at the paperwork. "Maxim."

I let out a breath. "Okay," I said.

"We're ready," Anja added.

Glancing over at Tori, I saw that she was pale but her posture was straight. She looked at me and gave me a short, firm nod. Then I looked at Anja again. Her skin was practically leeched of all color but she also gave me a nod. I linked my fingers together with Tori's. Whatever the results were, we'd face it together.

The doctor cleared her throat and looked down at the paperwork again. My pulse raced.

"The DNA shows conclusively that you, Stefan Zoric," she said calmly, "are not Maxim's father. Your DNA is a 0% match."

"Wait. Are you positive?" I couldn't help asking.

"Positive," the doctor said, not a sliver of doubt in her tone, and I suddenly realized why she put on such a serious face for these appointments. "We ran two independent tests, with two different lab technicians."

I let out a breath, feeling my shoulders slump with the release of so much tension. Despite the confidence of the doctor's assertion, it still took a long time for her words to sink in. It was a shock. I wasn't Max's father.

There was a soft, muffled sound, and I turned to find that Anja had her head in her hands and was crying. Tori let go of me and went over to Anja, rubbing her shoulders and back and murmuring soft comforting words.

I felt numb.

"I'll leave you alone to process this. Take as long as you need," the doctor said, picking up the file and heading out the door, shutting it firmly behind her.

Not Max's father.

I took a breath and leaned back in my chair, my head resting against the wall. I didn't know how I felt. Relief, yes, but also disappointment.

Max was a good kid, smart and inquisitive and fun—and I had really enjoyed spending time with him. Regardless of the paternity issue, I cared about him. And I hadn't minded the idea of being his father. I'd even started embracing the concept. Looking forward to what lay ahead.

At least the disappointment was mine and Anja's alone. It had been smart not to introduce me to Max right away as his father. For all he knew, I was just a friend of his mom's. And now, a friend of his as well.

I couldn't help thinking that for all of my brother's flaws, all of his drinking and immature behavior, Luka had done me a favor by expressing doubt about my paternity.

Because if I hadn't asked for a DNA test, I never would have known the truth. None of us would have.

But now, after all this hardship and strife, my relationship with Tori had been given the gift of a clean slate. As saddened as I was to lose my biological connection to Max, I took comfort in knowing that Tori and I wouldn't have to navigate that complication any more. Now we could focus on our marriage—on our family. Maybe start thinking about a baby of our own.

Glancing at Tori, who was still comforting Anja, it was easy to imagine her as a mother. To picture her glowing and pregnant with my child. It was something I wanted, I realized.

Maybe that could be the next step in our lives. Once my father had been brought to justice and his illegal business dealings dismantled, Tori and I could focus on having a family.

Anja was still crying, with Tori crouched on the ground beside her chair, holding Anja's hand.

"I'm so sorry," Anja said when she realized I was watching them.

"Don't be," I said. I reached over and pulled some tissues from the box on the doctor's desk. She was well-stocked; no doubt used to getting strong emotional reactions from clients.

"I hoped so much that it was you," Anja went on tearfully, dabbing at her eyes. "All these years, I never even allowed myself to consider that it wouldn't be."

Tori and I exchanged a look. I could see the relief in her eyes, but I could also tell that she felt bad for Anja, who she had grown close to.

"You didn't know," I reassured her. "It's not your fault."

I didn't blame her anymore for the part she had played

in my father's endless game of chess. We were all just pawns to him, a means to an end. Anja had gotten swept up in it just like the rest of us, only my father had managed to maintain near complete control over her life.

"Maybe that's why I stayed away so long, honestly," Anja said. "Because I didn't want to confront the possibility that you weren't Max's father. I wanted it to be true so badly, because it would mean he was a product of love, but I guess...I guess I was just fooling myself."

Her tears were welling up again, and Tori pulled her into a hug. I didn't want to push Anja when she was already so upset, but I knew that we couldn't have any more secrets.

"Anja," I said softly. "Do you have...any idea who Max's real father could be?"

Tori shot me a look, but I had to ignore it. I knew she was thinking of Anja's feelings, but it was important to try to figure this out. Not just for me or for Anja, but for Max.

"I think so," she said, lifting her head to look at me. "I only had one client back then who refused to use protection sometimes." She let out a breath. "He always gave me a fake name, but I recognized him once from the news on TV."

"From the news?" Tori repeated, frowning.

"So you know his real name?" I asked.

Anja nodded slowly. "Yes," she said. "He was a politician. From here. Senator Mitch Lindsey."

TORI

CHAPTER 20

"Psst...Tori."

A little origami crane made out of notebook paper landed on my desk and I glanced over at Diane, snapping out of my daze.

"You okay?" my hippie friend whispered.

Faking a smile, I nodded. But I wasn't okay, and I knew Diane would see right through me. Luckily, we were sitting in our Psycholinguistics class, and there was no way for her to grill me when Professor Dhawan was deep in the middle of a review for our upcoming final exams.

"Let's grab a tea after this," she suggested. "You seem—"

"Ms. Vergara," Professor Dhawan called out, one hand on her hip, "I can only assume you're talking during my class because you're just as excited as I am about the written portion of your final regarding the applications of language acquisition within the field of artificial intelligence."

Giggles echoed around the room, and Diane immediately blushed. "I'm super excited, actually," she said. "Really looking forward to it."

"Moving on," Dhawan said drily, "there will be an additional short answer question worth ten extra credit points for those of you who skipped ahead to the chapter on the neurolinguistics of bilingualism..."

Her voice faded into the background as I struggled to copy her notes off the board. She was basically listing every single concept that would appear on the exam, and I was grateful. I'd only missed a few days of classes when I'd fled to Springfield, but my timing had been awful. I knew I'd have to cram like crazy if I wanted to ace all of my finals. Unfortunately, with all the upheaval in my life and Stefan's, I'd been having a rough time reacclimating to school.

I'd felt a whirlwind of emotions since finding out that Max wasn't Stefan's love child after all, but instead my half-brother. I had a *brother*. It was surreal. Three days had passed since the DNA results had come in, but although I'd been doing my best to catch up with school and help Gavin's brother get all the information he needed to bust Konstantin and the agency, all I could think about was Max. He'd looked uncannily familiar to me from the first day I saw him. I just hadn't realized it was because I'd been seeing my father—and myself—in his eyes.

And then there was the ugly side of it. The fact that my half-sibling had been conceived because my father had been in the habit of hiring the same sex worker and frequently refused to use condoms. Every time I thought about it, my stomach started to turn. I hadn't been on speaking terms with him for awhile now, and this new development had only made my feelings of estrangement toward him grow even stronger.

Stefan and Anja hadn't even discussed telling him about Max yet, and they still hadn't broken the news to Konstantin, either. As far as my father-in-law knew, we were all operating under the assumption that Stefan was

Max's dad. For now it was better to have this card in our hands. Keeping Konstantin in the dark gave us an advantage. Anja had also asked for some time to adjust to the situation, and Stefan and I were happy to comply. We needed to process it all, too. But now it was Thursday, and I knew I couldn't stand any more inaction, just sitting around waiting for everyone to feel better about Max's parentage. He was *my brother*.

There was no way I could keep pretending that he wasn't now a part of my life, my own flesh and blood. Stefan had gotten the chance to spend time with him already—now that I knew that he was actually my half-brother, why shouldn't I get to see him as well?

I had to see him.

After class got out, I weaseled out of Diane's tea invitation by promising her a lunch date soon, then made my way across campus with my phone pressed to my ear. I'd called Anja the second I was alone, and now I was anxiously listening to the ringing on the other end of the call.

"Hi, Tori," she answered, her voice a little husky.

"Hey," I said. "I'm just calling because, um...I guess I was wondering if I could see Max?"

She didn't answer right away and I started to feel anxious, gritting my teeth as a stiff breeze blew through my knit hat. It wasn't until that exact moment that I realized how desperately I wanted a chance to get to know my brother.

"I was thinking we could all have a playdate together," I went on in a rush. "All four of us—you guys and then me and Stefan."

"What did you have in mind?" Anja asked cautiously.

"Well, I don't have classes this afternoon and there's this really cool kids' play area in the lobby of our apartment building. There's a jungle gym and a ball pit and everything..."

"Max loves a good ball pit," Anja said warmly. "Though they are little germ factories."

"Then I'll have to bring a bucket of hand sanitizer and a couple of plague masks," I offered. "It'll be tons of fun. Trust me."

We both laughed and then worked out the details.

"I think he will like you," Anja said, and I found myself grinning.

"I think I'll like him too." I was practically kicking up my heels with excitement as I waved down a taxi.

On my way home I called Stefan, begging him to leave work early and meet us at the condo. It wasn't hard to convince him. Ever since our uncomfortable Zoric family dinner, Konstantin had been making life hell for everyone who worked at KZ Modeling's offices. At least Stefan could take comfort knowing that his father's reign would soon come to an end.

I hung up and tapped on the divider between me and the cab driver.

"Can we make a stop?" I asked. "I just need to run into a store real quick—you can keep the meter running."

A few minutes later we pulled up to a curb in front of a toy store, and I tumbled out of the car and rushed inside, only to immediately find myself overwhelmed. What did one buy a seven-year-old? I had no idea, so I just started grabbing things willy-nilly. Board games, stuffed animals, Lego sets, a remote-control triceratops, a candy kit to make your own gummy worms.

Within ten minutes, I had a massive load of toys spilling from my arms. After the cashier rang me up, she paged an employee to go outside and help pack me and all my purchases into the cab. The driver laughed at all the bags, but helped me rearrange everything in the backseat before we got back on the road, heading toward the condo.

I'd probably gone overboard, but I couldn't help it. The thought of giving all these things to Max, of showering him with all this fun stuff, gave me a warm feeling inside. I knew Stefan would probably be a little exasperated at the bill I'd just racked up, but I also knew he'd be happy that I'd taken so much joy out of spoiling the kid. Anja and Max had spent the last seven years under my father-in-law's thumb, and everything they had ever gotten from him had probably come with strings attached. But these gifts had no strings. I just wanted my brother to like them—and me—and to be happy.

When I arrived, Anja and Max were waiting in the lobby. They watched with amusement as I staggered out of the cab, laden with bright colored paper bags and struggling to carry everything at once.

"What is all this?" Anja asked, her eyes wide as she helped me into the lobby.

Max was already staring at the toys spilling out of the bags, his gaze laser-focused.

"Things got a little intense at the toy store," I confessed to Anja, lowering my voice to a whisper. "I just felt like... I've always wanted a sibling. I can't imagine not spoiling him now. Plus, I've already missed so many birthdays and holidays, you know? I hope it's okay."

There were tears in her eyes and she flung her arms around me.

"He is very lucky to have a sister as generous as you," Anja said, making sure to keep her voice quiet as well. "Of course it's okay."

We hadn't told Max anything yet, and I didn't know

when we planned to. Not only was my father a high-ranking politician with a reputation to uphold, but he was also up for reelection this year. If news came out that he had fathered a child with a prostitute seven years ago, his chances of reelection—or any kind of continued future in politics—would likely be destroyed.

I pushed all thoughts of my father out of my head and forced a smile. I was here to get to know Max. To get to know my brother. Nothing was more important to me in this moment.

Putting down the rest of the toys, I looked down at Max and took a deep breath.

"I'm Tori," I said.

"I'm Max," he said seriously, holding out a small hand.

I shook it, thinking how little it was compared to mine.

"It's very nice to meet you, Max." I gestured at the bags. "I brought you some things to play with. Your mom said you can keep them if you want."

His eyes widened. "All of them?"

"Say thank you, Max," Anja scolded gently, putting a hand on her son's shoulders.

"Thank you!" he said, his eyes darting around at the piles of toys and games.

I felt a surge of joy.

"There's a really fun playroom down the hall," I told him. "Do you want to help me take these toys there so we can open them and play?"

"Sure!" he said, his eagerness making me laugh.

"Great," I said. "Let's get to it."

Together, we gathered up all the bags and headed to the playroom. Just as we had managed to pry open a bucket of Legos, Stefan came into the room to join us. He frowned a little as he took in the amount of brand new toys surrounding us, but I saw a smile playing on his lips and when he caught my eye, he gave me a wink.

While Anja and Stefan supervised, Max and I settled down on the floor mats and began building a city of Legos for the remote-control dinosaur to plow through. It soon became clear that Max was both creative and curious. He reminded me a lot of myself at that age.

The four of us played all afternoon, cycling through the toys one by one, playing the games we liked and setting aside the ones that were too easy. Max was quick to learn, and I felt a surge of pride. After a few hours, Stefan stepped out to make a work call and Anja settled into a chair with her e-reader, leaving me to bond with Max by myself.

"I heard you went to the zoo recently," I said. We were rebuilding the Lego city after it had gotten clobbered by the lumbering triceratops. "That's pretty cool."

"Yeah," Max said, his head bouncing up and down in an enthusiastic nod. "We saw ALL the animals."

"All of them? Wow." I couldn't help grinning. "What was the biggest animal you saw?"

He thought about it for a moment. "You mean the tallest or the heaviest?"

"How about the heaviest?"

"The elephants," he said, very sure of himself. "The giraffes were the tallest, though."

"Makes sense," I said. "What was the smallest animal you got to see?"

That took a little longer to figure out, but I could see him thinking hard, his tongue sticking out of one side of his mouth. "The spiders," he finally said. "But we saw some pretty big spiders too."

"Gross," I said with a shiver, eliciting a laugh from him.

"So, do you think you liked the big animals or the little animals best?"

"I like *all* animals," he said with a shrug. "Big and small."

My heart clenched with love for him. He was so charming.

How could my father have this beautiful, brilliant child and not even know about him? He'd done some undeniably selfish things in his life, but this was seriously next-level.

Despite our estrangement, I still loved my father because he was my father, and he'd raised me with love...but part of me couldn't forgive him for the way he'd chosen to live his life. He had cheated on Michelle, who was the closest person I had to a mother. He had slept with Anja, and probably other prostitutes, and he had done so without protection, putting everyone's health at risk. And he was actively working to protect Konstantin and the trafficking ring that KZM supported. I didn't know if I'd ever be able to talk to him again, or if our relationship was even reconcilable.

Max let out a yawn and I looked at my watch and found that it was later than I'd thought.

"Do you want to get him home for dinner soon?" I asked Anja.

"Let's get a pizza," Stefan suggested, coming over to help us clean up all the toys.

"I love pizza!" Max said. "With all the toppings! Can we stay, Mom?"

Anja laughed. "We can stay for dinner, sure."

Upstairs in the condo, Stefan called in our order while Anja set Max up in the living room with some animated adventure movie with talking animals. When the pizza arrived, she brought him a slice and returned to eat with me and Stefan in the dining room.

"He's really great," I told Anja.

She beamed. "He is, isn't he?"

"So smart," I gushed. "And sweet as pie."

"I'm glad you called. It's nice for Max to get to know his family." She paused. "But honestly, I still don't know what to tell him about you. Or his father."

I nodded. "I understand."

Reaching over, I took Stefan's hand. While playing with Max, I had thought a lot about what I wanted, and how I could be involved in my brother's life. I couldn't just act like he didn't exist, or that we weren't related. He was a part of me. A part of my family. Nothing could change that.

"I realize this is all really complicated for everyone," I told Anja, "but I want to be in Max's life, however I can be. If you're comfortable telling him that I'm his half-sister—when you think it's the right time, I mean—I would be thrilled."

Anja smiled, but I could tell that she was still hesitant.

"We don't have to tell him anything if you don't want to," I quickly added. "Or if you want to wait until he's older..."

"No," Anja said. "I would love to tell him. I think it would be good for him, and it's obvious that he likes you very much." She cleared her throat, looking down so that her hair fell in front of her face. "But I'm worried. I don't know what the senator will say. Or do."

"Honestly, you have every right to be nervous," I said. "I'm sorry to say so, but my father won't be happy to learn about Max's existence, I can tell you that."

Anja's face fell, but she didn't look surprised, just disappointed.

I continued, "Not only will it be a huge bombshell for him personally—and also my stepmother—but this is an election year."

"An illegitimate child could ruin him professionally," Stefan agreed.

"But he needs to know," I added. "And I think the world also needs to know what kind of man he is. No more secrets."

Anja was nodding. "No more secrets."

Stefan squeezed my hand. He knew how hard this was for me. How hard it would be for my family. But whatever happened, he'd be by my side. That was the most important thing.

"So would you be able to...get me an appointment with the senator?" Anja asked us.

"We can do that," Stefan said.

"He's out of town right now, in DC," I told her, "but he'll be back soon."

"As soon as he's back then," Anja said firmly. "Only, I have to ask..." She looked at us pleadingly. "Will you come? I don't want to be alone with him when I break the news. And I don't think he will try anything if you are there. It will make things easier, safer. Please."

"Of course," I said, knowing I spoke for both myself and Stefan. "We'll set up the meeting with my father and be with you every step of the way. We're happy to do it."

"That's what family is for," Stefan added.

STEFAN

CHAPTER 21

After dinner, Tori and Max returned to putting together the huge Lego set that Tori had gotten while Anja and I remained in the kitchen, cleaning up. I could tell that she was putting on a brave face, but it was obvious that her concerns about the future weighed heavily on her mind.

"Everything's going to be okay," I assured her, wiping pizza grease off the counter. "Regardless of what the senator says, Tori and I have your back. We'll figure it all out."

My ex nodded, but I could see that her eyes were filling with tears. She swiped them away as she turned to load the plates from dinner into the dishwasher.

"What is it?" I asked, worried that there might be something else she hadn't told us yet.

Anja was silent for a long time before she looked over at me, her eyes red.

"You've been so good to me, Stefan," she said. "Tori, too. I don't deserve it."

"It's water under the bridge," I said, gesturing for her to sit back down. "Sure, I wish things had happened differently, but I believe that you did what you thought was best—I can't imagine it's been easy for you all these years, being a single mom and trying to stay in hiding."

I went over to the cupboard where Tori kept the tea kettle and filled it with water, then set it on a burner to heat. My wife often liked having a cup of soothing chamomile tea before bed, and maybe it would help Anja unwind as well. One more thing they could bond over.

Anja shook her head. "This isn't about how I ran away when I found out I was pregnant with Max, though I am sorry for the way it all went down." She took a deep breath. "The truth is, I didn't come here intending to tear you and your wife apart. I was misled."

"By my father?" I guessed, knowing full well that he had orchestrated both Anja's original disappearance and this recent return with Max. "What did he tell you?"

"He said that your marriage was on the rocks," she admitted, looking ashamed. "I was told it had been arranged for political reasons, but that you were both unhappy."

"Half of that is true," I said. "But my wife and I are very happy together."

Anja smiled sadly. "He told me that Tori was on her way out anyway...but it was a delicate situation and you'd need a really compelling reason to divorce. He was sure Max and I could be that reason."

The tea kettle screamed, and I wanted to scream along with it. Anja jumped up and took it off the stove, and it was my turn to sink into a chair as she rifled through Tori's tea selection.

"My father really is some kind of evil genius," I mused, my jaw clenching in anger.

Anja laughed. "I guess I can't disagree with that. Maybe 'supervillain' is more accurate?"

"He does have all that money," I conceded. "And all those charcoal turtlenecks."

All jokes aside, I felt sick realizing my father had stooped so low yet again. I knew he'd wanted to get rid of Tori because she was defiant and headstrong and hated KZM's trafficking business—and therefore would always be a potential threat to it—but now I knew exactly how he'd managed to convince Anja to come back to Chicago with Max. By pretending that the two of them had a new life waiting for them here, with me. How fucking cruel.

Anja sat next to me, the scent of lemon wafting from her steaming mug.

"What else did he tell you?" I asked.

She frowned, thinking back. "He said...just that if I came back, we'd all have a chance to be a family together. That I owed it to Max to finally meet his dad. Give him all the opportunities I never had. I mean, your father was generous with us, but our life wasn't...like this."

Looking around the kitchen, decked out with its gleaming marble countertops, high-tech appliances, stupidly luxurious fixtures and all kinds of bells and whistles I barely even used, I didn't have to ask Anja what she meant. I had the wealth and resources at my fingertips to care for and spoil Max in ways Anja could currently only dream about. It was easy to understand why she'd bought into my father's tempting lies so quickly. All she cared about was her son.

"Tori and I are committed to helping you and Max in whatever way we can," I said.

"I know. And I can't thank the both of you enough for that," Anja said, pausing to sip carefully at her tea. "God, I can't believe I fell for his lies all over again. I should have realized it sooner, considering the man he was when I worked for him. I don't know why I ever trusted him to begin with."

"Don't blame yourself," I said. "You're far from being the only person he's taken advantage of. He's a master manipulator. And you were barely sixteen when you arrived in the US—it wasn't about being naïve; you had to take whatever opportunity came your way."

I could only imagine how hard it must have been for Anja. All alone in a foreign country, undocumented and impoverished, knowing she was the only hope that her family back in Romania had for financial survival.

But she was shaking her head. "There was more to it than that, Stefan. When I met your father I was young, yes, but I knew what I was doing. Some of the girls—the other models—they were bullied into the sex work, threatened with deportation. But coming to the States, I'd already figured that without papers or an education and not much English, it was pretty likely that the only work I'd get would be hooking. So when Konstantin said he'd help me get modeling jobs too, it seemed like a dream come true."

She was smiling bitterly, and my heart ached for the younger Anja who had been through so much, and who'd had to learn to be so strong.

"I'm so sorry," was all I could say. "You deserved better."

No matter how many countless times I'd heard some version of this story before, from other KZ models, it never got any easier listening to these survivors tell their tales of my father's evil. I also knew from experience that it was cathartic for the women to speak, so instead of filling in the rest of the story for Anja, I simply waited for her to get it out.

She took a long drink of her tea, and when she lowered

the cup I saw fresh tears streaking down her face. I reached for a few napkins and passed them her way.

"As time went on," she continued, "KZ expected me to spend more and more time on my back, and less on the runway. My life started to feel like a nightmare. Until I met you."

"We had a good run," I told her. "No regrets."

We shared a smile, nostalgic for our younger selves. The selves that no longer existed.

Anja went on, "I knew you loved me, and I loved you too. But I was convinced that I wasn't good enough for you. That we could never truly be together. That's why it was so easy to walk away when KZ gave me the offer—because I knew a woman like me wasn't worthy of a man like you."

"You're worthy," I told her vehemently. "You were *always* worth more than you thought. I knew exactly what kind of work you did, and I never thought you were anything less than a queen. No man deserves you if he doesn't think the same."

"Thanks," Anja said quietly.

I got up and took down Tori's favorite mug, putting together a tea tray for her. Then I turned back to Anja, who was staring out the window at the cityscape and sniffling into a tissue.

"Don't ever let a scumbag like my father define who you are and what you're worth," I said. "I wish things had been different for you. But you got Max out of it, and…I hope it's okay to say that I think he probably makes your whole life feel worthwhile."

"He really does," Anja said with a smile.

"I know I've said this before, but Tori and I will always be here to help you and Max, in whatever way you need. We care for both of you, and that's not going to change.

Even if the relationship between you and me is on different terms now."

"I understand," Anja said. "And I'm so grateful."

It was hard not to grieve for both of us. For the kids we had been and the people we had become. Still, I didn't regret the way things had worked out—how could I when it had gotten me a life with Tori?

"I should bring this tea to my wife," I told Anja, picking up the tray.

She followed me out of the kitchen and through the dining room, where we hung back and watched Tori and Max through the doorway for a minute, both of them deeply involved in constructing some kind of multi-towered castle in the middle of the living room floor.

"She is very special," Anja said quietly. "I'm glad my son will have a sister like her. Max deserves to grow up around people as smart and kind as he is."

"He does. So he's lucky he has you for a mom," I told her. "Make no mistake: he turned out the way he did because of how you raised him."

Her eyes grew teary again.

"You're a good man, Stefan," she said. "Knowing who you were as a teenager and listening to you now, I can't believe I ever worried you'd turn out like your father. He's been grooming you all this time, but it's obvious that you've been playing him."

"I don't know if I'd say that," I murmured, trying to keep my voice casual.

I cleared my throat, hoping to avoid giving anything away. Anja always had been able to read me like an open book when we were face to face. But things could get dangerous fast if I admitted that I was in the process of working with the feds to dismantle KZM's operations.

"Well. Maybe I'm wrong." Anja shrugged. "But if there's ever anything I can do to help stop him—and keep him from hurting other women—just say the word."

"Will do," I said. "But there's nothing going on."

"Of course. But if there is...I promise not to say anything," Anja added. "I can be very discreet."

"Sure," I said, bustling into the living room with the tea.

"Oooh, is that for me?" Tori squealed. "And are all those Oreos for Max?"

"They're to share," Anja cut in, "but you two can decide who gets how many."

As the other three fought over the cookies, I ruminated on everything Anja and I had just discussed. Clearly she suspected I had plans to dismantle my father's operation from the inside, but although I was grateful for her offer of help, I hoped I wouldn't need it. Frank Chase had led me to believe that my father's arrest was imminent. In the meantime, the wait was killing me.

"Looks like Max is ready for bed," Anja said, and I followed her gaze, watching as Max yawned, half a cookie in one fist. "I should probably get him home."

"Stefan's driver can take you," Tori offered.

"Good idea," I said, already pulling out my phone.

Tori and I helped Anja gather up Max and his bags full of toys and get them in the car before we headed back upstairs together. Tori was practically glowing from the playdate she'd had with her brother, and though I was happy for her, I couldn't help being distracted by all the information that Anja had given me tonight.

While Tori showered—and I could hear her singing happily in the bathroom—I sat on the edge of the bed, undressing and thinking about what Anja had said. Although I wasn't at all surprised to have confirmation that my father had attempted to split me and Tori apart, it didn't stop me from being furious.

Did he really believe that Tori was such a threat to his business that she needed to be removed from the equation? The irony was that he was right to worry—but the real threat was actually me.

Even though the last thing I wanted to do was speak to my father, and it was probably a lost cause anyway, I decided to confront him about all of this soon. After all, there might be other reasons Anja was a key player in his schemes. It couldn't hurt to try digging deeper.

Undressed, I leaned back against the headboard, waiting for Tori to come out of the shower. My body tightened with the anticipation of being with her—holding her, kissing her, fucking her—I never tired of it. I didn't think I ever would.

And there was one good thing that had come out of Anja's reappearance. For the first time since she had disappeared, I finally had closure to our relationship. No more wondering where she was, or whether she was safe or drugged up in some foreign brothel. She was one more model who no longer had to sell herself like that to please my father. To fill his pockets.

I wouldn't rest until all the other women working for KZM were free, too.

TORI

CHAPTER 22

"Mitchell Lindsey's office," a brisk female voice said.

I took a deep breath, my mouth suddenly bone dry despite the fact that I'd practiced for this conversation over and over again in my head.

"This is Victoria Lindsey," I said. "The senator's daughter. May I speak with my father, please?"

"He's en route to the airport in DC at the moment," she said politely, giving no indication of whether I'd been blacklisted from his contacts or not.

So he was still out of town. "Flying into Springfield?" I asked. The flight usually took about three hours, so I figured I could try him again after my first class let out today.

"Chicago, actually," she said. "He'll be at the office there for a few days before he heads home."

"Got it," I said, my mood lifting instantly. His schedule couldn't have been more convenient for me and Anja. "I'll call him back this afternoon then. Thanks for your help."

"Actually, I can try to patch you through to his cell if you like?" she suggested.

Guess I hadn't made the blacklist after all. "That'd be great," I told her.

The line started to ring and I tapped my fingers on the kitchen counter in time with the quickening of my pulse, wondering if he'd even pick up or purposely leave me hanging so I'd be forced to choke out an awkward voicemail.

I couldn't help feeling anxious. We'd been estranged for nearly two months, and hadn't spoken a word to each other since the day I'd found out he was involved in KZM's trafficking coverup. This was the first time I'd be hearing his voice since then. And since the recent revelations of his infidelity. His lying. The way he'd treated his bed partners.

I took another long drink of coffee to fortify myself, just about to hang up, when—

"Tori? What is it?" he asked in his usual gruff way. "I'm about to get on a plane."

At first I froze, unable to form the words. My anger about Max and Anja made it hard not to start flinging accusations or demanding he take action to correct his past wrongs.

"Tori?" my dad barked. "First class is boarding."

"I...need to talk to you," I finally managed, my voice sounding extremely formal.

"Obviously. Well, make it fast," he demanded. "I assume you've finally come to your senses."

I narrowed my eyes. It was obvious he thought this was an apology call. How dare he speak to me this way, after all he'd done. But of course, he didn't know what I knew. He thought I was still the same naïve, sweet, innocent daughter he'd always known. Calling to beg his forgiveness for my behavior on the day I'd told him he wasn't my father anymore.

He'd be wrong to think that. But it didn't mean I couldn't play into those assumptions.

"Actually, I was hoping to speak with you in person," I said in a gentle tone. "Your assistant said you're on the way to Chicago, so maybe I can see you while you're in town."

I felt bad about what this confrontation would do to my stepmother, but I hoped that she would understand and forgive me. Arranging this meeting was something I owed to Anja and to Max, but I was doing it for Michelle as well. She deserved to know who my father truly was.

"What's this all about?" he asked impatiently. "I have back-to-back meetings both days, and my fucking doctor's still telling me I need to be 'resting.' As if the country's problems can wait just because I feel a little under the weather."

Even though I was furious at him, even though I knew he was a liar, I still felt a twinge of pity. My father was not good at facing anything that reminded him of his own mortality.

"What about after work hours?" I asked. "Surely you can spare an evening for your only child? It's important."

I was laying it on thick—and with the knowledge that by the end of our meeting, he would know that I wasn't his only child anymore—Anja needed resolution, and the longer we postponed this confrontation, the more likely it would be that the news about Max would get to my father some other way. Or that Anja would back out, maybe flee and go into hiding again. I couldn't risk that.

Through the phone I could hear the boarding announcement repeating something about priority seating and families with children.

"Please, Daddy?" I said, hating that I had to resort to little-girl speak but knowing he'd be powerless against it.

He huffed. "Fine. Why don't you come over to the

condo after dinner tonight? I can spare maybe an hour. I gotta go."

"Thank you!" I crowed, feeling triumphant. "Fly safe. I'll see you later."

We hung up.

I had conveniently left out the part about bringing other people with me.

After I got home from school that night, Stefan and I called our private car and picked up Anja, who was leaving Max with the same babysitter Gretna had recommended the night of our family dinner. Max had basked in the older woman's grandmotherly doting on him, and didn't even put up a fight at being left home with her and his pile of new toys, courtesy of me.

Then, somber and tense, we drove over to my father's condo, prepared to confront him with the consequences of his actions from all those years ago.

Anja was twisting the hem of her sweater into knots, so I gently took one of her hands and squeezed it. She was shaking a little, and I didn't blame her. I was so nervous that I could actually feel the thumping of my heart in my chest.

At least Stefan seemed calm and collected. Just being near him, my leg pressed against his, made me relax. A little.

The car pulled up in front of the building, and for a moment none of us moved.

"Are you ready?" Stefan finally asked.

He had directed the question at Anja. Her face was pale, but she nodded, her gaze steely.

"I'm ready," she said. "Let's do this."

The three of us got into the elevator and with each floor, I could feel my anxiety build. Stefan and Anja were silent and fidgety, respectively, so I guessed they were feeling the same. Seconds after ringing the doorbell to my dad's place, I heard footsteps. I held my breath.

The door swung open, revealing my father's tired face. Before he could register that I wasn't alone, Stefan elbowed his way past, pulling me and Anja into the condo along with him.

"Evening, Senator," Stefan said.

My father's mouth drew into a firm line, but still he closed the door behind us.

"What the hell is this?" he demanded, following us into the sitting room.

He was very purposefully not looking at Anja. I had seen the flare of shocked recognition in his eyes when we'd pushed our way in, the way he'd looked immediately stricken at her presence.

Not just recognition—panic, too. Even though I'd never doubted Anja, my dad's reaction to seeing her in the flesh basically confirmed everything she'd told us about their relationship. But if he thought we were here about his infidelity alone, he had quite another thing coming.

"You remember Anja Borjan," Stefan said, gesturing in her direction.

Anja was standing tall but her face had gone pale, her eyes locked unwaveringly on my father. I went over and put her arm around her, causing my dad's eyes to bulge out of his head.

"I've never seen this woman before," he said, darting his gaze at her. "You're mistaken."

It was a terrible lie.

"You can drop the games," I deadpanned. "We all know what Konstantin's business is all about, and we also know why you have a vested interest in the...not-so-legal endeavors."

"If you think you're going to blackmail me, you can all get the fuck out right now," my dad said, starting to turn red. "My lawyer will ensure this slander never sees the light of day—"

"Just stop!" I interrupted. "This isn't even about that. It'll be easier for everyone if you just admit you know her, so we can move on to the real reason we're here. Now please, sit."

He did. Noticing a half-finished drink on the table beside the sofa, I handed it to him. He downed the rest of the alcohol in a single gulp. Finally his shoulders slumped and he looked up at me, seeming older and smaller than I'd ever seen him before.

"I'm not corroborating anything you just said," he stated. "But yes, I do know her."

"Anja," I prodded.

"I know *Anja*," he repeated, annoyed. I could see the woman's posture relax a little at hearing my father finally say her name out loud.

"Thank you," she murmured.

In my opinion, she had nothing to thank him for. Acknowledging her shouldn't have required this much pulling of teeth. My father really was a bastard.

"Now just get on with it and tell me why this woman is standing in my living room." He glared at Stefan and I before directing his full attention on Anja. "If you're looking for some sort of pay-off, like I said, you can leave right now. I'm not paying you a cent.

"In fact, go ahead and tell the media I was with you, for all I care. Who do you think the public will believe? A long-time, respected senator with a great track record, or some foreign hooker that just popped out of the woodwork?"

Stefan's fists clenched, and I could feel the outrage radiating off of him, but I pulled my husband back as Anja stepped toward my dad, her head still held high.

"It won't just be my word against yours, Senator," she said. "I have proof. Our seven-year-old son."

My father went completely stiff.

"You're a liar and a whore," he rasped, newly invigorated. "There have to be dozens of men out there who could have fathered your child! You're trying to pin it on me so you can get notoriety and child support, but it won't work. You think I haven't dealt with your type before?"

"Maybe I am wrong," she said calmly.

"You see?" my dad shouted triumphantly, gesturing in frustration to me and Stefan.

Anja went on, "And that's why we need you to agree to a paternity test."

My father scoffed. "There's no way in hell I'd agree to something like that."

I stepped forward. "You don't have to," I said. "If you don't give them a sample of your DNA, I'll give them mine. It might not be as significant a lab result, but it will prove that I'm related to Anja's son. And it will be enough to take to the press."

My father scowled at me in disgust.

"I can't believe you're buying into this woman's lies—and over the word of your own father," he raged.

I didn't say anything, just looped my arm through Anja's in a show of support. My father's gaze shifted accusingly to Stefan.

"And you. You're supposed to be keeping her in line! What kind of husband can't keep his wife from running around and colluding in these kinds of bullshit conspiracy theories?"

"The kind of husband who trusts his wife's rationale," Stefan answered drily.

"It's not bullshit," I insisted. I'd had enough.

Pulling out my phone, I scrolled back to a picture I'd taken of Max the other day. The one where he looked almost exactly like a dark haired, more boyish version of me at that age. Same upturned nose with its spray of freckles, same exact brows and eye shape. There was no denying he also looked a hell of a lot like my dad's old elementary school photos.

"Look at him," I said, thrusting my phone in his face. "Look! His eyes are blue-green like Anja's, but they're shaped *just like* yours and mine. And that chin? That's definitely yours. His hair even curls up like yours when it starts to grow out. How can you pretend he's not yours?"

My dad pushed my hand away, stood from the couch, and went to the bar at the other end of the room, where he poured himself a fresh drink. I knew his doctor had said my dad wasn't supposed to be drinking excessively, but I kept my mouth shut. The only thing I wanted in this moment was to get him to admit that he had fathered an illegitimate child.

After draining half the glass, he turned his attention back to me.

"Jesus, Tori. I can't believe you're doing this to me," he ranted. "I'm in the middle of an election, for Christ's sake! How could you possibly think it was a good time to approach me about something like this?"

He was visibly sweating, a light sheen on his forehead, and he looked exhausted. Not for the first time, I thought to myself how much he seemed to have aged over the last few months.

"This isn't about your career," I said. "I just want you to do the right thing."

"You're going to ruin my life!" he shouted at me. Then he pointed at Anja. "This is all your fault, you conniving whore."

Stefan stepped between my dad and Anja and me, shielding us from his unchecked rage.

"I suggest you calm down, Senator," Stefan said, his voice steely calm.

"Don't tell me to calm down!" my father spouted. "I'm going to have all your asses thrown in jail! I'm invincible! I have friends in the Department of Justice!"

So did we. But my father didn't know anything about that yet.

I'd never seen my dad so angry before. He was leaning back against the bar, his heavy breaths becoming ragged. It looked like he was struggling for air. Was it a panic attack?

"Dad?" I cried out, starting to move toward him.

Suddenly he fell to the ground, his hands clutching his chest.

TORI

CHAPTER 23

Even though I was wearing a sweater, I couldn't stop shivering as we sat in the hospital waiting room, my ass already numb from sitting so long in the uncomfortable plastic chairs. Hours had passed, and I hadn't seen my father since they'd loaded him into the ambulance outside his condo, his face covered with a mask, his limp body strapped to a gurney.

Anja had been the one to call 911 as I had knelt beside my father's prone body, my hands reaching for his, trying to find a pulse. But I had been in too much shock to be any kind of help, and Stefan had his hands full trying to calm me down and pull me away from my dad. The EMTs had arrived quickly, but everything after that was a complete blur. I didn't even remember getting into the car with Stefan and Anja.

My husband had already called my stepmom, and she was on her way, speeding here in her little roadster. The drive from Springfield was a long one. Still, she should be here any minute. I looked forward to Michelle's comforting southern accent, her soothing words.

"You hanging in there okay?" Stefan asked softly, his eyes full of concern.

I offered a weak smile. "I don't know," I answered honestly. "I still love him, even after everything he's done. I never got a chance to tell him that." My voice broke.

"He knew you loved him," my husband assured me, passing me a few tissues.

"All families fight," Anja added. "The love remains."

She was sitting across from us, trying to read the same trashy celebrity gossip magazine that had been in her hands since we got here, her gaze unfocused. We were all shaken by what had happened, and had settled into silence after we arrived at the hospital. Surely I wasn't the only one who feared that confronting my father had been what triggered his second heart attack. He was in surgery now, the nurse at reception had told me. She had no other news.

We were coming up on hour number four.

I didn't know what to do with myself. There was a TV in the waiting room but it was on mute. Whenever I glanced up, my eyes were so teary I couldn't even read the closed captions.

Glancing over at the reception desk, I searched the faces of the nurses, as if their expressions could tell me something. As if they weren't handling dozens of other cases, as if they were even thinking or talking about my dad at the moment. I hated all this waiting. The not knowing. The déjà vu was strong. It felt like I had just been here with him during his last heart attack. I was a mess.

Despite the fact that I was still mad at him, this wasn't how I wanted my dad to go, with both of us up in arms with each other. I prayed I'd get another chance to talk to him and tell him how I felt, despite all his flaws and past mistakes. I also prayed he'd have the chance to do right by

Anja and Max—not because he thought it was the only way to avoid blackmail or litigation, but because he chose to. Because he wanted to do the right thing. Maybe he'd even want to be an active part of Max's life, as I did.

My stomach twisted as I remembered how he had hit the floor. My shaking fingers hadn't been able to find a pulse, but I could still remember how cold his skin had felt. The whole thing kept replaying in my mind like a horrible movie that I couldn't turn off.

I watched a doctor stop at the nurse's station and I straightened, somehow knowing in my gut that this woman had information about my father. Sure enough, the nurse gestured to where we were sitting. I held my breath as she approached, adjusting the lapels of her white coat.

"Are you Senator Lindsey's family?" the doctor asked. She was older, exuding calm competency, with a regal bearing and a kind face etched with wrinkles and deep laugh lines.

"We are," I said, managing a nod.

"You can come with me now," she said gently.

We followed her silently out of the waiting area. At first I thought we were going to be led to a hospital room, where my father would be lying there in bed, pale and hooked up to machines but still alive, just like he had been several months ago, right after my honeymoon.

Instead, we were taken to an empty room.

"I'm so sorry," the doctor said once the door closed behind us. "I know there is a lot of press hanging around out there and I wanted to give you your privacy."

I didn't quite understand and stared at her, confused.

"And my father—?"

Her face said it all, and I felt myself sagging against

Stefan already. Her words sounded like they were coming from very far away.

"...has passed away, unfortunately."

My blood was rushing in my ears, my body going numb, and I struggled to listen to the rest of what the doctor was saying.

"...initial heart attack...sudden cardiac arrest during surgery...everything in our power, but ultimately it was fatal. I am so sorry."

Anja sank into a chair, silent tears streaming down her face. I knew they were not for her, but for me and for Max. For the tragedy that her son would never get to meet his father. The doctor handed her a tissue and held the box out for me. I shook my head.

I had no tears. Not yet. They would come, for sure, but right now I was still in shock.

The door closed and suddenly I looked up and realized that both the doctor and Anja had left the room. I turned to Stefan, confused, but he just took my hands.

"They thought you might need to take some time," he said.

I nodded. "It doesn't feel real. He can't just be...gone. This doesn't make sense."

"I know," Stefan said, pulling me tight against his chest.

Then my phone buzzed in my pocket. It was Michelle.

Where are you? her text read. *I just got to the ER entrance. What's the room number?*

My stomach turned over and I showed the text to Stefan.

"I don't even know what room we're in right now," I told him.

He gave me a firm nod. "Don't worry. I'll find her and bring her back here."

I grabbed his arm before he could leave.

"Don't tell her what happened," I told him. "Please. She deserves to hear it from me."

"Are you sure?"

"Yes," I said, even though I wasn't. "I should be the one to break the news."

When he left, I dropped into a chair and let out a deep breath. The reality of the situation was finally sinking in. In just a few moments I was going to have to tell my stepmom not just that her husband was gone, but that he had left behind a previously unknown son. I would have to tell her everything.

I put my head in my hands, hating that I had to do this. Hating that my father had left this mess for me to deal with.

Finally there was a soft knock on the door, and when I looked up, I saw Stefan peering through the crack he'd opened up.

"Michelle is here," he said.

"Okay." I stood and gestured that he should let her in.

She tore into the room, eyes darting around, tear tracks down her face and her hair disheveled and windblown. It was obvious she'd just driven the four hours from Springfield at breakneck speed, probably crying the whole way. My heart broke for her. I was about to make this day one of the worst of her life.

"Michelle," I said, voice wavering, opening my arms. She came toward me, enveloping me in a hug. Her heart was beating so hard and fast that I could feel it pounding against me.

"Tell me what happened," she choked out, clinging to me hard. "Where is he?"

As hard as it was to do so, I pulled away and led her to a

chair. We both sat down and I took her hands, barely able to meet her eyes.

This might be the hardest thing I'd ever had to do.

Although I barely remembered anything about my birth mother, Michelle had been a constant in my life since I was little. She'd been a true friend to me ever since that first day we'd met and made s'mores together. It couldn't have been easy, being such a young woman herself and coming into an already-made family, expected to be a trophy wife and a perfect politician's spouse, as well as a parent to a precocious child. I couldn't speak to the marriage she'd had with my father, though I knew he held her up as the ideal in many ways, but she had been a wonderful mother to me. She was family, and I loved her. And I was about to break her heart.

"I'm so sorry," I began, my voice husky. "He had another heart attack. We rushed him right here but then, during surgery, he went into cardiac arrest. He...he didn't make it."

She closed her eyes, and her shoulders started to shake with the force of her sobs. The sight almost broke me, but I was far from finished.

"I should have taken better care of him," she choked out. "I tried to get him to eat better. To stop drinking. But he was so stubborn. He didn't want to change."

"This isn't your fault," I said, rubbing her back. "There's nothing you could have done. That any of us could have done. You can't blame yourself."

I passed her the box of tissues. Ever elegant, even with her makeup smeared, she pulled a compact out of her purse and carefully blotted her face, fixing it until it looked as perfect as it could. Still, her eyes were red and puffy, already welling up again. She cleared her throat.

"I'll call his PR person and put together a statement from the family," she said firmly, transforming into the politician's wife she had been trained to be. "Does the media know yet?"

I shook my head and took a breath, tapping into my reserves of anger over the situation in order to keep from falling apart. I was barely hanging on. "There's more."

"More what?" Michelle asked, searching my eyes.

"There are some...things I learned recently," I said slowly. "Things that Dad has done over the years."

Michelle pressed her lips together, leaning back. She looked wary, but not surprised. No doubt, my father hadn't been able to keep all of his misdeeds a secret, and under her sweet accent and manners and charm, Michelle was sharp as a tack, and nobody's fool. I'd bet anything she was well aware that my dad had stepped out on her during the course of their marriage.

Still, I imagined the details would come as a shock.

But she had to know.

"There was another woman," I said haltingly, taking her hand in mine again. She only nodded. "Her name was Anja. They met through Konstantin—Stefan's father."

I didn't say anything about the trafficking—I didn't know if it was safe for her to know too much about what was happening behind the scenes at KZ Modeling—but I told her everything else. About my father's indisputable infidelity, and how there was a child.

"He refused to submit to a paternity test, and he swore Max wasn't his, but..."

Michelle's hand flew to her mouth when I showed her the photo—the same one I'd shown my dad. But instead of ignoring it or shoving it away as he had done, she gently took my phone from me and looked down at the screen with affection and awe.

"He looks just like Mitch," she said. "And like you did at that age. He's beautiful." Her finger traced the boy's face in the picture.

"He's a really cool kid," I told her. "Sweet and smart and...I kind of love him already."

Michelle shook her head, looking devastated. "I knew your dad fooled around, and I accepted it, but...it's just a damn shame his last act was to deny his son."

She handed my phone back to me.

"I think it was kind of a shock, to be honest," I admitted. "Maybe if he had more time to get used to the idea of Max, I don't know...it could've been different."

"Oh, I have no doubt," Michelle agreed. "I think he would have realized how much he'd always wanted a son and embraced him full stop. You know, we tried to have a baby back in the early days, thinking it might be fun to have a bigger family—of course we loved you to pieces—but we stopped after a few years went by. I just wasn't able to get pregnant."

"I'm sorry," I said. "I never knew."

"I bet Max would have filled a hole in the family that always existed," Michelle finished. She blotted the corners of her eyes. "Well. Maybe I never was cut out for motherhood."

"You were great at it," I said firmly. "You still are. I'm lucky to have you."

Tears began to fill her eyes again.

"As much as it breaks my heart that your father didn't step up for the boy, I'm not going to let that be his legacy. Just because there won't be anything for Max in the will, it doesn't mean I won't support him financially and emotionally. And his mother, too. As far as I'm concerned, they're part of the family."

We hugged and then went to find Stefan, who told us that Anja had gone home to be with Max. Michelle mentioned that she would like to meet him—if and when Anja was ready.

"I think she'd be open to that," Stefan said. "It's been just the two of them for so long, and to be honest, Max has welcomed all the new faces lately with open arms."

The three of us went back to our condo, and Stefan helped me set Michelle up comfortably in our guest room. On the drive over, she'd already started making calls to my father's staff, breaking the news and telling them to start preparing a statement.

I made a tray of tea and toast for Michelle and left it with her in the guest room, where she was still dealing with the logistics of everything. It wasn't until I was in bed, makeup off, pajamas on, Stefan in the bathroom taking a shower, that the reality of the day finally sunk in.

Tears welled up in my eyes as I grappled with the drowning flood of my conflicting feelings. My dad was gone, and I hadn't even been able to say goodbye. We'd long had a complicated relationship, and it had only become more difficult and strained in the past months. I'd been mad at him for a while. He'd proven he was a not-so-good man, and he'd done a lot wrong over the course of his marriage and his life. He was as flawed as any human could be.

But even though he was a tyrant of a father, he *was* my father. He'd given me everything—even though it sometimes came with strings—and I loved him despite his flaws.

What was harder was trying to forgive his connection with my father-in-law and KZ Modeling's illegal business practices. To forgive how he had treated Michelle and Anja and probably countless other women, and how he had denied Max. Maybe I'd never be able forgive those things.

Still, the tears flowed hot and fast when I thought about the fact that he'd never have a chance to make things right, to reconcile things with Anja or meet his son. He and I would never have a chance to mend our relationship.

I heard the shower shut off and I dried my tears, grateful that Stefan would soon step into the room and slide into bed with me. I knew that he would hold me close when I cried, and that he would bring comfort to me when I needed him the most. I'd never been more thankful for his presence and his strength.

TORI

CHAPTER 24

With a sigh, I kicked off my black shoes and sank onto my bed. I'd been standing in them for hours all day and my feet and back ached. Everything ached, from the arches of my feet to the insides of my cheeks, which I had taken to biting when I wanted to hold in my tears.

The funeral had ended several hours ago in Springfield. Michelle had offered to let us stay at the house another night since the drive back to Chicago would take so many hours, but all I wanted was to be home so I could sleep in my own bed again. Stefan and I had been away too long already—helping Michelle with the funeral arrangements, reaching out to friends and family and colleagues, making sure that things would be perfect and go off without a hitch.

It was hard to remember everything that had happened in the past week. The morning after my father died, his staff (under Michelle's supervision) had put out a press release informing the public that Senator Mitch Lindsey from Illinois had suffered a fatal heart attack. Since the news of his first heart attack had been kept fairly under wraps, the news came as a shock to many people. Especially his constituents, who had always bought into my father's image as a man of quiet, but resilient strength.

The truth about his final moments at his condo during the confrontation with me and Anja and Stefan—and the knowledge of Max's existence, as well as his history of involvement with KZM and its sex workers—was going to stay in the family. My father's name would remain untarnished. There was no point in dragging it through the mud now. His darkest secrets would never see the light of day.

Michelle had been incredible throughout the entire process, from fielding interviews to releasing carefully-worded statements to planning the funeral in his hometown of Springfield. She was the very picture of poise and confidence. I had to admit there was something satisfying about watching her, a woman who had remained on the sidelines for most of my father's career, stepping out and standing in the spotlight. And doing a damn good job of it.

She'd managed everything from the memorial's flowers to the venue to hosting the catered reception for VIPs at the house afterward. The entire affair was a huge deal, since my father was a US senator. Even the President made a brief appearance, embracing Michelle and me and offering us the kindest condolences. My stepmother had succeeded in orchestrating the perfect event to pull off the delicate balance of grief and deference to other people's need to be seen attending. There had also been press everywhere, and when I closed my eyes I could still see the flashbulbs from the hundreds of photos that had been taken.

Before the funeral this morning, she'd pulled me aside for one of her trademark pep talks.

"This isn't about us," she had reminded me. "It's about

honoring his memory and offering the public closure. So as hard as it's going to be, we've got to keep our chins up."

"I will," I'd said.

But the only closure there seemed to be that day was to my father's service. Everything else, everything to do with his personal life, still felt unresolved.

Then she'd handed me a huge pair of Dior sunglasses.

"Just in case. And I'll have about five hundred tissues in my purse, so don't hesitate to reach in there if you need one. But you can only let a few tears slip out in front of the cameras. The rest you hold in. Can't be making any of the VIPs feel uncomfortable, can we?"

"Sure," I said, but I caught her impatiently swiping away a few tears of her own.

Still, I figured I'd be okay following Michelle's lead in decorum. The uncontrollable sobbing only hit me at night. The days were easier for some reason.

I sat on the bed, watching her put her makeup on. A touch of foundation, a hint of blush. We'd both opted for simple black dresses, almost identical sheaths with long sleeves and boat necks. They were demure but form-fitting. Michelle had said we should look like we were appropriately in mourning, but also not like we were too devastated to pull ourselves together.

"People expect a show, so we'll give them one," she went on as she pinned her hair into a neat bun. "But I'm sticking to the script. Nothing more. I won't let this be a media circus."

My own hair hung in a loose ponytail, also at Michelle's request. She said I needed to look a little younger than my eighteen years, to emphasize that I was the senator's daughter. We needed to look similar, but not too similar. His surviving family, grieving in quiet dignity.

She'd worn simple diamond studs in her ears and a platinum bracelet my father had given her. I wanted to wear my wedding rings, but Michelle had vetoed the engagement ring.

"The diamond is too big," she'd said sympathetically. "Beautiful, but that means it'll catch the eye. We don't want people distracted by your wealth, or Stefan's. Just wear the band."

I agreed, and once we were in the private car taking us to the church, I asked Stefan to hang on to the ring for safekeeping.

"We won't wail or carry on," Michelle was saying. It was her mantra. "We can be sad, but not overly emotional. A few tears, at the most, and we'll save them for the funeral itself."

"We'll do our best," I told her gently. "And I'm sure it will be fine, either way."

I knew to anyone else, my stepmom's words might seem cold or unkind, but I was grateful for them. And while I doubted I'd actually break down crying in front of the press and all my father's political connections—my tears were private, and I'd excuse myself if it really came down to it—I was glad Michelle was laying out some guidelines to follow. I also took comfort knowing that I could watch her at any point during the day and follow her lead.

The second we pulled up outside the church, her eyes began to well with tears again. I watched her take a deep breath, dab her eyes with a tissue, and then carefully touch up her face.

"Here goes nothing." She snapped her compact shut and straightened her shoulders.

As soon as the driver opened our door, the flashbulbs started. Just like she'd said.

Standing next to Michelle inside the church doors to greet people and have them sign the guestbook, I realized how grateful I was for my stepmother. The past week she'd been a constant source of support, and I was so glad to have her at my side. I couldn't imagine going through this without her.

Once we got home to the condo, I'd expected to climb into bed and pass right out, but now that I was lying in bed in just my slip, my mind and heart wouldn't stop churning with emotions. I wasn't ready to deal with any of them.

As drained as I was in every possible way, though, I was too sad and anxious to sleep. I needed something to distract me. To make me feel good. Or at least feel anything other than this overwhelming grief that stole up on me every single night when things got quiet.

Sitting in the church had been the hardest part. So many people had spoken, but their speeches all seemed to blend together. I was glad no one had requested that Michelle or I speak; it seemed a given that we would be too distraught to say anything. I hadn't been able to stop staring at my father's casket the entire time. It was black and gleaming under the lights of the church, at least the parts of it that weren't covered in beautiful white flowers. But it was still a box. It seemed so...final. The thought of him in there...

I was crying when Stefan entered our bedroom with a tea tray for me. He'd brought me my favorite chamomile blend, I could tell by the smell wafting from the steaming cup.

"Tori," he said gently, setting the tray down and taking me in his arms. "Let it out."

But now that he was holding me, I found that I didn't want to cry anymore.

We'd slept in my childhood bed every night for the last

week in Springfield, but it had all been chaste—Stefan pulling me close and rocking me when I fell apart after long days dealing with the funeral home or my father's staff—and my body was hungry for more.

I didn't want to be held or stroked or touched tenderly. I wanted to be fucked. To be completely diverted from my feelings and to have my husband take me the way I wanted to be taken. Hard. Rough. Relentless.

When I slid my hand down inside his boxer briefs to wrap my hand around him, my pulse sped up. My husband was so gorgeous. It made my mouth water just feeling his cock in my grip.

"You're exhausted," he said, gently moving my hand.

"No," I told him. "I want you."

It was obvious that he wanted me too, judging by the fact that he was already hard, but still, he shook his head.

"I don't expect this, kitty cat," he said. "Let me tuck you in and I'll hold you."

I got up off the bed to slowly pull my slip over my head, then let it drop to the floor. As I slid my panties off I locked eyes with him. Soon I was wearing only my thigh high stockings.

"You're beautiful," Stefan breathed. "But—"

"Shh." I came toward him, putting my finger over his lips. "I don't want to be held," I told him. "I want to be fucked. I want to be touched and tasted and dominated."

Desire sparked in his gaze, and I crawled onto the bed and pressed my mouth to his. He instantly opened to me, and as we kissed I let my hands trail down his shoulders, raking his abs with my fingernails, stroking him through the fabric of his briefs.

I needed to feel connected, needed an outlet for the complex feelings roiling inside me.

THE CHOICE

"I want you too," he growled, rolling me onto my back and hovering over me.

"Then give me what I need," I said. My life had been a rollercoaster for the last few weeks, and I needed a release. Needed him to give it to me.

I wrapped my arms around his neck and pulled him down toward me for another kiss, arching my body against his, shamelessly grinding on him until he let out a soft groan.

"I want to take care of you," he protested.

"Then take care of me like this," I said, reaching up to grab the waistband of his briefs and tugging them down. We were both naked now. I could feel his control starting to break.

"Please, Stefan," I pleaded as I looked up into his eyes, knowing he could never say no to me when I begged. "Please fuck me."

We kissed again but it was different this time. More aggressive, more raw. His hands fisted in my hair and he plundered my mouth, his cock already driving against the wet lips of my pussy. I moaned with relief. This was what I wanted. This was what I needed.

Spreading my legs, I angled my hips to give him better access.

"You want this?" he demanded, reaching down to trace my opening with the tip of his dick. God, he felt good.

"Yes," I panted. "I want it. I want you."

He pulled away and dragged his hand roughly up between my thighs, slipping a finger into me where I was slick and hot and ready for him.

"You're so wet for me," he groaned, adding another finger and pumping in and out.

"Fuck!" I cried out, already close to an orgasm. It had

been too long, and I needed him so bad I could barely see straight.

He fingerfucked me roughly, pushing deeper, three fingers now, stretching me out in the most delicious, perfect way. I was panting his name between breaths, grinding hard against his hand. So close now. His thumb found my clit and he pressed it hard as his fingers continued to thrust. I was right on the edge as he leaned over to kiss me, his tongue stroking deep into my mouth, matching the pace of his fingers inside my body, and just like that my whole body crested the wave of ecstasy and I was coming right in his hand, shuddering with the power of my release.

I clung to him as I moaned, pressing my teeth into his shoulder, my knees going weak.

"Are you ready for more?" Stefan asked, positioning himself between my thighs.

"Yes," I whimpered. His cock was nudging at my soaking wet pussy. "I want you."

I arched up toward him, but he kept himself still.

"Tell me exactly what you want," he ordered.

"I want you to fuck me with that hard, perfect cock," I said, one orgasm hardly enough to satiate the intense desire I felt for him. "I want you to fuck me hard and fast. Please. I need it."

He didn't drag it out like he usually did, but instead rammed his cock into me with one brutal, perfect thrust. I gasped as he filled me, his hips rolling against mine, his length stretching me wide. It was exactly what I needed, exactly what I wanted.

Immediately he began to move, fucking me hard and fast like I'd asked, his hands spreading my thighs so wide the muscles ached so he could go even deeper. Then, without warning, he lifted my legs up, looping my ankles around his neck as he fucked me.

I gasped at the intense pleasure this position gave me, the exquisite fullness I felt. He had never been this deep inside me before, had never fucked me like this before.

My head fell back on the bed as he thrust into me over and over again, pounding out a rhythm, his grip now tight around my thighs. So tight I thought I might have bruises tomorrow. The thought of his fingers imprinted on my skin just made me hotter, more desperate for release.

"More," I gasped, my head thrashing back and forth. The pleasure was building inside me again, pulling me inexorably closer to another orgasm. "Please, Stefan. Make me come."

"You're gonna come for me," he commanded. "Fuck yes. I'm gonna fuck you hard, fuck you until you come. Until you scream. Come for me, Tori. Let everything go except how good I make you feel. Let it feel good."

He drew his hand between our bodies, pinching my clit in the most delicious combination of pleasure and pain. It was exactly what I needed.

"Oh my god," I cried, my moans turning into one long wail as I came, my body clenching around his, the climax so hard and deep it practically blinded me with white-hot pleasure.

"Fuck, I'm coming," Stefan groaned, his body jerking as he came in a rush, filling me up with his hot release. I would never tire of the feel of him coming inside of me, the way he'd relax into my arms afterward, our bodies still connected, our ragged breaths slowing in time.

I could feel his heart beating hard against mine. We were both completely spent.

"I love you," I sighed, my own orgasm still humming through me.

"I love you," he said, rolling over and pulling me close to spoon his body around mine.

Relaxing against him, satisfied beyond words, it wasn't long before we were both drifting off into a peaceful, dreamless sleep.

STEFAN

CHAPTER 25

Striding down the hall of the KZM building toward my father's lavish corner office, I straightened my jacket and tried to keep my breathing calm and even. What I really wanted was to kick the door open and drag him out of his chair by his tie, but I knew losing control around my father was the last thing I should be doing right now. There was too much at risk. I couldn't afford to give him any indication that an investigation was happening or that I was a true threat.

Not that I expected this to go pleasantly, regardless of my attitude.

Amidst all of the overwhelming circumstances of the past week and the logistical and emotional intensity of the before, during, and after of Senator Lindsey's memorial service yesterday, I'd barely had a chance to think about my own father. There was no way I could let his actions slide, though. And now that I was back at work at KZM, I was finally ready to confront him about the fact that he'd gone behind my back and tried to break up my and Tori's marriage. Call him out for the way he'd manipulated Anja and used her and Max as his pawns.

My adrenaline was pumping. Far from being nervous about speaking with my father, I was eager. Spoiling for a fight. It was time to let him know once and for all that he didn't get to control my life—that nothing he said or did would keep me from the path I had chosen. Just as I had done at the family dinner at our condo, when I'd reaffirmed my commitment to Tori.

Despite everything that was happening with my father, and everything that had happened with hers, I was beyond grateful that the two of us were finally on solid ground. We were a team. I was confident that after we survived whatever was coming next with the investigation into KZ Modeling, we would be unbreakable.

I was ready to put this dark chapter of my life behind me.

When I reached my father's suite of offices, I didn't even bother to check in with his assistant. Why give him the opportunity to turn me away, knowing he viewed every interaction with me as a dick-measuring contest? Instead I breezed right past her, despite her protests, and flung open the door to my father's inner sanctum.

He looked up from the pile of paperwork on his desk, projecting an air of annoyance.

"I'm busy," he barked, the very picture of self-importance.

"Good to see you as well, Father," I said formally, shutting the door behind me and walking toward him. "I think we need to have ourselves a chat."

Unsurprisingly, he made a big show of ignoring me until he'd finished looking through the file in his hand. I'd bet he wasn't even reading it—just wanted to make me wait, and drive the conversation himself. Finally, he set it aside and looked up at me, his expression bored.

"Well? Are you going to lurk over me all day? Sit down and speak up!"

"I'll stand, thanks," I said flatly. "I'm here to let you know that your attempts to break up my marriage are going to stop now."

The bastard actually laughed. "Is that what you think?"

"It's what I know," I said.

He folded his hands across his wide stomach and looked up at me, a smirk spreading across his face. I was glad I had been forced to stay away for a week, because if he had smiled at me like that right after I'd discovered that Max wasn't my son, I doubt I could have been held accountable for my response.

"You've expended a lot of time and effort trying to cause tension between me and Tori," I told him, "and I know you brought Anja and the kid back thinking you had an ace in the hole. But I gotta tell you...you didn't just fail. If anything, my marriage is stronger than ever now."

"Bullshit," he shot back, his cool demeanor cracking.

"I should be thanking you, actually," I said, unable to resist needling him. "Without Max showing up, I'm not sure Tori and I would have started talking about starting a family of our own so soon."

"How about that," my father said nonchalantly, rising from his chair to stroll over to the window. Looking out at the million dollar view of the cityscape, he went on, "You think I regret any of it? I don't. And I don't know why I should. I'd do it again a thousand times over."

"And you'd fail a thousand times," I said, moving closer. "Again."

He shrugged. "Now that Senator Lindsey's dead, the

poor bastard, my only regret is that I ever introduced you to Tori to begin with."

My fists clenched at my sides, but I refused to take the bait. "The way I see it, I lucked out."

"Don't be cute," he snapped, looking me full in the face. "This whole situation's turned into a damn shit show." He shook his head, calming back down. "No matter. The fact is, without the senator in our court, Tori is useless to us. Worse than that, with everything she knows, she's a *liability* now. I know your heart's in the right place—god knows you've never been smart when it comes to women, Stefan—but it's time to let her go."

It was my turn to smirk. "Not likely."

Lumbering over to the phone on his desk, he hit the intercom button. "I need an espresso in here, Darlene."

"Just one, sir?"

He looked up at me but I shook my head.

"That'll be it, sweetheart," he said. "And shake a tail feather, I've got a conference call with OmniVia in five."

Some days I wondered how Darlene kept herself from waltzing into my father's office and dumping the entire pot of coffee into his lap.

"Listen," he said to me, picking up where he had left off. "We're in a tight spot now, and with Lindsey gone, we're going to have to figure out another way to legitimize the business."

I nodded, trying to seem like I was still on his team. "Sure. That makes sense."

"I'm serious, kid." He was pacing in front of the window now. "You like your condo, your car, your cushy job? You'd lose it all in a heartbeat if KZM goes down. You want to keep working for the company, you need to get your ass to a lawyer, file for divorce, and start working on securing some new political allies. Especially considering my plans for the future."

And on he went. I clenched my jaw, watching my father pace and bluster. I'd had it with him and his demands.

I was so close to walking out and never looking back. Fuck the money, fuck the job, fuck the lifestyle. None of it was worth being complicit in my father's vile empire, swallowing his disrespect day by day, being treated as nothing more than a pawn in his game. But I also knew that the feds were finally closing in, and that my role as the man on the inside was crucial.

"What next stage?" I asked, my ears perking up at the last thing he'd said.

He waved his hand dismissively as Darlene entered with his espresso. "You'll know when I need you to know. But trust me, it's gonna be big."

It was impossible not to sweat what he'd just said—or not said. Hearing that he had some big plan on the horizon made me worry that the DOD needed to quit dragging their feet and get in sooner rather than later. Before my father could make his next move.

"If I'm supposed to be inheriting KZM's operations, I need to be kept in the loop," I pushed as soon as Darlene had left us alone again. "What exactly are you planning?"

But my father was not about to be baited.

"You haven't proven yourself worthy yet," he told me, settling back down behind his desk with his coffee in hand. "Let's see a real show of loyalty. Maybe then we can talk about your role in this new development."

With that, he picked up his phone, told Darlene to patch him through to the OmniVia call, and spun his chair away from me, already yucking it up with the executives on the line. It was as if I wasn't even there. As if, despite everything I'd participated in, and regardless of all the years I'd put my ass on the line for KZM, I was still small potatoes as far as he was concerned.

I let myself out of his office, nodding curtly at Darlene's sympathetic half-smile, seething and scheming the whole way back to my own desk.

There was no way in hell I was going to let my father get away with whatever he was planning. I'd figure out a way to get all the details and then I'd pass that new information along to Gavin Chase's brother and the feds. My father was going down. He'd never see it coming.

I buried myself in work all day, waiting for my father to go home. He was conniving, manipulative, and incredibly clever, but he was also arrogant—so arrogant, in fact, that he'd never expect anyone at the company to be smart enough to hack into his computer files. But I knew that if there really was anything to find, I could do it. I just needed access.

He left just after six. I called Bruce.

"I'm on it, boss," he said by way of greeting. "Red Bentley, heading west toward I-90."

"That's him," I said. "Call me if he goes anywhere besides home. If he leaves the condo at any point tonight, I want to know right away."

"Copy that," Bruce said.

The office was deserted, everyone else long gone as I snuck into my father's office.

It didn't take much to get into his computer—he had left it on, and his password was easy enough to crack, being a version of Danica, my mother's name, with a few of the letters swapped out for the @ symbol. I navigated over to his emails and began reading the messages in his Outbox, scanning for any keywords or coded phrases that might jump out at me.

Within minutes, my guts were churning.

Sitting in the dark, with the glow of the computer screen my only light, I read about my father's plan to shift his operations from sex trafficking to full blown slavery. He was ready to move beyond the prostitution ring, and I found evidence that he was already in the process of arranging to buy and sell people on the international human market. As 'property,' I knew they could be forced into labor, domestic service, criminal acts, marriage, and of course sex work.

I sat back, my heart pounding in my ears.

The shock took my breath away. I couldn't imagine that the late Senator Lindsey, for all his flaws, would have ever been on board with this. My father's Anja plan was diabolically brilliant in that regard—if Tori had left our marriage over the existence of Max (and before she could find out about the slavery), our divorce would have looked like an embarrassing but clearcut issue of irreconcilable personal matters. The senator couldn't have accused my father or me of backing out of our agreement on purpose. A few large donations to the Lindsey campaign later, and the wrecked marriage would have been mere water under the bridge between the two patriarchs.

With a few clicks of the mouse, I started printing some of the emails detailing the plan.

As the pages started stacking up in the tray, I realized that my father really was a supervillain, like Anja had said. It was sickening how well he had planned all of this.

I kept searching through his emails, knowing that even the ones I'd printed might not be incontrovertible enough to prove that my father planned to start selling people as slaves.

Finally, I landed on some hard evidence. Something that the feds could use to get my father, once and for all. Because he had already booked flights for his new merchandise. Scores of future victims from impoverished countries, who had probably been told they were coming to the United States to work and be given life-changing opportunities. They had no idea what my father truly had in store for them. They wouldn't just be prostitutes. They'd be slaves.

I printed it all, making sure the names of the individuals were on each confirmation page.

My father didn't think I was ready to take over the business—and he was right.

I was ready to take it down.

STEFAN

CHAPTER 26

The moment I walked in the door last night, I had told Tori everything.

"We have to stop him," she'd said, flipping through the stack of printed emails with shaking hands, her jaw clenched.

"We will," I had promised her.

Getting those documents to Gavin Chase's brother at the DOD would go a long way toward making that happen. It was lucky I'd been able to get all the pertinent information before ducking out of my father's office—names and flight numbers, dollar amounts and rendezvous points. Even with the coded language, it was clear that he was involved with illegal trafficking.

Within an hour of Tori leaving the condo for her morning classes today to pass off the information to Gavin at school, I got a call from the feds.

"This is everything we need to make an arrest," Frank told me, sounding more confident than he ever had. "I've been waiting on the higher-ups for the green light, but this blows all that bureaucracy and red tape to shit. We're gonna move fast. No more tiptoeing around."

"Thank fucking god," I said, relief washing over me like a tidal wave. The nightmare was almost over. "How soon?"

"You don't have the security clearance to know the details," he said, dropping his voice to a lower register, "but off the record, this might be the last night KZ spends outside a cell."

When Tori came home, I gave her the good news.

"So you're thinking tomorrow morning?" she asked.

"That's what it sounds like," I said. "I'll head into work early just in case."

Her jaw dropped. "Are you serious? You can't go to the office tomorrow."

"I have to," I told her, pulling her into my lap. "I need to see this through."

"Stay home with me," she begged. "I don't want you anywhere near your father when the shit hits the fan. Who's to say he won't do something drastic when he's cornered?"

"Like what? Go out shooting?" I said. "He doesn't keep a gun at work."

"Maybe not, but those agents will be armed. What if he tries to take you down with him? You're not bulletproof."

Her chin started to tremble, and I cupped her cheek and kissed her long and slow.

Once she'd relaxed in my arms, I leaned back and said, "I understand that you're worried—you have every right to be. My father is a dangerous man with a volatile temper. But I've waited years to see him brought to justice. I need this closure. I promise I'll be safe."

"You can't promise that." She was blinking back tears. "You're making a mistake."

"I'm sorry," I said gently, "but it's not fair for me to leave everyone at KZM to deal with a raid without me there. Plus, my father might think something is up if I don't go in. I don't want to give him any reason to suspect tomorrow is anything but another normal day at the office."

She let out a sigh and wrapped her arms even tighter around me, resting her head against my chest. I held her close, stroking her hair.

"You're a good man, Stefan," she said. "Please be careful."

The next day—as planned—I woke up early, made love to my wife, showered and dressed and drank my coffee, and went into work. I'd given Tori an extra long kiss goodbye, promising to call her as soon as I had news.

It was impossible to concentrate on anything once I was in the office, though. Sitting at my desk responding to emails, I tensed every time I heard footsteps coming down the hall. My knuckles were white as I clutched a pen, staring blankly at a stack of papers, trying to give the illusion that I was vetting a pile of modeling contracts.

In reality, all I was doing was waiting.

The minutes dragged. The ticking of the clock seemed to echo in my brain as I struggled through a few calls that were scheduled on my calendar. Beneath my desk, my foot tapped impatiently. Nervously.

Then, at practically 10:00 am on the dot, just as I was turning the corner to enter the employee lounge, the doors to the agency burst open and swarms of black suited men poured in.

It was immediate chaos.

Through the glass walls of the lounge, I watched them infiltrate KZM. I could hear shouts of confusion, a few screams, the sounds of filing cabinets being opened, the clang of them vibrating throughout the building. Word of the raid spread like wildfire, going from office to office, and a few people began freaking out and scattering, running for exits with phones pressed to ears and keys in hands. Most of them were unaware of what was really going on, having only worked for the legitimate side of the agency's business, but there were a few more senior employees darting back and forth through the hallways, shifty-eyed and clearly in a panic.

Meanwhile, KZM's main receptionist stood at her desk, her dark skin gone ashy, clutching her purse to her chest and looking around in confusion.

"Mr. Zoric? What's happening?" she asked, spotting me through the glass.

"It's okay," I reassured her, finally coming out of the lounge to stand near her desk as agents began storming in our direction. "Just give them whatever they ask for."

They wouldn't find anything in her desk or my office, and I didn't think they'd look that hard. What they wanted was my father—the person in charge. The rest of this was a charade. Everything they needed was already in their hands.

I headed back to my office, figuring it would be best to stay out of the way. As I walked down the corridor I could see, through office doors flung wide open, executives who were rifling through the contents of their filing cabinets or screaming into their phones.

"If you don't keep your mouth shut, I'll make you wish you'd never been born," I heard one agent hiss into his cellphone as he shoveled papers into his shredder.

"You *whore*," another was shouting at someone he had on speakerphone. "If I find out you're responsible, you can consider your career a dumpster fire!"

Part of me wanted to stop and bash their faces in, or at

least drag them to the nearest federal agent and offer them up for handcuffing, but I kept going, taking solace in the knowledge that the DOD would bring all the guilty parties to justice.

None of them would be getting away scot free.

My father's office door was closed, and suddenly my stomach dropped at the thought that he had somehow escaped—but then I was grabbed from behind and pulled into an empty office.

Turning around, I found my father and brother standing there. Luka looked confused and terrified, while my father just looked purple with rage. I kept my own expression neutral.

"What's happening?" I asked. "Who are these guys?"

"We need to get the fuck out of here," my father yelled, ignoring my questions.

"How? They're everywhere," I pointed out, my tone affected by genuine anxiety.

"Stefan's right," Luka said, eyes darting left and right. "We're trapped."

"We'll duck out through the back of the conference room," my father said. "There's a staircase that goes down to the basement, what used to be an old freight shaft. Let's move."

As he turned away, I saw the dark flash of a gun on my father's hip, under his suit jacket. Tori had been right to worry.

"Come on," Luka said, tugging my arm.

I had no choice but to follow.

In the conference room, door locked securely behind us, my father was babbling again.

"There's already a car waiting for us. It'll take us

straight to a private jet, and we'll be in the air before they even realize we're gone. The fucking bastards."

He was sliding over one of the soundproof panels off the wall, revealing an ancient-looking steel door that I hadn't even realized was there. Though the office building had been renovated into a sleek, modern style, underneath it all the original architecture was still intact.

Fuck. I had known my father would be prepared, but I didn't realize how prepared.

"We'll start a new life—a new business—in another country," he was saying. "South America, maybe the Bahamas. I have the passports and money all ready to go." The door swung open, revealing only darkness behind it. My father motioned impatiently for us to follow him.

"Wait. I don't understand," Luka said. His eyes were wide and he looked like a little kid.

I hated that he was caught in the middle of this, hated that I hadn't been able to protect him from our father. But I could take care of him now. Because there was no way in hell I was going to let my father take Luka out of the country—there was no way I'd let him get away.

"Christ, but you're slow on the uptake," my father sneered at Luka. "You want to stay here and rot in prison, or get the fuck out of here and start a new life?"

My brother hesitated. "I—I don't know."

Scrubbing his hands over his face in frustration, my father managed to flash his gun again. I could see Luka had noticed it, his eyes wide as he looked to me for help. For guidance.

"We can't just drop everything and leave," I said, trying to stall. There was no way I was going to tell my father that it was over for him—that I'd given him up to the feds—when he had a gun on his hip. "What about Emzee? And Tori?"

"Your sister's not involved. They'll leave her alone. And don't tell me you're still hung up over your god damn self-righteous bitch of a wife!" my father spat. "Has it not occurred to you that this could all be *her* fault?"

"She's got nothing to do with this!" I lied vehemently. We were both breathing hard.

If I could just get him to stay in the building a little longer, the agents would find us. They had to be making their way to us even now, I just knew it.

But fuck if I wasn't frustrated and pissed. They should have found my father first, gotten him into custody before they ever tried to spread out and take control of the entire office. Instead, I was the one who was going to have to keep him from leaving the country.

"Suit yourselves if you're too brainless to save your own skins!" my father exploded. "I'm getting out of here."

He ducked through the door, into the dark passageway beyond, sliding the wall panel back into place behind him.

Luka's eyes bounced back and forth between the misaligned wall panel and me.

Swearing under my breath, I knew I didn't have a choice.

"You go first," I told Luka. "I'm right behind you."

Quickly, I pulled out my phone and texted Tori.

911

kz escaping to garage in secret tunnel

tell agents now

Then I stepped over the threshold and pulled the wall panel closed behind me. I could only hope that she would get the message and alert the feds in time.

STEFAN

CHAPTER 27

Through a tunnel and down the stairs we went, the only light coming from our cell phones. It was a steep descent, steep enough to keep our pace on the slower side, lest we miss a step and go hurtling down into the pitch black. If my father was correct, the tunnel would take us through the bowels of building and spit us out somewhere in the parking garage. That was the only place we'd be able to get into a car without being noticed.

I could hear my father panting in the darkness, Luka sniffling back tears.

"You fucking useless drunk," he was hissing, mid-shuffle. "Stop stepping on my heels. You want me to break my god damn neck? I'll bet you'd like that, wouldn't you?"

I heard a slap and knew that my father had struck my younger brother. I balled my hand into a fist, praying that when we got to the other side, justice would be waiting. The winding stairwell seemed to go on forever, but I was grateful it was taking so long to navigate in the dark.

Finally, I heard my father slapping his hands against the

wall. Luka was waving his phone around as a flashlight, trying to help my father find the exit. I braced myself for what we'd see on the other side, holding my breath as he finally found a rusted metal door handle.

"Keep your head down and run straight to the car," he said, his voice low. "Once we're all in, we'll be off."

I could hear the glee in his voice, the confidence that he was going to get away with everything and escape to some tropical paradise to start up his criminal activities all over again. I felt a shiver of fear at the possibility that my message might not have reached Tori or that she might not have gotten in contact with the feds in time. No matter what happened, though, I wasn't getting on that plane with my father. I'd never leave Tori, even if I got shot in the process.

"Now!" my father hissed, pushing the door open.

Light streamed into the dark passageway, and for a moment I was blinded. I put my hand up, blinking against the brightness. But I didn't need my eyes to hear my father cuss under his breath. Standing in the parking garage waiting for us was a gang of heavily armed federal agents in heavy gear, their weapons pointed at all three of us.

I couldn't have been more relieved.

Luka dropped to his knees in shock.

"Hands in the air!" someone ordered.

My brother and I complied. I had known I was going to be arrested today—it was part of the deal, that I would be brought in with my family, even though I had been assured that I would not be charged. Thanks to my involvement, I had full immunity. This was all for appearances.

Meanwhile, it seemed as if my father was in a state of shock, his arms hanging limp at his sides. For a moment, I thought he might reach for his gun, but then his hands slowly, falteringly went into the air instead. Even from my position behind him, still half in the dark, I could see that he knew he was outmanned, with no way out. He knew that he had lost.

The gun was taken from my father and all three of us were cuffed. Only then was I able to breathe freely. It was over. It was all over.

Still, it wasn't enough.

I wanted him to know.

As we were led to separate police cars, I called out to my father, and his face turned in my direction. He looked old and weak, his skin ashy and his posture stooped, as if he had aged twenty years in the past few minutes. I felt no pity.

"This was me," I yelled to him. "You're going down because of me."

Prison wasn't as bad as I'd anticipated. Though I was sure the treatment I'd gotten was far better than what my father was receiving. Despite my immunity, I'd still been kept in a cell until the government raid operations were complete and the necessary release paperwork was dealt with.

I had ample time to work with my lawyer preparing a statement that would go out to the press. It stated, explicitly, that the illegal arm of my father's company had been run solely by Konstantin Zoric and a few select executives, all of whom were now in custody. The rest of the family—myself, Luka and Emzee—were not involved in any of the criminal activities that had taken place. Furthermore, KZ Modeling would continue to operate, but only as a legitimate talent management agency. In my new role as President and

CEO, I pledged to work with the feds to make sure that the back door business of the company was completely dissolved. KZM would also be rebranding itself in the coming months as well.

As my lawyer had warned me, the press took to the story like sharks to chum. Both my legal counsel and KZM's public relations department were inundated by requests for interviews and tell-alls. But I'd already informed my team that the prepared statement was the extent of my public speaking on the matter. I'd be focusing on strengthening the business going forward.

I was so relieved that everything was over, that I'd finally be able to stop working double-time to effectively run one crooked company alongside my father while simultaneously attempting to launch another, better company behind the scenes—and all of this labor for the same agency. It had been indescribably exhausting, mentally and emotionally, and in many ways my single focus since I'd left college. When I walked out of police custody, knowing that I was officially done leading two lives, it felt like I was walking on a cloud.

And for the first time ever, I'd be able to make time to focus on my personal life. I could finally be truly present for Tori. Give my wife all the attention she deserved.

Suddenly, I couldn't wait to be home with her. I'd been missing her since the arrest, and we'd spoken on the phone, but the need to see her, to hold her, to touch her, became an overwhelming desire that had me even more anxious to gather my things from the prison's holding area, slip my wedding ring back on, and get the hell out of there.

Maybe we could even take a vacation together. Me, her, and some tropical deserted beach. Nothing but Mai Tais and hammock naps for the both of us. Clothing optional. My imagination began to work overtime, imagining all the things I wanted to do with Tori. All the ways I wanted to be with her.

I sincerely thanked the officers who escorted me through the thick security doors and out into the light of day. When I emerged, however, it wasn't Tori who was waiting for me. It was Luka. He stood next to a black Town Car, waving. Flashbulbs were going off behind the barbed wire fence, and I cringed to think that the media was capturing this intensely private moment.

Approaching him cautiously, I wasn't sure what to expect. I knew he'd been released earlier than me, as he'd had even less knowledge of how KZM's underground business had worked, and under interrogation my father had immediately (and shockingly) absolved Luka of any involvement—but other than that, I had no idea how my brother was doing.

He looked a hell of a lot better than the last time I'd seen him. His face had lost some of that puffiness that had seemed as ever-present as the drinks that were always in his hand. In fact, he appeared to be freshly showered, shaved, and well-rested.

"Free at last," he said with a wry smile, pulling me in for a quick hug.

We stepped apart and stood there, staring at each other for a moment.

"You look good," I told him.

"Yeah," he said, rubbing the back of his neck. "I'm trying the twelve-step thing. Getting my act together. Only been to one meeting so far, but...it's going okay."

A broad smile stretched across my face. So he had

finally decided to get help. To get better. I felt a surge of pride at the way he'd taken responsibility for himself. It was unfortunate that it had taken such an extreme wake-up call in the form of the KZM raid and our father's arrest, but I was glad it had shocked him into action.

"That's great," I told him. "You stepped up. Couldn't be more proud, brother."

We settled into the back of the private car and got on the road, heading toward the condo.

"I just wanted to say..." he trailed off, looking embarrassed, before forcing himself to turn back and make eye contact. "You inspire me. I'm ready to build a life. Like yours."

I had to look away and blink the sting out of my eye.

"You've been through a lot," I told him, clearing my throat. "We all have. But I'll be with you every step of the way."

"All twelve of them?" he joked, and we both laughed at his lame attempt at humor.

"You're gonna do great things," I assured him. "Just take it one day at a time."

"I haven't been very adult about any of this," Luka said, shaking his head. "When I found out about everything—about who Dad really is, the kind of business he was running—I didn't know what to do. I just stuck my head in the damn sand."

"It's not your fault," I told him. "You just reacted poorly to a bad situation. But it doesn't define who you are. What defines you is how you get back on your feet, and look at you now."

Luka smiled. "You think well of me. Which is good news, because..." He took a deep breath. "The thing is, I didn't used to think I wanted any part of the company—even before I knew about the trafficking stuff, I always thought Dad was a tyrant who didn't treat his employees well. But now that he's gone, I was thinking...I want to be involved.

"I want to work for you. Help the agency thrive. Branch out into more diverse models, start promoting inclusivity, rebrand ourselves as true advocates and allies of our talent. I have ideas, Stefan. I'm ready to do this. I mean, if you'll have me."

I leaned back against the seat, mulling over my brother's breathless proposal. If Luka was willing to come on board and do some of the heavy lifting, bringing with him all the enthusiasm he'd just shown me, I'd be able to step back from agency's business even more. Spend more time with Tori, maybe start working on building a family. The thought was thrilling.

"Let me be honest with you, Luka," I told my brother.

I could see the apprehension in his eyes.

"You handled the truth about Dad and the models way better than I did. Maybe it looks like I'm some kind of hero in all this, but it took me *years* to work up the balls to reach out to the DOD. I've known about KZM for a lot longer than you have. And for so long, I did nothing."

"You were figuring out a plan," Luka said, defending me.

"That's the worst part," I said, still disgusted with the naïveté of my youth. "I *wasn't*. I stood by the prostitution for years, because I told myself they were willing. That it was a great way for them to make extra cash to send home to their families. I made excuses on top of excuses, as if I actually believed any of these women had a choice."

"I'm sorry," Luka said.

I let out a breath. "You know what finally changed my mind? When Dad made Anja disappear, right before I left for U Penn. If I'd been a better man, I would have cared about the models because what we were doing to them was wrong, not because *I* got hurt."

"What matters is that you made it right in the end," Luka insisted. "You took him down. It's over now."

The car had gotten hot and uncomfortable, or maybe I was just overly worked up. I cracked a window and let the ice-cold Chicago air flow over my face. Thinking about all the time I'd wasted, how many lives had been ruined before I started making moves against my father.

Luka was staring at me, silent but waiting.

"You're right. It's over. The nightmare is over," I echoed him. "I'm glad you have the same ethics I do. And I'd be honored to have you by my side from now on. In fact, I've been considering how to move forward to rebrand the agency, and I'm leaning toward a new name."

His brow creased. "What is it?"

"Danica Rose Management," I said. "Has a nice ring to it, don't you think?"

"Mom's name," Luka murmured. A grin spread slowly across his face. "She'd be proud."

It was a lot of emotion for the two of us to share, so I think we were both grateful to leave it at that and spend the rest of the ride in silence. When we got to my condo, I stepped out of the car and turned back to Luka.

"See you at the office tomorrow bright and early," I told him. "We've got a fuck ton of work to do."

He laughed. "See you there, man."

There was a light in his eyes that I hadn't seen in a long time, a fire that I had missed. I grinned at him, glad that I finally had my brother back and fully present. Glad that we'd be cleaning up this mess together. Who knew, maybe Emzee would want to join us as well.

As I headed into the building, laser-focused on seeing the woman I'd missed most while I was in prison, I realized that I was finally ready to start my new life.

TORI

CHAPTER 28

Today was the day. The reading of my father's will. Stefan held my hand the entire ride down to Springfield, while I leaned against him, staring out the window of the Town Car and occasionally resting my head on his shoulder.

My husband and I had hardly left our bed in the two days since he'd come home from prison. If it was up to me we would have stayed there forever, but we were expected that afternoon at an appointment with my father's lawyer. He and Michelle had already rescheduled the reading due to all the pomp and circumstance of the funeral, and then the KZM raid immediately following, which had hit me pretty hard. There was no more postponing it. It was pretty much the one thing that could put a damper on my desire to seduce my husband.

During the drive, I was a huge ball of nerves. This would be my first time back at my father's house since the day of the funeral, and I braced myself for an overwhelming rush of unresolved feelings. Of grief.

But when I saw the house, and Michelle standing in

front of it, all I felt was relief at seeing her. She looked better than she had in years. She was still the same Michelle, of course—classy, polished, the very picture of composure—but something about her seemed softer. More at ease. Stepping into the house, I could sense the change inside as well. There were no staff members running to and fro in their uniforms, the huge vases of formal white flowers had been switched out for bouquets bursting with color, and I caught a whiff of lavender and vanilla.

The house projected an air of welcome and warmth. For the first time, it felt like hers.

My father's lawyer met us in the library, and I couldn't help noticing that Michelle had taken the dark, heavy curtains down—allowing bright light to pour into the room. She also had a diffuser going in the corner: the source of the lavender smell. The usual thick scent of cigars no longer lingered, and I noticed the windows had been cracked open as well.

"I love what you've done in here," I told her. "It feels nicer. Less like a cave."

"Thank you," she said, smoothing back her hair, which was down for a change.

I would bet my father had rejected all her decorating suggestions when he was alive, given how obsessed with appearances he'd always been.

We settled onto the sofa while the lawyer pulled my father's will out of his briefcase and adjusted his glasses on the bridge of his nose.

"The document is fairly straightforward," he said, looking up at all of us. "Mrs. Lindsey, Mitch left you the deed to this house, along with some funds—" here he passed a sheet of paper over to Michelle, "—specifically set aside for your sole use, at your discretion."

I wasn't sure what was on the page Michelle was looking at, but she'd let out a little gasp. I couldn't imagine she'd been left anything less than a high seven figure number. My father had always given her a generous allowance and I was sure he'd made certain that she would be taken care of for the rest of her life.

"It's...too much," she choked out, her voice raspy with emotion.

"Don't worry," I told her. "I'll help you spend it."

She let out a tiny laugh at my joke and I gave her hand a squeeze. I knew the money couldn't come close to making up for all the lies and infidelity my father had put her through during their marriage, but at least now Michelle could live on her own terms. Maybe she could even sell the house and start over. Or do some of the traveling she'd always dreamed of.

There were tears in her eyes, but she managed to hold it together, giving the lawyer a firm nod before handing the page back to him.

He turned to me next, and Stefan tightened his grip around my shoulder.

"Victoria Lindsey," he began.

I swallowed hard. "Yes."

"Everything else is willed to you. Cash, stocks and bonds, as well as personal property, vehicles, and some real estate, including the apartment in Chicago and some acreage in Florida."

"Are—are you sure?" I sputtered. "There are no...amendments?"

"No amendments. It's all yours," the lawyer affirmed.

I was genuinely shocked. After I had married Stefan, I half-expected my dad to either completely write me out of his will, assuming my husband would take care of me, or do something archaic like add stipulations to the inheritance, or leave it all to my husband.

"Wow," I breathed, and this time, it was Michelle who squeezed my hand.

"Your father loved you," she said. "I know you two hit a rough patch a few months back, but he loved you just the same. This is what he wanted."

So he hadn't been holding a grudge when he passed. He could have easily changed his will at any time—hell, I knew he kept his lawyer on speed-dial—but he'd chosen not to. I felt a huge weight lift off my chest, and I leaned into Stefan with tears stinging my eyes.

"This is an itemized list of each and every asset," the lawyer said, passing over another sheet of paper. "At the bottom you'll see the total cash value, should you choose to liquidate."

My eyes widened as I scanned it. I was suddenly battling a host of conflicting emotions.

If he had died at any other time, this inheritance could have been used for absolutely anything I wanted, including my education. Even a divorce, if Stefan and I hadn't fallen for each other. It went a long way toward helping the bitter taste I was left with in my feelings toward my father. He'd been controlling, and he'd made some bad choices, but he had loved me.

Not only that, but by way of my arranged marriage—whether intentionally or not—my father had given me Stefan. When I looked over at my husband I saw a brilliant, beautiful man who had opened his heart to me. A man with integrity, who I trusted implicitly. Our marriage was a gift I would forever be grateful for.

"Thank you, Daddy," I whispered, dropping a kiss on

the page in my hand that now contained a whole world of possibilities.

After the rest of the will was read, Stefan and I had lunch with Michelle before heading back to Chicago.

"How do you feel?" he asked as the car pulled away from my father's house. What was now Michelle's house, I reminded myself. Perhaps I'd send her a house re-warming gift.

"Overwhelmed," I answered. "I'm grateful for everything my dad left me, but I don't know what to do with it. The cars, the stocks, the real estate."

"You'll figure it out," he said. "I'm just glad he decided his ultimate legacy would be to take care of his family. To do the right thing."

A lightbulb went off in my head.

"I have an idea," I told him, before asking our driver to head to the Four Seasons Hotel in Chicago, instead of going straight to our condo.

∼

ANJA GREETED us at the door to her suite when we arrived, Max hanging back shyly behind her. After the raid on KZM, they'd been forced out of my father-in-law's apartment. Stefan and I had set them up at the Four Seasons until things got settled, but we still hadn't decided what their next move should be.

"Is everything okay?" Anja asked, frowning with concern. "How did the lawyer go?"

She looked like she hadn't been sleeping very well, with dark circles under her eyes. I couldn't blame her. The whole ordeal must be taking a toll on her, and I knew she was doing her best to protect Max from everything that was going on.

"It was good," I told her as we went into the suite, taking a seat on the couch. I'd brought the thick manila envelope that my father's lawyer had given to me. Inside it were various legal documents, including a copy of the will and the list of assets I now owned.

Anja settled into a chair across from us, Max dropping onto the ottoman beside her.

We still hadn't informed him about who his real father was, or the nature of my relationship to him, but I was hoping that would change soon.

"The thing is...my father left me a lot more than I expected," I confessed. "Not even just money and cars and *stuff*, but also his condo here in Chicago."

Anja smiled sympathetically. "It sounds like a lot to deal with."

"It really is. And that's why I was thinking you could help me out," I continued.

"Of course," she said. "I'm not much for bookkeeping, but I can make some calls, help you figure out how to go about liquidating the assets. What can I do?"

Stefan nodded imperceptibly beside me, and I leaned forward and smiled at Anja.

"Actually," I said, clearing my throat, "I'd like to give the apartment to you and Max."

Anja let out a little gasp, her hand flying to her mouth.

"To us? But why? We could never—"

"Because you're *family*," I said firmly. "And I want you and Max to have a home here."

Max looked between his mother and me. "Are we going to live here forever?"

"I can't accept this," Anja said, shaking her head. "It's too much."

"Please," I begged. "I want you and Max to stay in Chicago. I want to have a chance to get to know him better. To watch him grow up. He's my—"

I stopped before I accidentally said the word. Anja looked conflicted. Max, seeing that his mother was upset, gave her a hug, looping his little arms around her neck.

"Don't cry, Mama," he said.

"I won't," she said, hugging him back. "Can you go play with your toys for a little bit?" she asked him. "So I can talk to our friends about some grown-up stuff?"

"Okay!" He got up and nearly ran across the room, flinging open a door to the bedroom and his stash of toys and games. When the door closed behind him, Anja burst into tears.

"This is too generous of you. Maybe we can work something out, I can pay—"

"No," I cut her off, going over to her with the big envelope in my hands. "Max is my father's son. My brother. It's only right that he gets part of the inheritance."

I rifled through the papers until I found the deed to the apartment, and I handed it over to Anja. Her hands shook as she took it.

"I'll have it transferred to you legally. And this isn't all," I said. "I'm going to have the rest of the assets split up evenly between me and Max. This isn't about charity or me being kind. It's the right thing to do."

Anja looked up at me.

"Max is very lucky to have you as his sister," she said, her voice thick with emotion.

"I'm the lucky one," I insisted. "I always wanted a sibling."

Her tears started flowing anew.

Reaching over, I gave her a hug. "It's the least I can do after everything you and Max have gone through."

Stefan moved closer to us. "Tori and I talked about it on the drive over, and we agreed that we want to be a part of both your lives," he told Anja.

"Max is family," I said, easing back from her. "And that makes you family, too."

Looking down at the deed to the Chicago apartment, I could see that she was considering it. Finally, she looked up at us and smiled.

"I can't thank you both enough," she said. "We'd love to accept."

We all cheered so loudly that Max came running out of the other room.

"What happened?" he asked, clearly not wanting to be left out of the celebrating.

"How would you like to stay here in Chicago, with our new friends?" Anja asked, pulling him into her lap.

Max thought about it for a moment. "Can we go to the zoo again?" he asked.

"Absolutely," I said. "You need to show me all your favorite animals."

Max smiled at me, and then at Stefan and then his mother. "Okay!"

Anja gave him a kiss. "Then this is what we will do, my darling. We will live here in Chicago so we can be closer to the people who care about you."

"About *both* of you," I said.

Anja nodded, clearly getting choked up again.

We stayed at the hotel for a few more hours, playing with Max and making plans with Anja to get them moved into the apartment by the end of the month.

When we left, Stefan pulled me into his arms, kissing me gently.

"I'm so proud of you. Of what you've accomplished."

I kissed him back, realizing that everything in my life was finally falling into place.

STEFAN

CHAPTER 29

Chicago disappeared beneath a layer of clouds as our plane reached its cruising altitude. I linked Tori's fingers with mine as we eased into our first class seats, relaxing completely for the first time in...ever. Things had finally started to settle down, one major thing after another reaching closure. So much so that I'd booked us last minute tickets to the Caribbean for Tori's Christmas Break.

The flight attendant came by with complimentary glasses of champagne and little squares of decadent chocolate. Without Tori having to ask, I slid my piece over and watched her devour it in a single happy bite that made me smile as I sipped my champagne.

She snuggled against me, and my heart felt full. I couldn't wait for us to get to our final destination, where she could throw her thick scarf and winter layers into her suitcase and not touch them for weeks. There'd be no need to wear anything but bikinis in the Caymans, and I had bought her a suitcase full of very revealing suits that I couldn't wait for her to model for me.

"Looking forward to the weather?" I asked as she leaned back in her seat. "It was nothing but sunshine and eighty degree days last time I checked."

"Yes," she practically moaned, letting out a sigh of relief. "I'm going to *live* on the beach. I was barely able to focus during my last exam—all I could think about was this vacation."

"How did the rest of your finals go this week?" I asked, having witnessed her round-the-clock studying over the past few weeks. I knew she hoped to end the semester on a high note.

"Good, I think," she said. Then she shrugged. "Though I don't know that I'll be looking at straight As this term."

"I'm sure you aced all the written questions," I told her. "Don't stress about your GPA."

"I'll try not to," she said. "But I'm going to work twice as hard in the spring."

"You're gonna kick ass next semester," I said. "But I don't want you to spend the whole trip thinking about school. Your homework is to just sit back, relax, and let me take care of you."

Raising my glass, I gestured for her to do the same. When we clinked, Tori toasted, "To a well-earned vacation. With my very sexy, very generous husband."

We drank our champagne, and then I tilted her chin up and kissed her. I wanted to do far more than that, but I knew it would have to wait until we got to the hotel. And even then, I had a few surprises up my sleeve. For now I settled for ordering us two more glasses of bubbly.

"What a year we've had," I mused, taking her hand. "Thank god it's over now."

"Six months," Tori corrected me in a low murmur. "But we got through it. Together."

"We did," I agreed. "And now we're stronger than ever."

She squeezed my hand tightly, looking over me to stare out the window at the thick clouds flying beneath the plane. I could tell she was thinking about her dad again, the way the little frown line formed between her brows.

Tori had gotten closure on her relationship with her father, and I knew his final gift had gone a long way toward healing the rift that had opened up between them over the last few months, but it was going to take a lot more time for her to process the sudden loss of him. Still, I'd be with her every step of the way.

I was lucky to have gotten closure on my search for Anja and the answers I'd sought about what had happened to her. Now she would be a permanent part of our lives, and I was heartened by the fact that she and Tori had grown so close. We'd also finally sat Max down and told him that Tori was his half-sister. Even though he was confused at first, and sad to know that his biological dad was gone, he had been thrilled to learn that he had such a cool older sibling.

I loved watching the two of them play together. Tori was such a natural with him and it was clear that the affection and awe they felt for each other was mutual.

"Did your lawyer have any news, earlier?" Tori asked, nervously twisting her hands.

My father was still in jail, so I'd been receiving updates on his upcoming trial whenever there was new information. My lawyer had called just before Tori and I had boarded the flight.

"He was denied bail again," I told her. "I was glad to hear it."

Tori nodded. "I think it's for the best."

"I heard from Gavin's brother as well," I continued.

"They were very strategic about his placement in the prison system so they could keep a close watch on him 24/7."

"You don't think he'll still be able to rebuild his network?" Tori asked.

It had been a major concern that I had shared with the feds from the beginning. My father was cunning and persistent. If there was a way to manipulate the system from in jail—to command a network of criminals on the outside—he would find a way. But his power to do that had been systematically disassembled, thanks to frantic negotiations between me and the feds, as well as a team of lawyers and law enforcement working together from across the globe.

"I think the right people have been alerted about my father's ability to make connections," I told her. "He's not gonna be pulling one over on anybody."

The relief was visible on Tori's face.

"My lawyer said it's likely he'll be in prison for the rest of his life," I added.

There was too much evidence, too many witnesses for my father to get away with his crimes. We'd built an ironclad case against him, and his ability to do harm was finally at an end.

"Too bad he took the company down with him," Tori sighed. "How is Danica Rose coming along? Have you signed any new clients?"

"Business is a little slow," I admitted. "But the scandal will pass eventually, get replaced with some other news."

Tori nodded. "I think it speaks volumes that the KZM models have all stood by you and signed new contracts with Danica Rose. The press releases have to be helping, too. Everything I've read says that they trust you, they're excited for the future with DR, and they're grateful for what you did. The public will come around soon enough."

"I think so too," I said. "And Luka's been amazing. Doing all the handholding with the models, taking their calls at all hours to answer their questions and address their concerns. If anything, it's because of him that we've only lost a few models."

"He told me he was helping them with their green cards too."

I broke out into a grin. "And compiling a directory of local therapists who specialize in trauma counseling. Can you believe it? He's practically a social worker himself."

"Sobriety looks good on him. I might have to set him up on a blind date with Grace one of these days," Tori said with a wink. "Either way, I'm glad he's doing so much better."

That was an understatement. I couldn't believe the progress my brother had made. Now that he was committed to staying sober, he was a new man. He was focused and determined, showing up to work every day as if he were trying to prove something. I kept telling him to take it easy and just focus on his sobriety, but he insisted that the work he was doing—helping me undo all the damage that our father had done—was a major part of his recovery.

It was incredible to finally be able to connect with my brother in the way that I'd always hoped for. Our father had made that damn near impossible, always pitting us against one other, always comparing the two of us unfavorably as a way to separate us and work up a rivalry. Now that he was gone, I actually had a chance to build a real relationship with Luka.

"He's been spending a lot of time with Anja and Max," Tori noted. "Every time I go over to see them, it seems like he's there, helping them get settled into the new apartment. Putting furniture together, unpacking boxes..."

"Playing videogames with Max," I interjected, and we both laughed. "Honestly, I think they like having him around. He fixes things and tries to be useful. It's good for everyone."

"I agree," Tori said. "It seems like we're all becoming a real family."

"All because of you, kitty cat," I told her.

She blushed and I wrapped my arm around her, pulling her closer. I couldn't wait to see the look on her face when she found out what I had planned.

∽

TORI

As we flew further and further from Chicago, I felt the stress leave my body. I hadn't realized how desperate I was for a vacation until Stefan had surprised me with it. Now we were off to spend the holidays in the Caribbean, leaving behind a city that was practically frozen over.

The next few weeks would be nothing but beaches, crystal clear waters, and ridiculous, fruity cocktails. I fully intended to spend the majority of my time soaking up the sun under a floppy hat with a book in my hand, ordering in lavish brunches from room service, and making love to my husband in our private bungalow.

I couldn't wait to land.

Stefan had closed his eyes and was leaning back against the headrest. I took a moment to admire him. The dark circles under his eyes were finally fading and I knew that after a few days in the Cayman Islands, where we had nothing to think about but each other's pleasure and needs, he would soon be well-rested and energetic again.

It was rare to see him not decked out in one of his designer suits. Instead he wore a pair of fitted dark jeans and a sweater that hugged his torso. I couldn't wait to strip him out of both the moment we got to our hotel room and could disappear completely from the rest of the world.

I picked at the tapas plate that one of the flight attendants had dropped off and tried to ignore the nakedness of my left hand, the pale white band around my ring finger reminding me that my wedding rings were still back in Chicago. I'd dropped them off for cleaning at Stefan's jeweler, along with his wedding band, a few days before our vacation. But when I'd gone back, the jeweler told me she was concerned about a loose stone on my engagement ring. She wanted to keep it longer to re-tip the prongs and check the tiny pavé diamonds on my wedding band as well. Of course I had agreed. The last thing I wanted was to lose my diamonds on vacation.

But now that I didn't have my rings anymore, I realized how accustomed to them I'd become. I felt incomplete without them. Even the few days of leaving them for a clean and polish had been uncomfortable, and I couldn't stop playing with the spot on my finger where they should be. At least I had the man who the rings represented right beside me, I told myself. That was what really mattered.

A few hours later, our plane began its final descent into Owen Roberts Airport on Grand Cayman. I looked out the window as we sailed through the clouds, the pristine white beaches and sparkling turquoise water coming into view. It was the opposite of the cold, frigid city we had just left behind. Even though I loved Chicago, I was eager to get a break from winter.

A private car was waiting for us at the airport and it wasn't long before we pulled up in front of our gorgeous resort hotel. I'd never been to the Caribbean before, but even my wildest dreams couldn't have imagined something as perfect as what I saw in front of me.

It looked like the screensaver on my laptop had come to life—nothing but lush green palms, lacy iron balconies, tall columns, and that unbelievably blue sky as a backdrop. The air was warm and fragrant, and I paused for a moment to take it all in, breathing deeply. Inside, the hotel lobby glimmering and spotless, with marble floors and huge open atriums.

"I can't wait to see our bungalow," I told Stefan, looping my arm through his as we followed the porter into our breathtaking suite of rooms.

"Do you want to check out the beach first?" Stefan asked. "The sun's setting in about an hour—it's going to be incredible. We can watch it from the sand."

He tipped the porter, who offloaded our luggage and then showed himself out.

"That sounds good," I told him, looking around at our lodgings.

I saw a huge king-size bed made up with crisp white linens and piled high with pillows. It faced floor-to-ceiling sliding glass doors that opened up onto our own private patio. The fragrance from a fresh flower arrangement scented the air, and the bathroom was loaded up with fancy spa products and fluffy Turkish robes. The best part was, the whole place was set apart from the rest of the hotel and even had a path leading down to the beach that was just for us.

I stripped off my sweater and boots and reclined on the bed. My silk camisole was slipping off my shoulder as I crossed my legs in my tight jeans, waiting for Stefan to pounce.

"Now that I'm lying here, I kind of feel like ordering room service and just staying in our room," I said, giving him a suggestive wink.

But he was staring out the window at the ocean.

"I really don't want to miss that sunset," he said, a wistful tone to his voice that I didn't hear often.

"There will be plenty more," I pointed out, hoping to sway him.

He turned around and smiled. "I know. But I want to start this vacation off right. This is the first day of the rest of our lives, and...I guess I'm feeling sentimental. If you really don't want to, though..."

My heart melted. This man.

"You win," I said, walking over to him to pull him into a tight hug. "Let's go."

I pulled a pair of sandals out of my bag and quickly changed into a light sundress. It was hot enough that the thought of wearing jeans for any longer was a minor torture. When I emerged from the bathroom, Stefan was down to his tight black T-shirt and he'd rolled up the cuffs of his jeans. I didn't bother hiding my stare. I couldn't wait to see him in a pair of swim trunks, emerging from the ocean, his body glistening with drops of water.

"You're sure you don't want to stay here?" I tried one last time, wanting desperately to start our vacation horizontal and in bed.

"Don't you worry, kitty cat. We'll be back in bed soon enough," he said with a wink, taking my hand and leading me out of the bungalow.

We walked down the private path to the beach and I

took a moment to soak it all in. My disappointment over Stefan not jumping my bones the moment we were alone faded quickly. We were in one of the most beautiful places I'd ever been and I had the man I loved at my side. We had all the time in the world to be alone and naked together.

When we reached the beach, however, my jaw dropped —as it became immediately clear why Stefan had been in such a rush to get here.

Standing on the sand was a group of our closest friends and family, arranged in what looked like a ceremony tableau. Anja and Max. Emzee and Luka. Michelle. Grace. They were all here, their faces lighting up when they saw us.

"Surprise!" they shouted at once.

My hand flew to my heart.

"What is this?" I asked Stefan.

But when I turned to face him, I found that he had sunk down to one knee. And he was holding out a ring. My engagement ring.

"You didn't choose this for yourself the first time, and I didn't choose it for the right reasons," he began. "But I've learned one thing, Tori. And it's that I love you. I want us to spend our lives together, and you'll make me the happiest man in the world if you want the same."

My eyes were filling up with tears.

"Tori," he said, his voice gone husky, "will you marry me again?"

"Yes," I choked out. "I will."

"Then let's do this and mean it."

He stood and swept me into his arms, kissing me fiercely.

I held out my hand for my ring, but before he slipped it

back onto my finger where it belonged, he showed me the inscription he'd had engraved on the inside of the band. It read, "the deal of a lifetime."

TORI

CHAPTER 30

As the sun set over the Caribbean in swaths of pink and gold, Stefan and I stood in front of our closest family and friends to renew our vows in an intimate, perfect ceremony. It felt nothing like our first wedding. That experience had passed in a complete blur, a performance that Stefan and I had been actors in, not participants. We'd had no control over anything.

This time was different. Like Stefan had said when he got down on one knee, this time we had the chance to truly choose each other. And we had.

I held his hands as the officiant he had hired spoke the words that were music to my ears.

When it came time to repeat our promises of love and devotion, Stefan pulled out both of our wedding bands—he'd thought of everything.

"There never were any loose stones, were there?" I teased.

"I may have arranged for my jeweler to intentionally mislead you," he admitted, grinning.

"What a sneak," I said.

He held out my ring to me. "Look on the inside."

I did. There was a new inscription on my wedding band, as well—this one said, "I'll always choose you."

My eyes were stinging with tears. "I choose you, too," I whispered.

"I love you," Stefan said, sliding it onto my finger alongside my solitaire. "You are my everything."

"And I love you." I slid his ring on him, and we were pronounced man and wife. Again.

Stefan wasted no time in sweeping me into his arms, and giving me a long, deep kiss that had all of our guests cheering, except for Emzee—who put her fingers in her mouth to let out the loudest whistle I had ever heard. Max was laughing and Anja had tears in her eyes. She mouthed "congratulations" to me, and I nodded.

After the ceremony, we all gathered further up on the beach where a beautiful spread of food had been laid out for us under palm trees draped in twinkling lights, and a string quartet was playing just for our party. I was so full of love and gratitude that I could barely eat, focused instead on trying to take in everything that was happening around me.

All of the people I cared about were here, together, to celebrate me and Stefan. It meant so much to me, after all we had been through, that we could have this time together. I watched as Michelle and Emzee and Grace talked, their heads bowed close together, no doubt discussing fashion or art, something all three of them were well-versed in.

Max was running up and down the beach, having a great time, while Anja looked on, laughing joyously. The most surprising thing, however, was Luka. I had fully expected him to be chatting up the many beautiful bikini-clad women that were walking along the sand, but instead, he kept close to Anja, occasionally joining Max, the two of them racing across the sand. Luka didn't even seem to notice the other women. I even saw him put his hand on Anja's lower back as he leaned closer to tell her something that had her burst out laughing.

Was there something between them that I hadn't been aware of?

"I think I spoke too soon about Luka and Grace," I whispered to Stefan, nudging him and gesturing in his brother's direction. "Are you seeing what I'm seeing?"

"I'm seeing my beautiful wife," Stefan said, tugging me out of my seat and gently pulling me back toward the sand. "Let's walk."

I'd have to find out about Luka and Anja some other time. Right now, I was happy to focus on my husband. The man who had made a deal with me all those months ago—a deal that had turned out to be the best deal imaginable.

We strolled along the beach, with the sound of the waves our only soundtrack. It was so beautiful here and I felt completely relaxed, completely at ease. I leaned into Stefan as we headed toward our private cabana.

My heart beat began to pick up as he unlocked the door to our room and pulled me inside. Finally, we were alone. Finally, I could do what I had been imagining all day.

He drew me into his arms and kissed me. It was like the kiss on the beach, at the wedding, but now that no one was watching, we were free to let our hands wander. His went immediately to my ass, pulling me up against the hard bulge of his cock. I moaned against his mouth, my own hands going down to his waist where I slipped my palms beneath his shirt, eager to feel his skin against mine.

Without warning, Stefan scooped me up into his arms.

"You deserve to be carried across the threshold properly," he said.

I laughed, feeling completely giddy as he navigated into the bedroom, toward the huge, soft bed I had been so eager to sink into. Stefan laid me down before covering my body with his.

I loved the weight of him over me, the way we fit together like puzzle pieces as he settled on top of me. I spread my legs so he could settle between them and align his hips with mine, the perfect, hard ridge of his arousal grinding into me exactly where I needed it.

Yanking at his shirt, I pulled it over his head and tossed it across the room. His hands skirted up my thighs, pulling my dress up along with them. I wiggled beneath him, and with a single smooth tug, my dress was up and over my head, leaving me in just my underwear

"You're beautiful," Stefan murmured, his hands stroking my naked skin.

All I was wearing was a tiny satin thong and matching bra. Stefan made quick work of both and then pulled my head back so he could kiss and bite and lick his way down my neck before heading even lower south.

I moaned as his mouth found my nipples and he began to tease them with hot flicks of his tongue. My hips writhed against the bed and I gasped with needing him so badly.

"Take off your clothes," I demanded between breaths. "I want you."

Stefan lifted his head and gave me a naughty look.

"I'm yours, kitty cat," he murmured, and heat spread through my body.

He knew exactly what that nickname did to me and I knew he did it on purpose. Leaning back, he undressed quickly and then settled back on top of me. I loved the feel of his bare skin against mine, hot and smooth and sleek.

His hand moved between my thighs and I opened for him easily.

"You're soaking wet," he said, giving me a dirty smirk.

"I'm ready," I told him, pulling his lips to mine and kissing him deeply.

His thumb found my clit immediately, tracing soft circles around the sensitive skin there.

"Yes," I moaned.

As his tongue thrust harder against mine, he began to stroke me in a matching rhythm, just the way I liked. Then he slipped another finger inside me, and then another. I gasped, grinding faster and faster against him as he skillfully fucked me with his fingers, the release I desired just agonizingly out of reach.

"Harder," I begged. "Harder. Harder."

I felt him smile against my mouth as he obliged. He was stretching me in the most delicious way, his hand moving faster, his fingers stroking deeper. It felt so good, so right, and as he bent his head to take my nipple into his mouth, sucking it hard, my body crested the wave.

The orgasm hit me hard, radiating from my center in shockwaves, and I arched on the bed as I moaned Stefan's name.

"I can't hold back," Stefan growled, moving between my thighs.

"Wait," I gasped, and before he could thrust into me, I placed my hands on his face. "I have to tell you something."

He lifted a brow, his mouth turned up in a curious smile. "I thought I was the one who had all the surprises today."

"Just one more," I said, barely able to concentrate as he pressed the head of his cock against my seam. "Do you remember how we talked about maybe...trying to start a family?"

"Yes..." He'd gone still, and for a moment I was afraid I'd said the wrong thing.

"Well, I—" I took a deep breath. "I stopped taking my birth control. So we can start trying. I mean, if that's something you still want."

Stefan was so quiet that I started to think I'd made a huge mistake, that I should have consulted with him first, that I might have just ruined our second wedding night. But then he cupped my cheek gently, and the expression I saw on his face nearly stopped my heart. It was full of such tenderness and love that it took my breath away.

"Yes," he said, leaning down to kiss me deeply. "God yes, I want that. A family. With you."

"Maybe we'll have a honeymoon baby," I said, smiling at him as relief washed over me. "Well, a second-honeymoon baby."

His smile turned wicked. "I guess we'd better get started then, huh?"

He was pressing into me again and I shivered with anticipation.

"Yes," I said. "Yes, please."

With one deep thrust, he plunged completely inside of me, deep and strong. It felt like we were one person, like we were completely, utterly connected.

"You feel so fucking perfect," Stefan moaned as he pulled back slowly before slamming into me again.

"Give it to me," I moaned, knowing he loved it when I begged. "Don't hold back."

Gripping my hips, Stefan rolled over and pulled me on top of him, forcing me back and forth over his cock. I cried out with the pleasure he gave me, letting him use me, loving the way he fucked me roughly. Once I picked up the rhythm, I leaned back so he could get a full view of my breasts bouncing as I met each hard thrust with my own. Both of us were gasping for air, reveling in the connection of our bodies. For a while I lost myself in it, closing my eyes and letting the pleasure overtake me.

"Fuck yes," I panted over and over. "Fuck me, Stefan."

When I started to feel myself get close I looked back at him and we locked eyes. A fresh wave of desire crashed through me knowing that he was watching me lose control, watching me get off on his cock. I leaned over him and gripped his shoulders for support, riding him harder, faster, wanting more of him. Wanting all of him.

"Yes," I moaned. "Yes, give it to me. Give it all to me."

Without warning, he shifted me so I was on my hands and knees. Then he moved behind me and ran his hand down the length of my spine before delivering a sharp, perfect slap to my ass. It stung in just the right way. He did it once more, and then drove his cock hard into me.

"Perfect," he was groaning with each thrust. "Perfect, you're fucking perfect."

I gripped the bedsheets in my fists as he took me hard, his cock pumping into me, back and forth, faster and faster, feeling so good I could only moan wordlessly into the pillow. As I did, I felt his thumb against my asshole, pressing, stroking.

"Yes," I cried, loving the sensation.

He shoved his thumb inside of me, all the way, until I was full—my pussy and my asshole completely owned by him. I pushed back against him, wanting more, wanting it all. He gave me everything I wanted, everything I needed, his body claiming mine now and forever.

There was only this—there was only us.

I felt my orgasm building, even stronger and more intense than before. Sparks were twisting inside of me, something deep in my core going taut and white-hot, and Stefan was fucking me even harder now, groaning as he started to reach the edge.

"I love you," he gasped.

Suddenly my release hit me in a hot wave, and I cried out breathlessly, my whole body vibrating as I climaxed. My pussy clamped around his cock, each contraction a shockwave of delicious ecstasy slamming through me, and I felt him lose control as I moaned his name. He thrust once more, deep, his fingers digging hard into my hips, and with a groan he spilled hot and fast inside of me.

We collapsed onto the bed, our bodies completely spent. Stefan gathered me into his arms, our limbs entangled. "I can't wait for what's next," I murmured. "I want to be with you always."

"Then let's make that happen." He held out his hand to me. "Is it a deal?"

It was exactly like it had been the first time we met. I took his hand in mine.

"Deal," I told him, knowing that this was one deal I'd never regret.

Tori and Stefan finally got their well deserved Happily Ever After. Are you ready to meet the notorious playboy, Luka?

Preorder The Sham.

Our marriage is a sham. I'm the first to admit it. Only privately, of course.

Notorious playboy Luka Zoric needs a wife, and the good PR it brings.

I just need the career boost being his top model will give me.

It's a win-win--on paper. But since when has real life been simple?

His jealousy makes me crazy.

The control he maintains over my body is unacceptable.

I really shouldn't be so turned on by it.

But there's more to both me and my husband than meets the eye.

And it isn't long before I'm wondering--which of us has made the bigger mistake?

The Sham

〜

Dear Reader,
Thank you so much for reading The Choice. I hope you loved the emotional conclusion to the Arranged Series. I truly enjoyed writing Tori and Stefan's story and can't wait for you to meet Luka and the woman who will hopefully

change his wicked ways. The Sham, book 1 in the Convenience Series, releases June 30, 2020!

Thank you again for reading Stefan and Tori's story. If you enjoyed the Arranged Series, I would greatly appreciate it if you let a friend or two know and leave a review. It's the best way to thank an author and just a few sentences is all it takes to show your support.

Sincerely,
Stella

∽

Want to be up-to-date with all my releases? Sign up for my newsletter!

ALSO BY STELLA GRAY

~

Arranged Series
The Deal
The Secret
The Choice

Convenience Series
The Sham - June 2020
The Contract - July 2020
The Ruin - August 2020

ABOUT STELLA GRAY

Stella Gray is an emerging author of contemporary romance. When she is not writing, Stella loves to read, hike, knit and cuddle with her greyhound.

Made in the USA
Coppell, TX
15 September 2020